head over feels

EMMA LEE JAYNE

FIDGETY FIREFLY BOOKS, LLC.

Head Over Feels

Emma Lee Jayne

Copyright 2023 by Emma Lee Jayne

This novel is a work of fiction. Names, characters, places and incidents are either the product of the author's imagination or have been used fictitiously and are not to be construed as real. Any resemblance to persons, living or dead, actual events, locales or organizations is entirely coincidental.

Cover credit: Ana Hard – anahard.com

Editor credit: Kate Johnson – zory.com

With regard to digital publication, be advised that any alteration of font size or spacing by the reader could change the author's original format.

✿ Formatted with Vellum

ping into her power & embracing herself. All via an internal monologue that is so damn witty that people *will* look at your for snorting in laughter. 10/10." - Kate, Amazon

★★★★★ "A wonderful, fun and entertaining friends-to-lovers story. There is great dialogue, laughs, banter and sweet moments. I love how Meg came into her own and fought for what she wanted...personally and professionally. A fun and fantastic read!" - Kristie, Amazon

TITLES BY EMMA LEE JAYNE

AUSTEN IN AUSTIN
Sense & Irritability
Pretense & Sensibility

TEXAS DIAMONDS
My Favorite Mistake
My Only Mistake
My Worst Mistake (coming soon)

His for the Holidays
Too Far Gone
In Too Deep
Love Letters to Tabitha

FROM SMARTYPANTS ROMANCE
Heart Smart
Smart Mouth

a note from emma

Dear Reader,

(Starting a note like that always makes me feel like Jane Eyre! But I digress...)

Head Over Feels is a very special book for me a ton of reasons. First off, it is a deep rewrite of one of my first published books. Very deep. Vantablack deep.

Since you haven't read this version yet, I won't spoil it by telling you all the things I changed (I hint at it in the acknowledgments at the end of the book if you're curious.) But basically, these characters (in some form or another) are old friends of mine. They've been in my life a very long time.

The second reason I love it is that it was edited by my dear friend Kate Johnson. She started as an editor and became a trusted friend while we worked on this book and other projects together. I love how books bring people together!

Finally, I just love Meg. She's funny, quirky, and so very

human. All my favorite characters are deeply flawed and insecure.

Speaking of flaws and insecurities … did you know I have ADHD? If this is the first book of mine you've read, you might not. But I write a lot of neurodiverse characters, so if this isn't your first book, you might know this already.

Like all personality traits, ADHD is a blessing and a curse. It makes me deeply perfectionist. And also practically unable to see typos and mistakes in my own work. If you find one (or more) of the inevitable typos, please reach out to me! I will do my best to wrestle it into submission. Typos might be missed words or weird breaks from me moving something around.

Please know, that these mistakes drive me crazier than they do you! I hire two copy editors for most books! And those pesky mistakes still sneak in! Ah well, consider it proof my books aren't written by AI.

Please follow me on social media and reach out (even if you don't find a typo).

Cheers and happy reading!

one

IT IS the truth universally acknowledged that a single man of good fortune must be in want of a friend who doesn't give a damn about his net worth.

Okay, so maybe it's *not* universally acknowledged, but I am convinced it's why Keegan McQuade and I have been friends for so long. And who am I to argue with Jane Austen?

To make matters worse, Keegan is single, rich, and ridiculously good looking. Which means everyone— women, men, little old ladies with walkers, over-eager golden retrievers ... everyone—falls all over him to get his attention, so he needs someone in his life who wants nothing from him and isn't constantly trying to hump his leg. I am lucky enough to be that person.

This is how our relationship has worked ever since we met our freshman year of college. I pretend he is an average guy, and he pretends I'm not an awkward nerd with a stutter who spends too much time in her own head.

For example, right now—a Saturday evening, during our normal weekly 'hang'—I'm pretending he has nothing

1

more exciting to do than order take out and lounge on my sofa.

And he is pretending that it's perfectly normal for a woman to lie on the floor glaring at a vacuum cleaner.

The vacuum in question is the latest model of the cordless Butler Steam Vac. It's a combination vacuum and steam cleaner with sleek lines and retro styling. In three days, the team I'm on at Forester+Blake ad agency has to pitch an idea for a new ad campaign to Butler.

I've worked on a three-person team at Forester+Blake for the past four years. Teresa is the team lead, and (I guess) sort of my boss. Tad, the youngest member, does all the tech stuff—putting together the multimedia and making things look great. I do all the preliminary sketches and, if I'm being honest, come up with most of the ideas.

And here is the crux of the problem. For this pitch, I got nada. Ziltch, zero, zip-zip-zipperoni.

Okay, not *nothing*. We have a pitch ready.

But what we have is just … blah.

My gut says it's not good enough.

I sigh.

I squint.

Behind me I hear Keegan, who is sitting patiently on my sofa, shift. I'm vaguely aware of him tapping away on his phone. Then the theme music from *The Good, the Bad and the Ugly* fills my living room.

I shift to see him holding up his phone, a grin on his face. I glare in return.

"What?" He chuckles. "I just thought, with the right soundtrack, maybe you'd draw your weapon and finally have this shootout with the poor vacuum."

I don't glare at him for long, but sigh and flop down on

the floor and stare at the ceiling. "I'm sorry. This sucks. I won't blame you if y-you want to ditch me for the night."

"What?" he asks in mock shock. "And miss this epic battle between good and evil? This showdown between woman and machine? This is the stuff of legend."

I grab a throw pillow and toss it at his head. He catches it.

"Besides," He turns his phone to show off the update from DoorDash. "Take out should be here in ten minutes. So whatever inspiration you're going to get, it needs to hit before then, or I'm starting the movie without you."

Despite our apparent differences—of which there are many—Keegan and I connect on a soul deep level when it comes to low-key hangs.

By which I mean we both love sci-fi TV shows, Asian takeout, cheap red wine, and post-punk music from the eighties.

I secretly suspect that Keegan also loves expensive red wine, but keeps his standards low to appease my bank account's ego.

By unspoken mutual agreement, we usually pretend that our income brackets aren't separated by several digits. Usually.

Even though he's lived his entire life in Texas, Keegan has the unmistakable vibe of a California surfer dude. He's tall and lean, with shaggy blond hair that falls almost to his shoulders and these intense gray-blue eyes. They remind me of pictures I've seen of the beaches in the Caribbean, where the water is so clear, you can see right through the depths to the reefs beneath.

He has one of those perfectly symmetrical faces. Between full lips and that little dip in his chin, he'd be almost too pretty if it weren't for the perpetual scruff on his jaw. Of course, he's got a surfer's perfect golden skin, so he always looks like he's just got home from the beach.

Once, not long after we became friends, I asked him if he surfed. He answered, "Only when I'm in Hawaii."

Who says stuff like that?

And, somehow, because he's Keegan, he didn't even sound douchey when he said it.

The closest I've ever come to Hawaii is my unflagging love of *Lilo and Stitch*. I love Stitch's ability to make chaos wherever he goes, and I admire a woman willing to make voodoo dolls of her enemies. Not that I've ever made a voodoo doll. You know, just in case law enforcement ever asks.

Somehow, despite our differences, Keegan and I have been friends since college, when we roomed together. After college, we drifted apart. Although we both still lived in Austin, he and my then-boyfriend, Ollie, didn't get along. Neither of them ever said it out loud, but I could sense it. Ollie didn't like that Keegan was there first, even though my relationship with Keegan was never romantic, and Keegan didn't like ... well, I don't actually know what it was about Ollie that bugged Keegan.

During the years Ollie and I dated and then lived together, Keegan and I hung out less, despite my best efforts. But the second Keegan heard that Ollie and I had broken up and I was kicking him out, Keegan showed up at my place with a rental truck, a dolly, and a half dozen mutual friends to help pack up Ollie's stuff and get him out of my life.

I am not exactly comfortable letting other people do favors for me. I don't think I could have accepted that help from anyone but Keegan.

He's offered to help me out a lot over the years. Everything from trying to coax me into trips to Hawaii to subtly stocking the fridge with my favorite foods.

I have always refused the trips (no matter how tempting, exotic, or needed), and as soon as I caught on to his shopping shenanigans, I started labeling all my food as soon as it came into the house.

What can I say? According to my mother, I have stubbornness issues. But I prefer the phrase "obstinate, headstrong girl," because Jane Austen always says it best. But I digress.

My point is, the breakup with Ollie is the only time in our friendship that I let Keegan help me. Sure, it's nice that he wants to give me charity. I just refuse to be the person who receives charity. Do you blame me?

Keegan needs someone in his life who doesn't want things from him. It might as well be me.

Now that Ollie is out of the picture, Keegan seems perfectly content hanging out at my place, eating takeout, and watching sci-fi. Tonight, it's *Galaxy Quest*—probably the best movie of all time. We've got a cheap AF box of red wine and take out from Ramen Tatsu-Ya.

In short, it's the perfect Saturday evening.

Or it would be if I had even a hint of an idea for how to sell this damn steam vac.

I give another dramatic sigh, rolling over to my belly, propping myself up on my elbows to glare at the vacuum again.

Keegan groans, and I can practically hear his eye roll.

I'm about to just give up and kick the damn thing to the curb, but before I can stand, Keegan lowers himself to the floor, mirroring my posture.

"Okay, Glasses. Lay it on me. What's bugging you about this one?"

I shift, rolling onto my side to look at my best friend. "Y-you don't have to do this."

"Nonsense." Once again he mirrors my posture, one elbow wedged under him, knees crooked as he faces me so that our legs almost touch. "We're in this together. If you're in a deathmatch with a vacuum, then so am I."

I kick my foot out to nudge his shin. "But you hate being on the floor."

"I work at a bar."

Keegan is underselling himself. He doesn't *work* at a bar. He *owns* a bar. And Hung Out to Dry is one of the most popular bars near campus.

I nudge his shin again. "Your point? Because I don't follow."

"The floors at the bar are caked with fifty years of spilled beer and vomit. If I burned the bar to the ground, I wouldn't want to sit on the pile of ash left behind."

"I thought there were health codes and vats of bleach involved?"

"I'm just saying, there's a reason I don't get down on the floor at the bar. I'm not afraid of getting hepatitis on your floor."

"Good point."

"Okay, break it down for me. You can write copy about anything. Why does this one have you stumped?"

So, so, so many reasons.

If I can nail this ad, I'm hoping to parlay it into a promotion. One in which I head up my own team and (hopefully) make more money. Money that will keep me from having to find a roommate. Ollie never contributed a lot of rent, since his income was less stable than mine, but money has been tight now that I'm footing the entire bill. Of course, I can't say that to Keegan, because he'll just offer to loan me money.

So instead, I slant a look at the offensive machine. "W-who needs a vacuum with features like this? Sure, parents with small kids who spill everything. But that's the obvious target market, right? If Butler wanted the obvious, they w-wouldn't be looking at a new agency. They want something fresh. In a world of R-roombas and automated cleaning, why would someone buy this? Why—"

I break off when I glance over at Keegan to see him grinning at me.

"What?"

He smirks. "You're cute when you're brainstorming."

I stick out my tongue at him. "Shut up."

"I'm serious."

"Sure," I snark.

I'm about to get back to glaring at the vacuum—after all, the clock is ticking until DoorDash arrives—when he reaches out and tucks a lock of my mousey brown hair behind my ear.

Awareness of how close we are, lying here on the floor beside one another, hits like a comet. Keegan is my friend. Nothing more.

Still, there are moments when even I can't pretend Keegan isn't stupidly hot.

This is one of those moments. When we're standing, he's more than six inches taller than my five-five and change. The bonus of all those extra inches is that I don't have a reason to gaze longingly into his eyes very often. But in this position, we are dangerously close to soulful-gaze territory. This close, I can distinguish each fleck of blue in his otherwise gray eyes. With a lock of blond hair dangling across his perfect cheekbones? Gah! I have to force myself to look away.

Unfortunately, when I drop my gaze, it lands on his bicep. The way he's propped up on his elbow makes his muscles bunch and his bicep looks huge. Like, strain-the-fabric-of-his-t-shirt huge.

Sure, he works hard, but he doesn't actually bench press kegs for a living, right?

"Hey." Keegan snaps his fingers in front of my face.

I look up to see him grinning.

"Eyes up here, Glasses."

Shit.

He caught me ogling his arms like one of those groupies that hangs out at the bar all the time, hoping he'll notice them.

Keegan and I are too close for me to be embarrassed, so I tease him back.

I reach out a finger and poke his bicep. "What's up with this? When did you get all jacked?"

He jerks back when I poke his arm because, although he hates to admit it, he's crazy ticklish. "Hey, watch it."

He tries to grab my finger in his hand, but I move on from his bicep to his pectorals, poking at his muscles like I'm checking the consistency of rising dough. Except his chest doesn't give at all.

He is one-hundred percent steely, hard muscles.

"Seriously. What's going on here? Have you started taking steroids? Do I need to watch out for 'roid rage?"

Keegan clears his throat.

My gaze snaps to his, surprised to see his pupils dilated. And to realize that I'm no longer poking his muscles like they're rising dough, but trailing my fingers along them as if I'm bewitched by his chest.

Shit.

I snatch my hand back, sitting up into a cross-legged position as if there's nothing weird about stroking my best friend's chest.

Keegan clears his throat again. "Meg, I—"

I hop to my feet, snatching up the offending vacuum, and carting it off. "W-when do you even have time to work out?" I call from the hall as I shove the vacuum into the closet by the stairs.

He makes a huff that sounds annoyed. "It's not like I have anything better to do. Besides, I've been a little frustrated lately."

I glance back to see him lying on his back, one knee bent, the other straight, his forearm draped over his eyes.

He looks relaxed, but there's a kind of tension in his body that indicates he's ... not.

"Your dad giving you a hard time again?"

His father is the CFO of McQuade Development, a local real estate company. He's always badgering Keegan to work for the family business.

Keegan scrubs a hand down his face and stands. He gives me a hard look that makes me think he's working up the courage to say something, but then he sighs. "Something like that."

Before I can ask for more specifics, an alert dings on Keegan's phone and he's heading down the stairs to the entry level of my townhouse.

"The take out is here," he calls out, stating the obvious.

"I'll open the wine," I answer back, trying to keep my voice cheerful and devoid of any incipient awareness of Keegan's undeniable hotness.

But who am I kidding? There's nothing incipient about my awareness of Keegan. I know he's hot. I've always known it. It's just something I try really hard not to think about. If I'm thinking about it now, then the stress from work must really be getting to me.

two

AN HOUR OR SO LATER, we're ensconced on my sofa, nibbling on the last of our dessert. Keegan brought Pocky for dessert. My box is empty, so I reach over and grab one of the chocolate-coated cookie sticks from his open box.

He swats at my hand. "Hands off."

I snag one anyway and he lets me. "It's not like you're going to finish all of them before the end of the movie, anyway."

He pauses the movie and shuffles his half-full box to his left hand so it's farther away. "You don't know that."

"The movie is almost over," I point out, burrowing my toes under his leg. "Y-you don't have time to finish your Pocky."

He pretends to fight me over them, but lets me snag a couple. There are several wonderful things about our decade-long friendship. Obviously, he lets me steal his Pocky (as well as assorted other treats). More importantly, he never makes me feel weird about the stutter I've had since childhood.

11

A stutter? you ask in surprise. *Don't most people grow out of those?*

Yes. Most people do. People whose parents can afford speech therapists. People who are lucky. People whose asshole fathers don't nag them relentlessly about it.

Even with all of those resources, some people just never do grow out of them. And, no, it's not a sign I'm stupid or slow or nervous. And, yes, when people make a big deal out of it, I do feel stupid, slow, and nervous. Which is why I love hanging out with Keegan, because he never makes me feel that way.

Ollie never went out of his way to make me feel insecure about my stutter, but he wasn't a guy who was comfortable with silences. If no one else was talking, he'd fill the gap. Which, in retrospect, should have been a red flag.

"Why are your toes so cold?" Keegan pushes playfully at my legs.

"Because it's winter," I mutter, pulling my throw to my chin and burrowing closer to him.

He laughs. "It's late March. That's not winter."

"Hey, that's winter in some places! And we're having this cold snap!"

"So turn up the heat. It's got to be—what? Sixty-five, sixty-six in here?"

Yes, I keep the heat at 65 in the winter, when I can stand it. A) because it's the environmental thing to do, and B) because my townhouse was built in the early seventies and is an electricity hog. My place is one of four tiny, three-story townhomes snuggled next to each other. Mine is in the middle, which means for most of the winter I can rely on the insulation the other two houses on either side provide. Plus, I have a little wood-burning fireplace. Which I never light, but Keegan does if he's over and it's cold.

This weekend we're having a bit of a cold snap—most likely the last of the spring—and because of its age, my condo feels every temperature swing.

"You know," I tell him. "If you're cold here, w-we could always do movie night at your place."

"Nah." He gives a tug to the blanket, pulling it closer over his side. I follow, burrowing next to him. "Your place is nicer."

"Bullshit." I bonk him over the head with my empty Pocky box.

Thanks to Keegan's trust fund and his family's real estate development, he owns a condo downtown that is, by every definition, nicer than my place.

I have never understood why he likes to hang out here instead of at his place, only that he calls his condo "soulless."

I've tried to remedy the problem by buying him pillows and cozy throws, but he still prefers to hang out at my quirky little townhouse, despite the fact that it's got three floors and too many stairs. Every time Keegan describes my townhouse as "cozy," I accuse him of having a stair fetish.

"If you want it to be warmer, you could start a fire," I suggest gently.

"Shush," he tells me, hitting play on the remote. "Don't talk over the movie."

I roll my eyes, since he's the one who started the conversation with his criticism of my cold toes, but I don't. Instead, I get lost in the movie. I bury my face in his shoulder during the big emotional scene where Tom Allen has to tell the Thermians that he's just an actor, because that part always kills me.

By the time the movie ends, it's so warm and cozy on the sofa, I have trouble summoning the energy to get up.

I need to though, because I have to pee and my wine glass is empty. I just can't make myself. For the first time all day, my toes actually feel warm, so I'm relaxed and sleepy.

Which must be obvious, because Keegan gives my calf a squeeze and says, "Are you falling asleep?" There's humor in his voice.

I free my toes enough to give his thigh a light, playful kick. "No."

"Yes, you were."

"So what if I was?"

He's openly laughing at me now. "It's only 8 o'clock. On a Saturday."

"Not all of us are cool, hip night owls who stay up all night managing bars and hanging out with musicians after."

This is the problem with having a best friend who owns a bar. Our schedules are so diametrically opposed. What's dinner for me is practically breakfast for him. Which is why our "shared" love of cheap wine works. He rarely drinks and probably pours himself a glass just so that I don't feel like I'm drinking alone.

"You know you never sleep well if you fall asleep on the sofa. And I don't wanna be the one listening to you complain about being tired tomorrow morning."

"It's not my fault I'm sleepy. I haven't slept well this week. That's all."

He shifts, turning to face me, as he pulls his leg up onto the sofa next to him and rearranges my feet so that they're in his lap instead of under his leg. Then he takes my feet in his hands and starts massaging my soles. "What's up?"

"Nothing," I say, dodging the question.

It's not nothing, but sometimes I worry Keegan gets bored listening to me talk about work. I don't blame him.

His job is inherently more interesting than mine. His bar is a favorite among the professors and the students alike. It's regularly on the best-of-Austin lists put out by the Austin American Statesman and the Austin Chronicle. Last year, the city asked him to join the Green Business Leaders advisory board.

So when he talks about work, it's one interesting antidote after another.

I work at an ad agency. I love my work—which is creative and challenging—but when I talk about work, it's all about demographic trends, emerging technologies, and metadata. I can't blame him for not being interested.

However, Keegan clearly knows me too well and hears the deflection in my voice, because he asks, "Trouble at work?"

At his prodding, I unapologetically open the can of bitch-fest flavored worms. "You could say that," I say with a sigh. "I've been there for six years now. I've gotten raises on par with my work, but no promotion yet."

He glances up at me, his gaze uncharacteristically dark. "And you want that promotion, don't you?"

"Yeah. Do you blame me? Sometimes, it just feels like I'm spinning my wheels." I love the creative aspect of my job, but success in advertising requires a certain style and confidence I simply don't have. I'm shy and dorky. I'd be at a disadvantage even without the stutter. Ergo, there are natural limitations to my success. "I love working at Forester+Blake. I don't want to work anywhere else, but I want more control over the work I do."

He sighs. "And it's the recognition you want, right?"

"I want more creative control."

Teresa is fantastic, but our visions don't always line up. And when they don't, she gets defensive. If I ran my own creative team, my work could be more innovative and I wouldn't have to fight so hard for the good ideas. Plus, as team leader, I would get a raise.

A raise would be really nice. Preferably one big enough that I won't have to rent out my spare bedroom. It's not that I don't want a roommate. I'm not opposed to other people, in theory, but have you seen the bad roommate subreddit? It's terrifying. I am not equipped to handle a roommate who poops in the shower.

Yes. I know. Not all roommates poop in the shower. They're not feral cats. For that matter, not even all feral cats poop in the shower. My point is, I've been enjoying being on my own since Ollie, and I don't want a roommate if I can avoid it.

He rubs his thumb up the arch of my foot, hitting some pressure point that seems to release all the tension in my shoulders, and I let out a groan.

His mouth quirks up in a little grin of superiority. As if he's proven something by being stupidly good at foot rubs.

"If you keep that up, I might just chain you to the couch and never let y-you leave."

His gaze darkens, and his lips twist into that smug little smirk of his. "Chained to your couch? At least I'll die happy."

Gah. That smirk does unspeakable things to my hormones. It always has. But I've known Keegan long enough to take his teasing banter with a grain of salt. He doesn't mean to blast me with his smolder, he just doesn't know how to turn down the intensity of his charm.

If the visual of him chained up and at my mercy is a little too vivid in my mind, then ... well, that's my own damn fault. Plus, I'm an expert at coyly sidestepping conversations and staying out of the smolder-blast-range.

The key is pretending I didn't even hear the teasing innuendo.

A moment later, I open my eyes to see him looking down at my feet in his lap, concentrating on that as if it's the most important thing he's ever done.

He shifts my feet in his lap and keeps kneading.

"I don't think they appreciate you enough there," Keegan mutters.

This has been the common refrain of our renewed friendship. During The Ollie Years, Keegan and I stayed in contact, but not enough for him to see the highs and lows of my job. Now that we're hanging out every week, there's a lot of under-the-breath muttering on his part.

"Yeah, yeah, yeah." I pull my feet out of his lap. "You trust fund kids don't know what it's like on the mean streets of Austin. Long hours, under-earning. Always one paycheck away from needing to pick up a side hustle with DoorDash."

He grabs one of my feet and holds my ankle, keeping me off balance until I look up at him. His gaze is dark again, but stormy this time. "You wouldn't dare."

I chuckle. "What? Work for DoorDash? I was joking."

He lets my foot go and blows out a breath. "Thank God. I'd never be able to sleep at night knowing you were out delivering food in the middle of the night."

I kick his thigh gently. "You work at a bar. You don't sleep at night, anyway."

"You know what I mean."

"I do. And thank you for caring, but I can take care of myself, thank you very much."

"Oh, I'm well aware." He slants me a look. "But if money's tight, I could always—"

I kick him again. Ever so slightly harder this time.

"Don't finish that sentence. Money isn't tight," I lie, swinging my feet to the ground. "The opposite, in fact. Money is loose. It's practically baggy."

Keegan quirks an eyebrow in a display of overt skepticism.

"I promise. Besides, w-who am I to complain when the eye candy is so good?"

That skeptical eyebrow drops into a scowl. "What eye candy?"

Relieved that I successfully averted his attempts to dig into my finances, I waggle my eyebrows salaciously. "Haven't I mentioned how hot my boss is?"

The scowl deepens. "No. That hasn't come up."

Amused by his reaction, I fluff the details. "Mr. Forester is" —I bring my fingers to my mouth to blow a dramatic chef's kiss— "Very tasty."

"Did you develop some kind of Daddy fetish? Isn't he like sixty?"

I blink, then guffaw with laughter. "Um. No. You're thinking of the original Mr. Forester, the guy who hired me right out of college. Who was fantastic, but not at all a tasty snack." It's a sign of how far Keegan and I drifted apart during the Ollie years that he's this out of the loop on my work life. And then I cringe, because this conversation suddenly seems weird and distasteful. "And he passed away two years ago. The tasty snack is Mr. Reid Forester, who took over as president of the company."

Keegan makes a grumbly, dissatisfied noise. "So, this guy is your boss?"

"Technically, he's my boss's boss's boss. Because Teresa is my boss, and Matt Blake, who is VP of creatives, is her boss. And when Reid took over as president, even though he's younger than Matt, he became Matt's boss. So I think there's enough space in the chain of command that it's okay for me to have a crush on him."

"You have a crush on this guy?"

His tone makes it clear he doesn't approve.

"When did you get to be such a stick in the mud?" I tease. "Is it smart to have a crush on my boss? Probably not. But it's not like anything is ever going to come of it. He probably doesn't even know I exist."

He taps the top of my foot until I look at him, then he says in a serious voice, "Trust me, unless the guy's an idiot, he knows you exist. Just be careful, okay? I don't like the idea of you flirting with this guy. The power dynamic is unbalanced."

I laugh again. "Um ... I don't think that's going to be a problem. You've clearly forgotten how much I suck at flirting."

"You're better at it than you think," he mutters.

Which is just adorable and proof of what a good friend Keegan is, always trying to bolster my self-confidence.

"Don't worry about it. It's a harmless crush. It's no different from the crush I had on you when we first met."

Keegan goes completely still. My feet are still in his lap, wrapped in his hands, but I swear he's so still he's stopped breathing. I look up to see a shocked expression on his face.

"What?" he asks, his lips parted in obvious surprise, and the intensity of his focus on me is unsettling. Something in the incredulity in the syllable sounds like a crack, like some sort of shift in power. Like some scale of balance is upset by my admission.

I'm not entirely sure if my offhand remark about the very-dead, very-over crush was a good or bad idea, but it seems like Keegan knows *exactly* how he feels about it.

three

I NEARLY LAUGH out loud at his expression. "Oh, my gosh. Don't look so horrified. It's not like I still have a crush on you."

"I just ... I didn't ... *What*?"

His confusion finally registers with me. I've *never* seen him at a loss for words. "Wait. You didn't know I had a crush on you?"

He slow blinks and then says, "You had a crush on me?"

"Yeah, I did. I mean, look at you." I gesture at him. "You're stupidly hot. And, annoyingly, stupidly kind and smart, too. You're like a crush equivalent of a triple threat. I thought my crush was pretty obvious."

"It wasn't."

He still looks so stunned it's all I can do not to laugh.

"Didn't you wonder why I was nervous around you all the time? Why I could barely talk to you?"

"You have a stutter. I just assumed that's what you were like. And you were shy." Keegan's gaze is roaming my face, looking at me like he hasn't seen me in years.

Something about it makes me uncomfortable, so I stand

20

and start gathering the remains of our takeout and bringing them into the kitchen.

"Yeah, sure, but I was also extra shy and stuttered even more than usual, *because* I had a crush on you." I scrape the dregs of our food into the countertop composter before loading the dishes into the sink and rinsing off the takeout containers. All to avoid having to look at him. I give another laugh, trying to make light of how awkward this conversation is, but this laugh sounds forced. "I can't believe y-you didn't know that."

"Why didn't you say anything?" His voice sounds suddenly serious.

I shake the water off the takeout containers and turn to drop them in the recycle bin, then rinse off my hands. Done with that task, I have no choice but to turn and look at him as I dry my hands off. "What should I have said? We were friends. And you're a good guy. Anything I would've said just would've made it weird. You obviously weren't into me and way out of my league anyway and—"

"I'm not out of your league." His tone is unexpectedly harsh. "If anything, the opposite is true."

"Pul-ease." Again, I keep my tone light. Keegan lavishes praise on all of his friends, so of course he's going to say that. "Keegan, be serious. You're gorgeous and rich. I was shy and dorky and nervous all the time. Obviously, you were out of my league."

He rounds the kitchen island to stand in front of me, cupping my shoulders with his hands. "Meg, you are smart, beautiful, and ambitious. *No one* is out of your league."

I wave aside the compliment, taking it for what it is. "Of course you think that. You see me through best-friend-colored-glasses."

Yes, I'm smart. And yes, I'm ambitious. My brains are

just the product of lucky genetics. My ambition is purely the result of growing up lower middle class, the third daughter of a single mom. But I am not beautiful. Not by society's standards, at least. I'm too curvy, with more extra padding than it is acceptable. No, I'm not a troll, but between my glasses, my stutter, and my general reserve, I've always just blended into the background. Mousey Meg.

And it's okay. I don't mind blending into the background. I don't particularly like being the center of attention, anyway.

Right now, for example, with Keegan focusing all of his attention on me, I feel … jittery. Like that time my chiropractor used a TENS unit on my back and slowly increased the electric current buzzing through my muscles.

Afraid I might actually die of electrocution if he keeps looking at me like this, I pull away.

"Best-friend-colored-glasses? What's that supposed to mean?"

"You know what I mean."

"Maybe you better explain it to me."

"You've essentially microdosed my presence long enough that you don't see my weirdness."

"I don't even know what that means, Meg."

"You're not exactly objective, are you? I'm like a homeless puppy you started feeding a decade ago, and now you can't get rid of me."

He rolls his eyes like I'm being ridiculous. "That isn't true."

"Don't get me wrong. I appreciate it. I love that you always have my back. And some day, when I'm ready for a real post-Ollie relationship, you will be the first person I call to give me a pep talk so I can work up the courage to get back into the dating pool."

Keegan makes a noise of either disbelief or frustration, and I can't quite tell which.

I turn to see him leaning against the island, his legs stretched out in front of him, his arms crossed over his chest in a way that shows off his biceps and his chest muscles.

Not for the first time, I wonder when he finds time to work out.

But I push the thought aside, because he's still just looking at me, something in his expression that I can't read but that rackets up my concerns about my potential electrocution.

After a long moment, he pushes away from the counter and walks over to me, his eyes still searching my face. Something in his expression makes me feel nauseated. It's that jumbled feeling you get in your tummy when you're on a roller coaster and it's about to reach the crest of the first big climb.

Which makes sense, I guess, given that I just admitted out loud for the first time that I used to have a crush on him. This is the roller coaster of untold secrets. The big drop is fraught with awkwardness. I know how this story ends because I've imagined it too many times.

He's not attracted to me and never has been. I don't need to hear him say it aloud. No, I can't stand to hear him say it. To hear the pity in his voice.

I hate being the object of pity. As someone who's stuttered my whole life, I've had more than my fair share of pity and it's the fucking worst.

So, yeah, this story ends with him feeling shitty and me resenting him.

How could we recover from that?

Short answer: we wouldn't.

I just can't let him say the words out loud.

When he stops in front of me, I blurt the first thing that comes to mind.

"Well, I guess you need to be going, huh?"

He gives me another one of those slow blinks, which makes me think I've made things worse.

So I just start babbling. "You need to get to work since it's Saturday night, and who knows what traffic will be like! Austin traffic is the worst. I swear it gets w-worse every day. Can you imagine how bad it will be in ten years? But maybe we'll have flying cars or something by then."

Keegan lets out a huff of laughter, his mouth quirking in that half smile of his.

Gah.

That crooked smile used to make me crazy. Back when I had a crush on him.

Thank god I'm past that. And at least he's chuckling now, instead of looking at me in the slow, steady way that I find so unnerving.

"Actually, I'm not working tonight. Roxy is handling the bar tonight."

"Oh." Roxy is his assistant manager. Sassy, smart, and super outgoing, she is the perfect person to manage the bar when Keegan isn't there. But I'm still surprised he's not going in. "What's up?"

He shoves a hand through his dirty blond hair. "I've been summoned to brunch with the family."

"Ah ..." I murmur noncommittally, because voicing my opinions about his family isn't particularly helpful.

My family is difficult too, so I know the unspoken rule of the shitty-family-support-network. You're allowed to complain about your own shitty-family, but you're not allowed to criticize anyone else's.

"I'm sorry," I tell him.

He quirks his eyebrow at me. "You could always come with me as backup."

"Um ... No way. Pretty sure your grandfather would have me tossed out by the management like the street urchin he undoubtedly imagines I am."

"I don't think he pictures you as a street urchin."

"Well, maybe not. But that doesn't mean he wants me swimming around in his pools of money either."

"Do you think my grandfather is Scrooge McDuck?"

"Maybe," I admit.

"He's not that bad," Keegan tells me, but I'm not sure if he's saying it to reassure me or himself.

I feel my resolve wavering. "I can come with you if you need me to. It might take all my courage, but I will brave Scrooge McDuck."

He laughs. "Nah. I got this."

I know he *has this*. I also know his dad is a dick and that tomorrow will be full of lectures about how he's not "living up to his potential" and should "stop messing around with that bar."

Just thinking about his family gets me riled up. I'm torn between wanting to punch someone (his father, obviously) and wanting to just hug Keegan.

So, naturally, I fluff the pillow to release my excess energy.

I give the pillow a couple of shakes to fluff it, then carefully place it in the corner on the sofa before giving it a whack on top to artfully dent it.

When I straighten, I see Keegan barely concealing a grin behind his hand.

"What?" I ask.

"I think you killed it, Glasses."

I look from him to the pillow and then back again. "What? I fluffed it."

"You karate chopped it. You're like Miss Piggy."

"No. I'm not. Besides, I'm pretty sure it's Ms. Piggy. And if it's not, then it should be, because Piggy is a feminist icon. I would be lucky to be Ms. Piggy."

"What did that pillow ever do to you anyway?" he asked, shooting me a thoughtful look. "Or were you imagining the pillow was my father?"

"Maybe." I make a show of walking away, then swing back dramatically to deliver a karate chop worth of the pig herself, yelling, "Hi-ya!" Then I straighten, nodding. "Yeah, that time I definitely imagined it was your father."

"He's not nearly as bad as you think," Keegan says, even though he's trying to repress his smile.

"Maybe not. I'm allowed to be unreservedly on your side on this."

He's openly laughing now. "What would I do without you, Glasses?"

I beam up at him. "Lucky for you, you'll never have to find out."

A few minutes later, Keegan heads out, and I'm left alone with my thoughts.

My mind trips back to that moment when I was so sure he was going to apologize for not wanting me the way I had once wanted him and I breathe a sigh of relief that he didn't get the chance. I cut him off at the pass. We averted disaster.

He will never have to feel bad for not wanting me. And I will never have to worry about losing my best friend.

I do, however, still have to worry about the pitch meeting on Tuesday, so I pull the vacuum out of the hall closet and resume my show down with it.

My gut tells me that this pitch is a tipping point in my career. If I can nail it, everything will change. I'll finally be team leader and solidify my position at the company.

27

four

UNREQUITED LOVE IS for foolish girls.

I am not foolish or a girl. I am an intelligent, well-educated, grown-ass woman. Ergo, whatever I'm feeling right now is not unrequited love, despite Keegan's fears that I am *in over my head*.

I refuse to be one of those silly girls who pines for some guy who is out of her league. I learned my lesson about that a long time ago.

Moreover, I'm not foolish. I have a degree from one of the best advertising programs in the country. I graduated magna cum laude, for Pete's sake.

I'm not silly. Okay, I'm a little silly.

My point is, I'm twenty-eight. I'm a competent, adult woman. I'm a homeowner. Buying my townhouse put me in crippling debt, but it's mine. It's close to downtown, and it's within biking distance of a Trader Joes. Basically, it's perfect. Not to mention, I saved enough for a down payment in this economy, despite the fact that Ollie rarely paid his half the rent. That shows how very mature I am, right?

That is how I know what I'm feeling right now isn't unrequited love.

Because no mature, competent, responsible woman falls into unrequited love with her boss. Her younger boss.

Just to be clear here, Reid Forester—the hot, twenty-six-year old son of my former boss, Jonathon Forester—is super hot.

But if I've learned anything from my friendship with Keegan, it's that there's no point in pining after some hot, unattainable guy I can't have.

If my life was a novel, the title would be: *Meg and the Unattainable, Unfortunately Attractive Guy*. Possible subtitles could include: "A brief history full of heartbreak," and "How to get your dream guy to notice you but still not fall in love with you," or possibly, "Is it still celibacy if you're masturbating?"

My point is, I know what I feel for Reid is pure fantasy.

But what am I supposed to do? I work at an ad agency. My imagination is my stock in trade. My imagination literally pays the bills. If I don't give my imagination free rein at least some of the time, it might break or stop working or ... whatever happens when creative people lose their mojo.

You know what happens to people at ad agencies who don't have good ideas anymore? They lose their jobs. Then, they go into debt and eventually lose their townhomes that they can barely afford as it is. After that, their credit sucks, and they have to move to the suburbs where they have to drive to a Whole Foods. It's all downhill from there.

My point is, fantasizing is a very important part of my creative process. Especially on a day like today, when we have a meeting with all the uppity-ups to pitch our idea for Butler.

The idea that is *still* absolute shite.

So instead of sitting at my desk and trying to polish the shite into a pearl, I go meditate.

Our office has a series of meditation rooms set aside for employees to use. Tad, the youngest member of the three-person team I work on, uses the rooms to nap off hangovers. Teresa, the team lead, actually meditates. I use my reserved time to fantasize. Not because I'm a perv who can't make it through the day without fantasizing ... but because it's good for my creativity. I get all my best ideas when I'm fantasizing. Plus, it's a documented fact that the theta brain waves you experience when dreaming are the source of creativity.

Okay, so, I can't point you to the actual documentation for that, but I'm sure I read it somewhere.

Frankly, I'm hoping those theta brainwaves will kick in and inspiration will hit.

Also, I need to clear my head. I'm still feeling unsettled by what happened Saturday evening with Keegan.

I settle into an easy cross-legged pose in the dimly lit meditation room and try to let my mind drift, but moments from Saturday evening creep back in ... Keegan stretched out on the floor next to me, facing me and propped up on his elbow ... my feet in his lap as we watched the movie ... his expression when I admitted I used to have a crush on him ... the sheer ... what?

What was his expression?

Confusion? Yes. Definitely. But not just confusion. There was something else there as well, and it's driving me crazy that I can't tease it out.

I'm not great at reading people's emotions. Probably because I spend so much time in my own head. Even with the people I'm closest to, I have to consciously queue up my thoughts and words. That means that sometimes I miss things.

Which is how I feel about Saturday night. Like I got distracted and missed something important, and my creative mojo has been off ever since.

Surely I'll get a great idea for the ad if I just let my mind wander a bit. I try to think about how broad Reid's shoulders looked this morning. I try to picture him stalking across a field in the early morning mist, wearing a greatcoat, a la Mr. Darcy. I even try to imagine him wielding a lightsaber, dressed in black, like Kylo Ren.

But my mind won't settle. It just keeps coming back to my best friend, lying on the floor beside me in a show of solidarity, trying to help with my work, even though it's got to be boring AF to him. Trying to help, even though he hates floors, because ...

The idea hits—fully formed—like it's downloaded into my brain directly from the creative ether. My eyes pop open.

I stumble to my feet, heart pounding, only to stand there in the center of the small room, looking around frantically for a moment, until my gaze lands on my drawing tablet.

Thank God I brought it in with me.

I grab the pad and then sink back to the floor as I flip it open and slide the stylus out. I start sketching as soon as a blank page loads. It's all short lines and imperfect angles. The roughest of sketches as I chase the images down and force them onto the screen.

Twenty frantic minutes of drawing later, and I have enough of it down that I can show it to Teresa.

When she's not at her desk, I check the break room first. Eventually, I find her in the conference room where our meeting will be. It doesn't start for another twenty minutes, but I'm not surprised she's already there, getting her laptop hooked up to the projector. That's Teresa in a nutshell. Always prepared. Always one step ahead.

And I know she wants the Butler account as badly as I do. We aren't the only team who is pitching ideas today, but she and I both know we're the best team.

She glances up when I enter. "Good. You're here. I was afraid I was going to have to go pry you out of one of those meditation rooms."

Forester+Blake is respectful of the creative process. I could spend all day in a meditation room and Matt, the VP of creatives, wouldn't say a word about it. Teresa, on the other hand, likes Tad and I to "be present" so we can function smoothly as a team. Which sometimes feels like code for "be available for me to boss around, even though I'm not technically your boss."

"Meg, can you go sit in the back of the room and make sure the lighting is right on these slides?"

"Sure. But first, can I sh-sh-show you this new idea?"

"Can it wait?" She doesn't even look up.

Why does she always blow people off like this? It's like whatever's going on in Teresa-world is somehow more important than the rest of us. But I need for her to hear me out before this pitch, so I try again.

I smooth my ruffled feathers and try again gently.

"It's for the Butler pitch." I offer, perhaps a little too timidly.

This time she arches an eyebrow. "The Butler pitch is in five minutes."

I look down at my watch. "Fifteen." I hold out my tablet to her. "And you and I both know what we have isn't good enough."

Teresa's gaze flickers over the image dismissively, and then she rolls her eyes. "Seriously, Meg? Now? Even if this brainstorm of yours is better than what we've been working on, we don't have time to rework the pitch."

"Just hear me out." I pause, queue my thoughts, and measure my words. "We're not pitching to Butler until Monday. That's plenty of time to rework the final pitch. Besides, w-w-what we've got now is hackneyed. Y-you said so yourself yesterday. Frazzled mom steam-cleaning? That's been done. This new idea is s-s—"

"Is sexy. Yes, I know. Meg, all your ideas are sexy, but we're pitching an ad for a steam cleaner. I just don't see how that can be sexy."

"Just look at it. Please."

Teresa sighs, but takes the tablet from me. "I'll glance through it."

A few minutes later, while we're waiting for upper management to show up—i.e. Reid, Matt, and Pete, Teresa's boss—I watch as Teresa flips through the sketches I made just a few minutes ago. Yeah, they're a little primitive, a little rough, but they're good.

I hold a breath as Teresa studies the last sketch. I know I have her when I hear her chuckle.

"W-w-well?" I lower myself to the chair beside Teresa and scoot it up to the conference table.

Teresa narrows her gaze to a playful glare, like she's annoyed with me because she likes it. "You know it's good. You wouldn't have brought it in otherwise."

"But?"

"*But*, we present in—" She glances at her watch, "—less than five minutes. I won't pull a fully developed pitch for a couple of sketches. What we have is solid, too."

What we have has been done a thousand times. "But—"

"No." Teresa flips over the cover of my tablet, putting it to sleep. "Look, Meg, it's my decision to make. When you're leading your own team, then you can decide."

I nearly groan in frustration. It always comes back to that: Teresa's the team leader. If I want more responsibility and more control, I have to show Matt that I'm ready for it.

And this is what I've been working my ass off for. It would be more money and more responsibility. More money would be great, obviously—and I'm not afraid of more responsibility—but what excites me is the additional creative freedom I'd have. I'd have the control to create amazing campaigns without having to fight so hard to push the envelope.

What terrifies me is giving presentations.

How can I accept a position as team leader when every time I open my mouth, my fear of stuttering cripples me into mute silence?

But this is exactly why I've been working with a speech therapist for the past year. When I was a kid, my single mom didn't have the extra money for it, but I do. I scrimp and save to fit it into my budget—which is already tight— but I make it work.

My speech therapist assures me I'll be ready to lead presentations soon. Until then, I can bide my time.

It's not even just my job that's at risk here. If I fumble a presentation, an important one, the company could lose a client. I love working here. This company has become a second home. I can't risk the good of the company just because I want more freedom to play with my ideas. I'm not ready to lead my own team yet.

All these thoughts are swirling around as I waffle between just letting this idea go, or pushing for it.

I should fight for this idea. Especially since I know I'm right. "Teresa, w-w-we—"

But—once again—Teresa doesn't let me finish. "What we show Reid and Matt today has to be flawless." There's a sort of pleading desperation in her eyes. "You know how important this presentation is, right?"

"Well, yeah." But even as I say it, I'm questioning myself. Do I really know? Teresa has her shit together in a way I don't. Sometimes I get so lost in my head that I don't pay attention to company politics and the dynamic in the office. She does. "Is there something else going on?"

Teresa lowers her voice. "Forester+Blake has lost three accounts in the past six months. You know what this industry is like. If we don't have clients, people get laid off. It's that simple."

Shit. She's right.

This industry can be brutal. Companies, even ones as solid and Forester+Blake, always have to hustle. And if a company isn't bringing in new clients, people get laid off.

"Okay, th-then—" I draw in a shaky breath "—that's all the more reason to show Reid and Matt my new idea. It's much bet—"

"No. And that's my final word."

I'm still reeling from that new information when the door to the conference room swings open, and Matt and Reid enter. Teresa does the thing she always does at meetings with the uppity ups, where she makes a round of introductions.

I've never known if she does this to remind them that she's the team leader or if she's circumventing the potential embarrassment if they don't remember our names.

Matt, one of the company founders, always looks amused when she does this. Reid, always the stoic, keeps his expression blank as he's introduced to me for what has to be the thirty-seventh time and I can't help but wonder if he remembers me from one meeting to the next or if he needs these introductions because I'm just one of nearly a hundred employees.

But then his gaze slides past mine. He's nodding and smiling to the other people in the room—that little half-smile of his, which always seems both confident and wry—and it's once again like I'm not even there.

I try not to stew over it. Thankfully, I never talk much at these meetings. Tad starts the meeting off, running through the initial research we did about the company and the success of past ad campaigns. When he finishes his bit, he sits down.

Matt leans forward. "We're looking forward to seeing what you've come up with. I talked to the people at Butler just this morning and assured them you're our most creative team."

Teresa smiles smugly. "Of course we are."

Matt rocks back in his chair with a laugh. "They just don't want to see another pitch about grape juice."

Teresa doesn't even blanch. Without even an instant of hesitation, she snaps the laptop closed and reaches for my tablet.

"We've got just what they're looking for."

I sit there, dumbfounded, as Teresa seamlessly switches tracks and pulls up my idea.

Well, shit.

I should be happy that my ideas will get to see the light of day, and I am. But I also feel a familiar burst of panic, which is what I always feel when people look at my work.

Of course, no intelligent person would look at the sketches and jump straight to the conclusion that I have elaborate fantasies about my boss. I am a mousy, plain, middle-aged woman. (Okay, twenty-eight isn't middle-aged. But I will be some day, and I've always *felt* decades older than most of my peers.) There is nothing about me that screams has-an-active-fantasy-life. That's the way I like it.

Isn't it?

A few minutes into the pitch, I hazard a glance in Matt's direction. He's smiling and nodding his head, pleased with the ad idea, just as I'd known he would be. A moment later, Audrey knocks on the door and enters the room.

She hands Teresa a message, then scurries away. Everyone in the room sits up a little straighter while we watch Teresa read the message. Audrey wouldn't have interrupted the meeting if it wasn't important.

Teresa skims the note, her face going white. Then she folds it neatly in half, no doubt trying to appear calm. For the first time in the years I've known her, Teresa's professional facade slips as she excuses herself from the meeting and accepts Matt's reassurances that we can continue without her.

Almost as an afterthought, she turns to me and asks, "You can finish up here?"

"Of course," I say, but I doubt Teresa even hears me. It doesn't matter either way. I can do this. I *know* I can.

I push myself to my feet and cross to the front of the room, everyone watching me.

Not just Matt and Reid, but also the three people on the secondary team. People I barely know. They're all watching me. Waiting.

Okay. I can do this.

Just finish the presentation.

I try to imagine my speech therapist's soothing voice encouraging me. All I have to do is take a deep breath, imagine myself speaking, and then say the words out loud.

"As y-y-y—" But the words clog my throat like trees caught in a logjam. I open my mouth to try again. "As y-y-y—"

Okay, Meg, I tell myself. *You've got this. Just a few short sentences. Just wrap it up.*

This time, when I open my mouth, not even one word passes my lips. The logs caught, piling one upon another.

And then I make the mistake of looking at the people around the table and whatever words I might have spoken finally splinter under the pressure.

I snap my mouth shut as failure closes like a fist around my heart.

I tear my gaze away from my drawing to find Matt has stood and crossed to my side. He places a comforting hand on my shoulder. "Don't worry. I think we've seen enough to approve the ad. It's good work."

Reid nods. His smile is kind. Patient and supportive. "Excellent work."

Supportive patience is the *worst.*

Humiliation burns through me as I watch them leave.

They loved the idea. I know this is a win, even if I bungled the bit where I was supposed to talk.

Still, I have a big knot of ick in my stomach.

This is what I hate the most: the pity. I hate how awkward people feel when I can't get words out. And I hate that all the work I've done lately hasn't helped me when I need it most.

I set aside my embarrassment. No matter how the meeting ended, it was still a win.

They liked the idea. My idea. The team at Butler will love it, too. I know they will. I can feel it in my gut.

I gather my things and leave the conference room. Once I'm back at my desk, I notice Teresa called and left a message on my cell asking me to call her back.

"What happened?" I ask soon as she picks up. I know it must be something big, because she wouldn't have left mid-meeting otherwise.

"It's Noah. The school nurse called. She thinks it's appendicitis."

"Oh, no!"

"She assured me it's probably not that big a deal, but she still wants me to take him straight to the doctor. He'll probably be fine. It's just—"

It's just that Noah is Teresa's only child, and since her divorce three years ago, any time Noah gets sick, the burden of caring for him rests solely on Teresa's shoulders.

"You don't have to explain," I reassure her.

"Thanks." Teresa draws in a shaky breath and when she starts talking again, she's erased the emotion from her voice. "Tell me how it went. They loved it, right?"

"I m-made a fool of myself, but they loved it." As business-like as she sounds, surely even she isn't this blasé about it. "What about you? Will you be okay?"

"If he has to have it removed, it'll be his first surgery. And I'll have to miss work. After we get off the phone, I'll need to talk with Audrey to see if Matt can do the Butler presentation."

"I'll do the presentation," I tell her.

The words are out of my mouth before I can second guess myself.

I don't even stutter once when I say it. Teresa must be

too worried about Noah to question me, because I'm sure that normally she would.

After we hang up, I stop by Audrey's desk and chat with her for a few minutes, explaining Teresa's situation. As always, Audrey's pert efficiency makes me a little nervous, which means my stutter gets worse talking to her.

Audrey dresses like an extra from The Queen's Gambit. She's pretty, stylish, and effortlessly cool in a way I have never been. Like, never, ever. It's doubly awful because we're the same age, and I somehow look a decade older than her.

Though she's friendly enough, I always feel even more dumpy when I talk to her.

On the other hand, Matt's presence is so comforting, I have to resist the temptation to put out cookies and milk for him like he's Santa Claus. Despite that, I have to tap down my anxiety as I tell him I'm planning on doing the Butler presentation myself.

He gives me a long, piercing look, and then nods, clearly pleased.

"Good. You'll do a great job. And you should be the one to present your own work."

"It's the team's work," I say.

He arches an eyebrow. "Those were your drawings, weren't they?"

"Yes, but I'm the artist on the team. I always do the concept sketches."

He chuckles. "Nice try, but I know a Meg Demeo idea when I see one."

I can feel myself blushing because I know what he means. My ideas are always the sexy ones.

And, yeah, it makes me uncomfortable that he knows that. The world expects hip, sexy ideas to come from women who look like Teresa or Audrey, not chubby, frumpy women who look like me.

I'm twenty-eight going on seventy-three. I'm a cat and some bifocals away from being a crazy cat lady. It's one thing to let Teresa pitch my ideas to a company. It's another thing entirely to do it myself.

But if Teresa can't do it, I need to step up. I can't rely on her to pitch my ideas forever. It's my time to shine—I mean, I hate that it's because Teresa's kid is sick, of course, but this is a perfect opportunity for me to prove myself. To show the company what I can do on my own. And to push myself creatively.

Right before I leave, Matt says, "I'll come along as backup. Just in case you need it."

Oh, God. How embarrassing would it be if Matt has to jump in and save me?

I can't let that happen. Which means I'm going to need help. The kind of help I can't get from Matt or Tad. I need girl squad help.

five

I TRY to buckle down and get work done after the meeting, but by three o'clock, even I'm willing to admit that the afternoon is a wash. I spend most of the time fleshing out the drawings I did for the Butler pitch, but I can tell it feels off. To make matters worse, Tad badgers me with offers to help prep me for the meeting. I manage not to snap at him, but just barely.

So at three, I log out of my office computer, pack up my tote bag, and head out. I text my friend Reb, who works for a gaming company up on the twenty-sixth floor. Reb and I met a couple of years ago and even though we have nothing in common other than we're both women in our twenties who happen to work in this building, we became good friends.

I'm clocking out early. Want to grab a drink downstairs?

Honeybun, I only got in two hours ago

And unless you want to come down here and explain to a mob of barely post-adolescent game designers that boob plate armor is stupid and potentially dangerous, I am stuck in this meeting for the foreseeable future.

Do I want to know what boob plate armor is?

No.

No, you do not.

Trust me on this

How did the pitch meeting go?

Great. I got a last-minute stroke of genius and saved the day.

And now they want me to give the presentation to Butler

That's amazing!

A confetti gif comes through next.

We'll celebrate later

We should go shopping this weekend so you can buy something badass to wear!

Will it have boob armor?

Def not

Back to the boob-armor-debate trenches for me

I shoot back the "Run Away" gif from Monty Python.

With Reb out of commission, I head down to the parking garage and drop my bag off in the trunk of my car. Then I walk to the French bakery a block over, where I buy a dozen macarons and add in banana nut muffins at the last minute because that seems healthier.

One of the best things about my office is that it's only a couple of blocks from Keegan's condo. Now that we're hanging out more, we both have apps that allow us to track one another, something Keegan insisted on now that I walk over to his place sometimes after work. *For my safety.* Insert eye roll here.

It seemed ridiculous at the time, but I've gotten used to being able to check and see if he's at home. According to the app, he's not at home, but it looks like he's stuck in traffic a few blocks away. So I walk over to his place, texting him as I go. He tells me he's on his way home and that I should let myself in. Keegan and I have had keys to one another's various residences ever since we shared an apartment in college. It annoyed the shit out of Ollie.

Even though I regularly come home to find Keegan stretched out on my sofa watching TV, I'm not quite comfortable enough to let myself into his place. So I ride the elevator up to the twelfth floor, where I make myself comfortable on the sofa in the small common area outside the elevator. I'm scrolling through Instagram, mindlessly eating one of the macarons, my box of pastries on my lap, when the elevator doors open.

I glance up to see Keegan stepping out of the elevator along with his neighbor, Selah. Selah is a cross between a Nordic runway model and a Southern belle. She's thin, gorgeous, and blesses my heart every time we run into each other.

Today she's got both of her hands wrapped around Keegan's bicep, and she's laughing up at him like they're auditioning for a Cialis commercial. They look so good together. It makes my stomach churn.

Not that my stomach gets to have an opinion on their combined beauty and perfection. I probably just ate too many macarons.

When Selah sees me, she flashes me a fake smile. "Keegan, someone left a package on your doorstep."

His steps slow when he sees me and he pries Selah's hands off his arm.

I refuse to acknowledge her jab and focus on Keegan. Paying people like her any attention is a waste of time. I stand, tucking my phone into my back pocket.

"Hey, Glasses," Keegan says, walking over to me.

There's something different in the way he's looking at me as his long legs eat up the distance between us. I shiver in response and mentally chide my body, something I've had to do hundreds of times over the years. You can't have a best friend like Keegan and not have physical reactions to his hotness periodically.

I blurt, "I brought macarons."

I'm immediately annoyed with myself for feeling like I have to explain why I'm visiting my best friend.

But before I can say anything else, Keegan takes the box of cookies in one hand and reaches up to thread his other hand into the hair at the base of my neck.

What the ...

And then his lips are on mine, and he's kissing me.

Keegan is kissing me.

Holy shit.

Keegan. Is kissing. Me.

My mind stutters to a halt as I get lost in the sensation of his lips moving over mine.

The hand holding the box of cookies snakes around my back, pulling me closer. Instinctively, I rise up on my toes, plastering my body to his, and he's all hard lines against my softness. My fingers grip the fabric of his shirt, and he growls in response. GROWLS!

Now my panties are drenched, and I may or may not be trying to figure out a way to climb his body. He angles my head to deepen the kiss, his tongue moving against my lips, tracing the seam of my mouth and sending a flurry of sensations dancing along my skin. I whimper.

Confused, I tamp down my response. I don't understand what's going on here and until I do, I don't dare let myself enjoy it.

Then there's a loud, obvious throat clearing from behind us.

I barely register it, but Keegan pulls back from me. Still holding me against him, his gaze on my face, he gives me the sweetest smile. My heart—my poor heart doesn't even know what to do with that smile.

"This is a treat. I didn't know if I'd see you today after Saturday night," he says.

He says *Saturday night* in a way that implies something way more salacious than a movie and take out. Which is weird. Though—obviously—not the weirdest part of this interaction.

I try to roll with it and say something that doesn't make me sound as frazzled as I feel

"Sorry if I taste like cookies."

Keegan's gaze darkens as it lingers on my lips. "You taste perfect."

Gah. How does he do that? How does he turn the

smolder on so effortlessly? Is it just genetic luck or did he take some kind of workshop?

I clear my throat. "I brought m-m-macarons," I stumble, wishing I had access to a smolder of my own I could whip out.

His lips twitch into one of those half smiles of his. "You didn't have to do that."

Behind him, there's another throat clearing. This time louder.

Keegan extracts his hand from my hair, slowly, like he's mesmerized by the texture of each lock. Then he turns to face Selah, keeping his other arm behind me and tucking me against his side, even though he's still holding the box of macarons.

"Oh," he says to Selah, as if he just now remembered she was here. "Did you need something?"

"I ..." she trails off, her gaze flickering from me to Keegan as if the sight of us together has fractured her understanding of the universe.

"You were saying something about a restaurant opening?"

The question is clearly aimed at her, but as he asks it, he nuzzles his nose into my hair at my temple, giving the unmistakable impression that he can't stop touching me long enough to talk to her.

Selah takes a step back, her cheeks flushing. "Um, no. I just ..." She lets out an annoyed huff of air. "Well, I guess I'll see you two around. Or not."

She turns and walks off down the hall, her long legs carrying her around the corner and out of sight.

Keegan keeps his arm around me as he walks to his door, then drops it as he unlocks his door and holds it open for me. Mind still reeling, I follow him in.

Once the door is closed, he leans against it and lets out a groan of relief.

"Thank you for that."

"For the cookies?" I ask … still sounding stupid. Still *feeling* stupid. Because what in the name of all that's holy just happened?

"For letting me kiss you." He pushes away from the door and walks over to the island counter separating his kitchen from the living area and sets the box down.

He's so casual and unaffected. Because of course he is. Meanwhile, I'm a confused, emotional, horny mess.

"Every time I've come home in the past month, I've run into Selah in the lobby. She keeps mentioning events she's going to and restaurants she wants to try. I'm exhausted from trying to come up with reasons to say no."

"That's why you kissed me," I say numbly, the puzzle pieces falling into place.

He opens the box and pulls out two macarons, holding one out to me. His gaze roams my face, like he's searching for something. Some hint of … I don't know what.

Then he flashes me a smile that's all smug arrogance. "Yeah. Sorry to pounce on you like that."

I'm sure he intends that smile to be just a normal friendly smile, but those lips were on mine just a few minutes ago, and I feel the effect of that smile all the way to my core.

I step closer and accept the macaron he's holding, trying to wrap my brain around the fact that Keegan kissed me. That it was possibly the best, most mind-blowing kiss of my life, and it was just for show. Not that I have a lot of experience with mind-blowing kisses, but still.

"A little heads up before having to channel my inner coquette would've been nice."

His eyebrow raises, "Inner coquette?"

"You know, the part inside of you that's flirty and attractive and you know ..." I feel myself start to color. I'm honestly talking to Keegan, of all people, about being a coquette. About being attractive or like ... sexual. On any level. My neck is becoming so hot I'm pretty sure it could fry an egg.

Mission abort.

Mission abort.

I clear my throat, trying again. "I mean, the coquette Meg is largely invisible and practically nonexistent, as you know. Due to how bad I am at the flirting." I force a chuckle. "But if I know it's coming, maybe I can be prepared. Maybe workshop some ideas for banter first."

He laughs. "You're thinking too much."

"That's me. Overthinking things is my superpower. But I can pull up a shred of flirtiness to help in a pinch. Like quarterly or something."

"So you're saying you have a quarterly sexy allotment I can access?"

I nod brightly, doing my best to shove away the very clear and sensual and x-rated images flooding my head of what Keegan *accessing* me would look like. "Anything for a friend!"

Then I realize how that sounds, and I shove the entire macaron in my mouth before I can say anything else stupid.

Just kill me now.

Keegan gives me another long look, his smile deepening.

As if he knows exactly how flustered I feel right now. Which sucks.

Because, yeah, I'm flustered. My unfortunately hot best friend kissed me and now I ... I have feelings about that.

Exactly what those feelings mean, I don't know. But I definitely have feelings. Which is possibly the most annoying thing ever, because I did not work for years to bury the crush I had on him, only to have it rear its ugly head now.

Even worse (or at least just as bad), my flustered-ness seems to amuse him.

That's me, the comic relief.

That's obviously all I'm fit for. Comic relief and fake kisses to throw avaricious runway models off his track.

"You know," he says as he rounds the island and flicks on his fancy coffee maker. "You could use your key to let yourself in. I wouldn't have given you a key if I didn't expect you to use it."

He is right, of course. He tells me that all the time. However, I would never just let myself in.

Keegan and I have been friends since college, when we both lived in the shittiest co-op in Austin, possibly the world. It was near the UT campus and cheap, but it was basically built of roaches and hepatitis held together with mold and cobwebs.

After a semester there, Keegan suggested we move out and share an apartment. I didn't learn until after we'd moved in together that he had a trust fund, and the only reason he'd lived in the shitty co-op was because it pissed off his father.

I couldn't imagine living in that pit for any reason other than financial desperation.

To this day, I'm convinced there are only three reasons we're friends: A) I am one of the few people who became his friend without knowing his net worth, B) our shared love of sci-fi TV (basically anything from Star Trek TNG to Firefly), and C) pity.

I mean, I mentioned that I was poor and living in a pit

when we met, right? Basically, our freshman year in the co-op he adopted me like some sort of stray dog and he's simply too kind hearted to kick me to the curb.

Not that he would admit to being kind-hearted, or that I'm his pity friend. Everyone else in his family views kindness and empathy as signs of weakness. Even though he devoted his adult life to being a thorn in their side and their reputation, there are some lessons you can't shake off.

Which means there might be a fourth reason we're friends: D) I don't harbor any expectations that he will "outgrow his blatant disrespect for the family name and reputation and join the family business," and also, E) his family doesn't like me, so his hanging out with me irritates them.

The point is, I learned a lot about Keegan during the years we shared an apartment. Including knowing that letting myself into his place on a random afternoon might not end well.

I'm certainly not going to judge Keegan or any woman he picks up for doing whatever they want to do in the privacy of his bedroom. I just don't want to know about it.

I don't want to know about it. I don't want to care about it. I certainly don't want to have feelings about it.

So I ignore his comment about using the key and ask, "How was brunch with the family?"

"Promises of wealth and power. The guarantee that I can create my position at the company. Mostly the same stuff as always."

"Mostly?" I ask.

Ever since I've known him, Keegan has been summoned to family brunch on at least a quarterly basis. I don't know how often the rest of his family meets for Sunday brunch, only that he avoids it until it is unavoidable. For years, his father has been pressuring him to grow up and come work for McQuade Development.

Keegan has his back to me, fiddling with his coffee maker—which I swear is more complicated than my car, and probably more expensive, too—as he coaxes it into producing a perfect latte. Because his back is to me, I don't see his expression as he says, "You know what it's like. Grandfather won't be around forever, so Dad and Aunt Joan are duking it out for dominance. Dad is convinced that if he can bring me back into the fold, Grandfather will leave him in charge."

The coffee maker gives a frothy sounding trill and a moment later, Keegan turns around, sliding a latte across the island to me along with a shaker of sugar.

I'm not sure exactly how to respond. Keegan isn't exactly private about his family, but he also isn't as proud of them as some trust-fund babies are. They just were what they were, and Keegan largely tried to stay out of it. I don't want to pry too much, but it seems like a golden opportunity to ask about Keegan's vision for his family's future.

"Is he right?" I ask, pouring sugar into the coffee he's made me.

"Maybe." Keegan shrugs. "Brunch was full of a lot of talk about how much I've matured over the past few years and how my bar is actually a sound business investment that adds local flavor to the family portfolio."

I snort. "Didn't he once threaten to buy your loan from the bank and demolish it with his bare hands?"

Keegan laughs. "You remember that, huh?"

I remember every shitty thing his father ever said to him. I think of myself as a pacifist, but if I could I would etch the words, *I will not bully my son,* on the back of

Jonathon McQuade's hand, like an avenging Delores Umbridge, I would.

I'm dying to ask who he thinks would be better to inherit—his dad or his aunt. Mostly because of what that would mean for him. For *his* future.

After so much time without Keegan in my life—and now that he's finally back—the idea of him getting swept away into the family business makes my stomach roil. And not in a fun, I'm-on-a-roller-coaster way. But in a terrifying, I'm-on-a-roller-coaster-and-forgot-to-buckle-in kind of way.

I can't lose Keegan again. I just can't.

six

I SIP my coffee in silence while Keegan makes his own coffee, my mind churning through the things that have happened in the past few days like a mental blender. All the pressure his dad is putting on him, plus the idea that Keagan may actually be considering joining the family business. And on top of that, Selah's unending advances.

Selah—beautiful, rich, and connected—is exactly the kind of woman his family would love to see him settle down with. No wonder he snapped and kissed me just to get some breathing room. Not that much breathing happened while he was kissing me.

When he turns back around, his own latte made, I say, "So what's the verdict on your dad's job offer? Did you tell him to go fuck himself?"

Keegan gives me a long look and then asks, "Would you hate me if I didn't?"

I blink. "W-w-what?"

"Would you hate me?" He takes a sip of his latte, not quite meeting my gaze. "If I didn't tell him to go fuck himself?"

Mostly when I'm slow to speak, it's because I'm trying to circumnavigate around any words I might stutter on. This time it's because I'm trying to find words, period. The words that won't hurt my best friend.

"I could never hate you," I eventually say. "But if you are thinking about going to work for your father, I would ..."

Basically, I no longer know what to think about Keegan's dad. So I finish my sentence with, "I would wonder if you were doing it for the right reasons. I would w-worry if you were doing what you really wanted to do or if you were doing what seemed easiest."

He gives me a long look, his lips twisting in a wry smile. "Let's not kid ourselves. There wouldn't be anything easy about working for my dad."

"Then why—"

"I can't work at a bar forever."

"You don't work at a bar," I remind him. "You own a bar. A very successful one. And when you add in the sustainability initiatives you've instituted—"

"That's just it."

"What's just it?"

"The sustainability initiatives. That's what my dad is offering to let me do."

"Oh." I sit back on my stool, lowering my coffee mug.

In the time he's owned Hung Out to Dry, his bar has become one of the most environmentally responsible businesses in the area. It started right after he bought the place when I talked him into putting in recycling bins. Those were a hit with the students—because students are always one of the most environmentally conscious markets—and his efforts have grown every year since then.

"Dad is putting together a bid on a property out in the Edwards Aquifer."

The Edwards Aquifer is one of the most environmentally sensitive parts of the state. The movement to preserve the aquifer is the cornerstone of environmentalism in Austin.

"I thought all that land was in trusts that keep it from being developed."

Keegan shrugs. "Most of it is. That's why Dad wants to bring me on board. He's convinced the only way McQuade Dev will win the bid is if I work up the proposal."

"That makes sense. You are the only McQuade on the Austin Sustainability Council."

"He swears I'll have carte blanche on the proposal, at least as far as the sustainability stuff goes, and if we get the bid, he'll let me oversee retrofitting our existing properties."

"Wow."

My perfect latte suddenly tastes bitter, so I shove a macaron in my mouth, thinking while I chew. I don't know whether to be impressed that Keegan's dad finally found something to use as leverage or suspicious of his motives.

I swallow the macaron, searching for the right response. Nervously, I crack a joke.

"Ah, tempting you with sustainability, he is," I say in my best Master Yoda voice. "The lure of the Dark Side is strong."

Keegan laughs, just like I knew he would. "All these years and your Yoda voice still sucks."

I shrug and smile. "Hey, I can't be great at everything."

He gives me a look I don't quite understand. "Pretty sure you are, though."

This isn't the first time Keegan's dad has made outrageous promises to lure him back into the family fold. I'm right to be suspicious. I know I am. But it's Keegan's family. Keegan's *life*. If he wants this, then who am I to talk him out of it? Yes, his dad has a history of berating him and belittling his accomplishments. But Keegan is a grown man. He can stand up to his dad. If he wants to.

It's that *if* that has me worried.

"W-what are you going to do?"

"You think it's a mistake," he breathes.

It's not a question, but an observation, and I curse how transparent I am to him.

"It's not my decision to make." I pick up another macaron, just to have something to do, but I don't eat it, not when the remains of the last one are still so dusty in my mouth. "If he gives you the free rein you're describing, it would be an amazing opportunity. A chance to do something you'd be proud of and to put your own mark on the company."

"If." Keegan nods, repeating the key word in my sentence.

"How will you decide?"

"There's a fundraiser this weekend for Dig Deep, which is this—"

"Oh! I know what Dig Deep is." It's one of the charities he supports as part of his work on the Green Business board. "They educate communities about green gardening practices and help them install community gardens in urban food deserts."

His lips quirk, his gaze moving over my face. "Do you know everything?"

I shrug. "*The Chronicle* named it one of the new and noteworthy charities a couple of years ago, and since food insecurity is a growing problem all over the country ..."

I let my words trail off, feeling oddly self-conscious about the way he's looking at me.

After a second, Keegan chuckles, ducking his head.

"They're having a fundraiser this Saturday at the Lady Bird Johnson Wildflower Center. My dad bought a batch of tickets. He wants me to go."

"Oh." I nod slowly, seeing where this is going.

"Apparently, it will be a chance to meet all the right people."

Listening to him, I'm struck by a single thought. This is the beginning of the end. This moment, right here.

Okay, maybe not *this* moment. But Saturday night, for sure.

This is when Keegan begins to grow beyond our friendship.

Some part of me always knew it would happen. He couldn't put off growing into a proper McQuade forever. He has the brains and the soul of a leader in business. It's in his blood. In the decade I've known him, he's played at owning a bar, but it's not like even that was just a bar. Almost as soon as he bought it, he started stretching his wings, looking for ways to make it more environmentally friendly, ways to meet Austin's sustainability goals, ways to make it a forerunner for businesses in the future. And he's been great at it.

Which means his father finally found something that might tempt Keegan to come work for him. My heart constricts in panic because this feels huge. This feels like I'm losing him.

I plaster a huge smile on my face. "That's amazing." God, I hope he can't hear how false my cheer sounds. "That's the perfect job for you! And I guess this means you're going to miss dinner next week."

Keegan looks at me, his expression bemused. "Actually, I was hoping you would come to the gala with me."

"With you?" A sound escapes me, half laughter, half hysteria. "Going to a gala as your date is even more ridiculous than that kiss in the hall."

Keegan pauses, his mug partway to his mouth, and gives me a heated look over the rim. "I didn't think the kiss was that bad."

Bad? Um ... no. Not at all, considering my panties may never be the same, and I'll probably be dreaming about that kiss for the rest of my life.

Since I can't admit that out loud, I roll my eyes. "Please. Stop fishing for compliments."

He chuckles. "Who says I'm fishing for compliments?"

"You know exactly how good that kiss was."

"Yeah." His gaze darkens. "I know how good it was for me. I'm asking how it was for you."

Mentally, I'm flailing. What is he saying? That he enjoyed kissing me?

What is happening here???

"My point is, the idea of me at a gala is ridiculous." I scoff to hide my discomfort, completely sidestepping his question. "Besides, y-your dad hatesss me. I'm pretty sure he will not want to hang out with me at this gala."

"Actually, I have tickets, too. So we wouldn't be in his party."

"Oh." The fact that Keegan has tickets to this event already only confirms what I was thinking just a minute ago. He was going to go to this event regardless of whether his dad asked him. It feels like I really am losing him.

"I think we both know I'm not really a gala gal." My awkward alliteration only drives home the point.

"It would mean a lot to me," he says simply. Before I can muster up any more protest, he adds on a simple, "Please."

God. Please? He's really gonna pull out that?

Keegan never asks for anything. Literally. He's never asked me for anything. He doesn't ask for money, obviously. He doesn't ask for favors. He doesn't need me to drive him to the eye doctors, or to catch a ride after he's dropped off his car for an oil change, or to water his plants when he goes out of town. Keegan is the kind of guy that the phrase generous-to-a-fault was invented to describe. He never asks for favors from anyone. So for him to say please is the equivalent of someone else getting down on their hands and knees and groveling.

Still, I struggle for a response. "I wouldn't know how to dress for a gala. I have nothing to wear."

"I'll buy you something." He shrugs dismissively, like the solution should be obvious.

"You know I'm not gonna let you do that."

Keegan is always offering to buy me things. Obviously, I never let him. Charity is a line I refuse to cross. Partly because I'm too proud. I don't mind admitting that. And partly because, as I said earlier, he has that small generous-to-a-fault problem. No way am I going to take advantage of that.

"You might have plenty of money, but that doesn't mean I'm going to let you spend it on me."

"You should let me buy you a dress. It's only fair. I'm going to make you go to this thing with me."

I cross my arms over my chest and grumble, but say nothing. I am probably secretly hoping that he comes to the conclusion I have. Namely, that I shouldn't go to this thing with him. My lack of gala-wear is the least of my concerns.

But he clearly knows how to hit me where it hurts, because he levels a look at me and says, "Don't make me brave these lions all on my own."

I roll my eyes. "Gah. Drama, much?"

"Whatever it takes, Glasses." He laughs, pulling out his phone and typing out a message. "I'll have my mom send me a list of places where you can find an appropriate dress."

"See if she can recommend one of those places that rent clothes or that do vintage and second-hand clothes," I suggest.

He shoots me a droll look. "If I'm paying, it doesn't have to be secondhand."

"If you're paying, then it *definitely* has to be second-hand." I glance around at the understated, no-nonsense opulence of his condo. With the view of Lady Bird Lake. Insert eye-roll here.

"Let me pay. You'll be doing me a favor."

"If you already bought the tickets, then, technically, y-you are paying. I mean, unless you want me to pay for my ticket?"

I leave the offer dangling there. Keegan clenches his jaw. "Why are you this stubborn?"

"I know you mean well, but look at this condo." I gesture to the hardwood floors and sleek leather furniture. To the stunning view of the lake. "Do you even remember how much you paid to have this place decorated?"

"What's your point?"

"My point is, you don't think about money. You don't have to. So if I let you pick out my dress and pay for it, you'll drop way more money than I'm comfortable with."

"So?"

"So, then I would be *that* person."

"What person?"

"The person who takes more from you than she gives."

He looks at me as if I'm speaking a different language, so I explain further. "You have so many people who just take and take from you and give nothing back. And I refuse to be that person."

"You could never be that person."

"Exactly. I can't be that person. The only reason our relationship works is because I don't expect you to spend money on me."

"That's bullshit. Our relationship works because you're my best friend." He stalks around the island to my side of the counter. There's something unsettling in his gaze. Impulsively, I down the rest of my latte. "Meg, I—"

I move away from him to put the empty cup in the sink. I feel like I need to say something, but I don't know *what* to say.

Everything about today has me unsettled. From the events at work—which I still haven't told Keegan about— to the way he kissed me out in the hall—which I know was just for show, but didn't *feel* like it was for show to me—to him asking me to come to this gala with him.

It's all too much. It all feels like I'm hurtling toward some catastrophic change in my life that I have absolutely no control over. And I hate not having control. My thoughts are a jumbled mess, and before I can get them into any sort of order, Keegan is once again at my side, gently turning me to face him. He keeps his hands on my shoulder in a way that I suspect is supposed to be reassuring.

"Meg, please let me do this. I'm asking you for a favor. If I'm gonna drag you to this gala with me, at least let me pay for the dress."

I search his face, seeing a hint of desperation there. "You don't have to—"

"I know I don't have to. I want to. If you're there with me, I'll be more comfortable. But only if you're comfortable.

If that means I buy you a dress and spend money that I won't even miss, then that's a reasonable trade for me."

It's his use of my given name that does it for me. Keegan has called me Glasses ever since that day I got locked out of my room at the co-op wearing only a towel and—you guessed it—glasses. So if he's pulling out Meg now, then he really is desperate.

I can't let him pay. It's just not in my nature to accept charity from anyone. Not even my best friend.

"Okay, I'll go with you," I agree, without committing to letting him pay. "But if your mom really is going to help, I truly would rather she look at one of those consignment places. It's more economical, and it's better for the—"

"And it's better for the environment." Keegan cuts me off, grinning. "Yes, I know. I was the one who got us tickets for that symposium on fast fashion, remember?"

"This is true."

And, faced with this example of all the times I've dragged Keegan along on weird adventures, I have to admit that I owe it to him. I have to go with him so that he doesn't have to face his family alone. I make a noise that I hope he interprets as excitement.

Who am I kidding? He knows me so well, I'm pretty sure he sees right through me.

Thankfully, he changes the subject. "Hey, how did the meeting go today? Did you ever come up with an idea to pitch?"

"Hmmm, yes." I can feel my cheeks heating up as I remember the bizarro fantasy that inspired my idea.

He raises his eyebrows and makes a gesture that I should keep talking.

But what can I say? I can't tell him about the idea, not

when it started with a fantasy about him kissing me. Not when I'm still so unsettled by him actually kissing me.

So, instead, I ignore his gesture. "We pitch to Butler next week." I make goofy jazz hands. "Yay."

He grabs a macaron. "I knew you'd come up with something."

A few minutes later, I leave Keegan's and head back to the Prescott Towers garage to pick up my car.

I try not to think about how vague I was about the presentation and the idea I came up with. I can't really explain why I didn't tell him about Teresa needing time off and that I'll have to give the big presentation myself. Partly, his news just seemed bigger, and I didn't want to make tonight all about me. Partly, I didn't want to have to describe the idea that I will ultimately pitch.

Mostly, I think I'm still just disconcerted by him kissing me in the hall.

Because wowza ... that knocked my socks off. And it was just *so* not what I needed today. Today I needed familiarity and normality. Instead, I got an earth-axis-tilting kiss from my best friend. Which he gave me only so that his neighbor would leave him be.

The bad news is, now that I'm thinking it through, this event on Saturday is exactly the kind of thing Selah would also go to. Which means Keegan wasn't being wholly honest when he invited me.

Yes, he wants me there to act as a barrier between him and his family. I know enough sustainability and ecology buzz words to hold my own with even the most adamant environmentalist. I will also be a layer of protection to scare off the Selahs of the world. Which means there will be more fake canoodling in my future.

Suddenly, the presentation I have to give on Monday isn't the most terrifying thing in my future.

It's not until I'm nearly asleep that I remember that, for once, Selah didn't bless my heart. Which is ironic, because I have the sinking feeling that, after today's kiss, my heart might actually be in danger.

seven

BY THE TIME I wake up Tuesday morning, I'm second guessing myself. About everything, basically. Why did I agree to do the presentation? Why did I agree to attend the gala with Keegan?

And I already have messages from Teresa asking for updates. I am tempted to chunk my phone across the room and go back to bed, but I put on my big girl panties and force myself out of bed. I drag myself off to the shower and start my coffee. Then I add an extra glug of heavy cream to my coffee. If I'm going to face today, I need to minimize the acidity in my stomach. And reinforcements.

I open up a new text chain between myself, Reb, and my dear friend Thea. I met Thea Jones years ago while volunteering for Austin Creative Reuse, a charity that accepts donations for used art supplies and resells them to fund art projects in local schools.

Thea was an it girl and model turned actress in the 70s. At some point in the 80s, she went from famous to infamous to obscure trivia-question-answer. At least, that's my impression based on my mom's reaction of salacious yet judgy disdain when I mentioned that I knew her. I did only the shallowest dive on Google after my mom's response, then quickly backed out of it when I saw how deep a rabbit hole it was. By that point, I already knew and respected Thea. The way I see it, friends don't read friends' bad press.

Basically, Thea has a past. And if she wanted me to know the details, she'd tell me herself. She tells a lot of stories about Hollywood, but very few about her own life. She has a story about everyone who's anyone, and her stories are too entertaining for me to care if they're true. Even more astonishingly, she's one of those people who can tell an outrageous story and still make everyone involved seem like a decent human being. But as far as I know, she's not close to anyone from that time in her life. Despite that, she seems at peace just being quietly fantastic.

In short, she's my icon. Both Reb and Thea have epic levels of self-confidence. If I'm going to rock this presentation to Butler and earn my own team, I need their advice.

> Yesterday's pitch for the Butlers Steam Vac ad went great. But they want me to give the pitch to Butler myself.

REB

> You got this!

THEA

> Congratulations, my dear!

> I need help! Any chance y'all are free for an emergency summit over lunch?

THEA

> Absolutely. Just tell me where and when.

REB

Definitely. Especially if we can go to HO.
I've been craving their fried cheese taco.

I was thinking of that salad place in the
building.

REB

REB

Please

The honest truth? I don't want to go to Hung Out to Dry for lunch today. After yesterday's fake kiss debacle, is it any wonder?

I'm still coming up with a plausible excuse when I get two more texts from Reb, both variations of the begging GIFs, and a final text from Thea that merely says "1:30 at HO?" Reb responds with a GIF of a cheerleader celebrating and ultimately I cave, giving Thea's text a thumbs up.

Okay, the situation isn't ideal, but it will be fine. After all, Keegan usually takes Tuesday off. And he works nights. Roxy, his assistant manager, takes the daytime shift most days. So chances of running into Keegan are slim.

In fact, why did I even bother suggesting a different restaurant? I'm sure I won't see him there. More importantly, it will be okay if I see him there. Because he's my best friend. Despite any weirdness yesterday with the kiss, that's all he is. And that kiss meant nothing, anyway. It was only weird because I didn't expect it. I didn't know he was going to do it, because I didn't know he was having trouble fending off Selah. Now that I know, I can mentally prepare for any fake-dating-shenanigans that might happen on Saturday.

Have I listed enough reasons why it will all be okay?

Yeah. I thought so.

Between all the texting and drinking my coffee, I barely have time to throw on one of the simple dresses that I wear most days.

I slip into a silk dress I thrifted several years ago.

It always felt decadent to wear silk, and the environmentalist in me always feels good knowing my clothing choices don't add to my footprint.

I once read an article in Business Insider about Matilda Kahl, an ad exec in New York, who wears identical outfits every day of the work week to free up her creativity for her work. I figured if it worked for her, it would work for me.

True, she's tall, blonde and gorgeous, so she'd look great in anything. And I am ... not. Still, I like my collection of black, shapeless dresses. I don't mind blending into the wallpaper.

By the time I make it out of the house, I'm running only a little late. Traffic in Austin is the normal interminable slog that leaves me questioning all of my life choices. Thank God for audio books and murder podcasts.

I make it to work on time and answer the slew of emails and messages that have inexplicably piled up overnight. I know for a fact that Tad was out with friends last night, so how the hell did he have time to message me five times?

When lunch rolls around, I meet Reb in the lobby, and we take a ride share to Hung Out to Dry, since neither of us wants to bother finding parking. As soon as we're in the car, Reb mentions the boob armor issue again, then argues about it with the driver for the entire ride. By the time he drops us off at the bar, I still don't know exactly what boob armor is, but I'm thankful that at least I don't have a job that random strangers feel inclined to comment on.

A decade ago, back when Keegan and I were at UT, Hung Out to Dry was an English-style pub called The Dog and Whistle, which, I think we can all agree, is a horrible name. When the guy who owned it put it on the market right before we graduated, Keegan snapped it up and the rebranding began.

It's been a bar in one form or another since the late seventies, which makes it one of the oldest continually operating bars in Austin. It's just east of campus, nestled up against a residential area full of what was once cheap college housing. The interior is small and packed with history. The walls are plastered with vintage concert posters that date back to Austin's origins as the self-proclaimed "Live Music Capital."

Even though smoking hasn't been permitted in the venue for more than a decade, the smell of smoke permeates the wood. There's a porch that wraps around the front of the bar to the patio along the side and back of the bar. Live oaks offer shade, and misters and fans keep the patio cool enough to sit out on it most of the year.

Of course, it's spring, and the weather is amazing today. Reb and I find Thea already seated at a table on the patio. She's ordered chips and guac and a frothy, pink drink that's almost as glamorous as she is. Once we're seated and have ordered, I fill in the details about the presentation to Butler—a.k.a. my impending doom—that I didn't share over text.

When I explain the situation to them, Reb is the first to respond.

"Why are you worried?" she asks with a wave of her hand. "You got this."

"I don't got this," I argue.

"Of course you do." She tilts her head in question. "You can't possibly think you are incapable of presenting your ideas—you're brilliant, Meg."

"Brilliant I might be, but not being able to t-talk is an issue."

She takes a gulp of the gingerbeer she ordered. "It's barely noticeable. Most of the time, I forget you even have a stutter at all."

I don't point out to Reb that—for all her many wonderful personality quirks and attributes—she is maybe not the most perceptive person. I'm sure she's brilliant at whatever gamer-y things she does, but she has less social polish than most do. So if she thinks it's barely noticeable, that's not encouraging.

I swivel to look at Thea. "What do you think?"

"Let me consider …" Thea says slowly, each word pronounced with a stage actress's care as she sits perched on the edge of her chair, sipping her drink dramatically. "The presentation is on Monday?"

"Yes. Which gives me four days, assuming I work through the weekend. Which I don't actually have time to do."

Reb snorts a laugh. "Right, because of your busy social schedule."

Yes, she knows exactly how not busy my social schedule is. "Stop acting like y-you don't work just as many hours as I do." I kick her under the table. "Besides which, I have a thing to go to this weekend."

"A thing?" Thea asks, archly. "What thing?"

Sasha, a gorgeous silver tabby that lives on the deck, weaves her way through the tables toward us. I lean down, stretching out my fingers toward her, hoping she will let me pet her. She doesn't.

"A fundraising thing." When they pin me with identical, curious stares, I elaborate, explaining that Keegan needs me to go to the gala with him to act as a buffer between him and his family.

I try to keep the details to a minimum because Thea is a self-proclaimed romantic and refuses to believe my friendship is only that.

"So," she says before pausing dramatically to sip. "You have a big presentation on Monday and a date with Keegan on Saturday."

"It's not a date," I counter. "I'm just attending an event with him. As a favor."

"Hmm," she murmurs noncommittally, her eyes gleaming with a cunning that would make a military strategist proud.

Reb jumps in before Thea can ambush me. "But the presentation is what's important. This is her career at stake." She looks back at me. "And Teresa took off work for the rest of the week?"

"Yes."

"Remind me again why someone else can't present for you?" Thea asks, as Sasha the cat saunters over to Thea's chair and stretches to put her paws on Thea's knee.

Thea barely glances down at the cat before giving her leg a pat. Like the traitor she is, Sasha leaps onto Thea's lap, shooting me a disdainful look.

Before I can answer, Reb holds up her hand. "I got this one." She twists on the sofa to face Thea.

"'Cause if she can do this presentation, it'll be good for her career and her confidence. Plus, she'll prove to herself that she can ditch Teresa, head up her own team, and generally look like a genius. Of course, if she fails, they could lose the account." Shaking her head, she turns back to me. "Which wouldn't be good for your career in today's market."

"Th-thanks, Reb, for your obvious faith in my abilities."

"No problem."

I stick out my tongue at her. She shoots me the finger playfully.

We pause as the waitress delivers our food. Hung Out to Dry has a limited, seasonal menu packed with locally sourced ingredients. They always have a few taco options, a few salad options, and some vegan options. Once I have a few bites of taco in me, I feel better.

Thea issues a thoughtful, "Hmm," staring into the near distance thoughtfully as she strokes a hand down Sasha's back, ignoring me and Reb.

I can't help but resent that Sasha has settled onto Thea's lap. All these years I've been coming here and Sasha barely tolerates me. Of course, that's a step up from how she treats everyone else.

Reb takes another gulp of her latte. "What I don't get is why you're so afraid of freezing up during the presentation."

"Because of my stu—"

"Right. Your stutter. But what's the big deal, really? So you stutter. As long as you don't freeze up completely—"

"But I do freeze up. All the time."

"Not all the time." Thea interrupts. "I see you talking to strangers all the time at volunteer events."

Thea, who believes the key to staying young is being active and giving back, lets me drag her along to all kinds of events—everything from planting community gardens to cleaning up the local hiking trails.

"You recruit anyone who shows up. Yes, sometimes you

stutter while you're talking with them. But you never freeze up."

Reb—who has only come with me a few times—jabs a finger in my direction. "She's right. I once saw you convince a group of high school volunteers that composting was cool. Composting! Why is this situation at work any different?"

"It just is." I open and close my mouth, searching for words, for an explanation I don't have.

When I'm volunteering, it's not about me. It's about the cause. It's about restoring the black land prairie or cleaning up Waller Creek. I'm not the center of attention.

But an ad pitch meeting is completely different. When I pitch one of my ideas, it's like putting a piece of my soul up to be judged by others. There's nothing else that makes me feel that vulnerable.

That's why I freeze up.

Or rather, why I've frozen up in the past. This has to be different.

"Freezing up isn't an option this time. I can do this, right?" I prod.

Thea's sharp gaze cuts to mine. "You want to know if you can overcome your stutter long enough to give an important presentation? And your job is at stake if you don't succeed?"

"Yes," I say, far more boldly than I feel, because, holy shit, hearing it out loud, it sounds so much worse.

Reb takes another bite of her tacos. "You got this."

I glare at her, though I'm not sure which I resent more, her blasé attitude or her ability to eat in a time of crisis. Though this is way more crisis-y for me than it is for her. "Could you at least try to be helpful?"

She sets down her taco. "You want my advice?"

"Yes. But only if it's something more helpful than 'You got this'."

"Okay, here's my advice. If you're really this worried, don't do it."

"I w-was looking for something a little more productive than that. Aren't you an exec at that gaming company you work at? You're a badass boss, right? Can't you, like, mentor me?"

She rolls her eyes. "Yeah. I'm a badass boss at a gaming company. Totally different skill set."

Resisting the urge to shake her by the shoulders, I practically yell, "What is wr-wr-wrong with y-you? For y-years you've been telling me to do something about Teresa. And now that I am, y-you have no advice?"

Reb gives me a long, hard look and says, "Look, I'm an expert on game design. Not people, not presentations, not dating. None of it."

"Who said anything about dating?"

She ignored my question. "But you're making this presentation into a big deal because you're avoiding something else."

"What's that supposed to mean?"

"You're going on a date with Keagan. Mr. McHotness himself."

"It's not a date."

"Are you sure?" she asks.

"Yes. I'm sure."

"Then why are you blushing?"

Shit. Why am I blushing? I don't have an answer to that, so I dodge the question. "Why does it matter? Sometimes people blush because they're sitting in the sun. Or they're having an allergic reaction to something they ate."

"Maybe it doesn't matter. Or maybe you have unresolved feelings for him."

I look from Reb to Thea and back again. Thea seems lost in thought as she strokes Sasha. Reb raises an eyebrow, clearly waiting for me to respond.

What am I supposed to say here?

Do I admit I used to have a crush on Keegan? Do I tell her about the kiss?

I could really use some ... clarity or something in regard to Keegan. Girl talk, maybe? Advice? I'm not sure what exactly I want, but just... telling someone. Letting my friends know it happened somehow makes it, I don't know, *real* in a way I could really use right now. Like if I could just talk about it, maybe I would feel less overwhelmed. Less ... Untethered.

Or do I steer the conversation back to what is actually important: the presentation that could make or break my career?

"Presentation. Let's refocus!"

I'm not ready to talk to anyone about that kiss that wasn't really a kiss.

I'm not even ready to think about it. Because the truth is, kissing Keegan made me feel things I'm not ready to admit out loud. It brought back all the yearning and angst from the first few months of our friendship. From that awkward time in my life when I wanted more from him than just friendship.

I can't go back to that place. Certainly not now when our friendship is finally back on track after the Ollie years.

Keegan and Ollie never got along. It sucks when your best friend dislikes your boyfriend. And it sucks even more when you realize he was right.

Ollie was never an overtly horrible boyfriend. There

were no blazing red flags. He wasn't controlling or emotionally abusive. Thank goodness. But he also wasn't the guy I thought he was when we got together. When we met, he seemed ambitious. Smart and full of big ideas. He was going to start his own company and create world-changing apps.

But somehow, his ideas never quite came together. The ideas always seemed great, but there was always ... something. Some reason why his plans didn't come together. Some person or situation that was holding him back. His partner was a sellout who left to "work for the man," some collaborator he was counting on left the country, the VC money he needed fell through. The failures were never his fault. The blame always belonged somewhere else.

Still, I stuck with it. I stuck with him. Covering his half of the rent. Buying the expensive half of the groceries. Loaning him my car even though he never filled up the tank. I was there. Until suddenly, the person "holding him back" was me.

I could put up with a lot, but even I saw that for what it was.

And when I needed someone to help me pick up my life when Ollie and I broke up, Keegan was there. He showed up. No questions asked. He held me as I cried. He brought me chocolates. When he found out that Ollie hadn't moved out yet, he helped Ollie pack up his stuff and move, for Christ's sake. At least, that's what I assumed happened. Because the day after Keegan found out that Ollie hadn't actually left, Reb showed up to take me to breakfast and when we got back, Ollie and all his stuff were just gone.

Point is, I just got Keegan back as a friend. I can't let myself question the boundaries of our relationship.

"I have f-f-four days to figure out how to give a presentation that could make or break my career. And between now and then, I also have to attend a friggin' gala that I do not know how to dress for or how to act at. Let's focus on those problems."

Thea gives a smile so bright I see the lingering star power that got her in movies. "Oh, I already have solutions to those problems."

"You do?"

"Of course I do." She practically beams. "It's Marion Davies."

I look over at Reb, who looks as baffled as I am. "Who?"

"The actress," Thea supplied. "Marion Davies. She's the key."

"Wasn't she William Randolph Hearst's mistress?" Reb asks.

"Oh, you are a smart one." Thea winks at Reb, patting her on the arm. "But she was so much more than that! She was one of the most talented actresses of the time. A true comedic genius. I met her once, you know. Just as kind and generous as—"

"What's this have to do with Meg?"

"Why, everything. Marion Davies spoke with a stutter. In the golden age of silent films, her stutter was never an issue, but when talkies came out, everyone feared her career would be over."

My heart spasms at the thought, making my chest feel tight and my breathing panicky. My situation is bad enough. What would it be like to have your entire career upended because the technology evolved, and suddenly you can't do your career at all?

"That's horrible," I say, surreptitiously rubbing at the spot on my chest where I'm pretty sure I'm developing heartburn from this story. I mean, at least it's distracting me (and Reb) from the drama with Keegan, but still ... "What did she do?"

"In nineteen twenty-nine, Marion starred in her first talkie, *Marianne*. Everyone who knew of her predicament was terrified for her, but when the movie was released, she sang, she danced, she even spoke with an accent. And she never stuttered once."

"I don't understand. Did they hire someone to do a voice over?"

"Not at all," Thea beams, clearly pleased with herself. "You see, Marion Davies stuttered, but her character, Mari-anne, did not."

"I don't understand. She just pretended she didn't have a stutter, so she didn't?"

"Exactly." Her eyes barely crinkled at the corners as she beamed at me, as if I were a star pupil. "All you have to do is create a character to play. An alternate persona, if you will. One who doesn't stutter."

eight

MY BREATH CATCHES in my throat as I process Thea's suggestion. Could it really be that simple? Could this really be the answer? After a lifetime of stuttering, of awkward silences and pitying glances, of avoiding words I thought might trip me up?

Reb snorts loudly. "This is the stupidest idea I've ever heard."

Thea shoots her a smug, sly smile. "You just don't like it because you didn't think of it."

"No." Reb gives another exaggerated pout. "Maybe. But also, it doesn't make sense. The idea is for Meg to impress these bigwigs at work, right? If she gives this presentation dressed up as some alternate persona, then won't her bosses just think she's mentally unstable?"

As Reb ticks off each of her objections on her fingers, I look at Thea, who merely chuckles, patting Reb's hand reassuringly.

"Oh, you silly girl, you've misunderstood me completely. I'm not suggesting she try to fool other people into thinking she's a different person. She only has to fool herself. Her persona will be all up here." Thea taps her temple. "If she believes she won't stutter, then she won't."

"Sure, I guess."

I draw out the word, wishing I felt more confident about this plan. "Is this going to work?"

"Of course it will work," Thea gushes with her normal over the top enthusiasm.

"You know, I think I read about a local newscaster with a stutter who does the same thing." Reb pulls out her phone and starts typing. A moment later, she mutters, "Yep, here it is."

She holds out her phone to me. I take it and scan the article. Sure enough, a guy I grew up watching on the evening news speaks with a stutter when he's not on air.

"Well, shit," I mutter. The article links to another article about other famous people. I automatically start reading names out loud. "Marilyn Monroe had a stutter? And James Earl Jones?" I look from the phone to Thea and then to Reb. "Mufasa. Fucking Mufasa has a stutter, and I didn't know it? What the hell? How is this even possible?"

"Actually, my dear," Thea says gently. "Mufasa, the character, didn't have a stutter. That's the point."

"I know, I just ..." I glance down at the list again. "I think if Emily Blunt and Julia Roberts both have stutters, shouldn't someone have mentioned this to me before now? Do you know how many times my mom made me watch *The King's Speech*? A lot. But somehow this never came up?"

Reb takes the phone and glances at the article. "Isn't this just a Wikipedia page?"

"What's your point?"

She hands the phone back. "Just that this is commonly available knowledge, I guess. Didn't you ever google famous people with stutters before now?"

When she says it like that, I just feel stupid, so I'm sure I sound grumpier than I should when I say, "No, I didn't. Obviously. Or I would have known the voice of Darth Vader had a stutter, too."

I can't help feeling annoyed at having to justify my ignorance on this issue. Reb knows my dad left when I was eight. She knows how tight money was when I was a kid, how sparse resources were in my family. Mom did her best, but as a single mother of three girls, her best covered only the barest necessities. We barely afforded things like food and rent. A private speech therapist was out of the question, and the one the school provided me barely scratched the surface.

Yes, recently I started therapy on my own, and my therapist is pleased with my progress, but I can't help feeling frustrated by the pace. By the feeling that I'm still waiting for my real life to begin.

Thea gives several sharp claps, and I'm not sure if she's determined to get my attention or if she's just that excited about her plan.

"You'll need a makeover," she says when I finally meet her gaze. "Of course you'll need a new haircut. New clothes. None of your current potato sacks will do. You'll need a whole new look, obviously."

A whole new look? A makeover? I don't know if that should make me nervous or excited. One thing is for sure, I'm too desperate to dismiss any possibilities.

I may be willing to get a makeover for the sake of this presentation. I don't love the way Thea says I need one. Like it's a foregone conclusion that my sense of style sucks.

While processing how I feel about that particular criticism, I reach for my drink. The ice sloshes against the glass as I tilt the bubbly lemon seltzer toward my mouth, the fizz tingling my nose as I sip. Tart lemon mixes with a vanilla simple syrup, creating a lemon-pie flavored drink I've been addicted to for years.

I can't take full credit, of course, since it's Keegan's place. Though I *was* the person who initially argued that he should explore offering custom sodas for the menu—non-alcoholic options that still are delicious. After presenting him with a few simple syrups, herb, and seltzer combos, Keegan became a convert, and the mocktail menu at Hung Out to Dry was born.

I tip the glass back a little more, catching a few nuggets of the perfectly crunchable ice the restaurant has had for years now—also one of my favorites—and chew, decimating the little bundles of frozen joy.

Good ice, craft sodas, and tacos. *Life is good*, I remind myself. *Even if your friends think you dress like a slug.*

The crunching is helping, the chill cooling the tinge of embarrassment that's threatening.

"Yes," I say drolly. "*Obviously*, I need a makeover." I've always valued comfort over style, and yes, my work "uniform" has a sort of Doby-in-a-clean-dish-towel aesthetic, but hearing Thea sum it up so succinctly stings a bit.

"Oh, a makeover! Yay!" Reb leans forward, clearly thrilled. "What are we talking? New hair? Glamorous clothes? What?"

Thea and I give Reb identical, skeptical looks.

My personal style might be drab, but at least it's consistent. Reb, with her bright purple streaks in her pixie cut hair, and her never ending rotation of geeky shirts, is not exactly someone I'd peg to help with a makeover.

"Um ..." I say cautiously. "I don't mean to criticize, but ..."

Reb looks down at her worn I-solved-the-Rubik's-Cube

T-shirt. She plucks at the blue raglan sleeve. "This is vintage."

"Uh-huh."

"Like, it's an *original* Rubik's Cube prize shirt. I paid five hundred dollars for this, and I was lucky to get it."

"Dear, you clearly have more money than fashion sense." Thea gives her a pat on the hand. "But never fear. I can help Meg with her clothes."

"Why does Meg need help with her clothes?"

All three of us turn to see Keegan standing beside our table.

When did he sneak up on us?

Aloud, I say, "I didn't know you were working today."

"Just got in."

The table we're at only seats three, since it's nestled against a live oak, but Keegan snags an empty chair from a nearby table and slides it in beside mine. I try to scoot mine over to make room for him, but since I'm on the tree side as well, there's not really anywhere for me to go.

Thea and Reb—who see Keegan less often than I do—chat for a few minutes, complementing the food and catching up. There's a brief discussion about boob armor, during which Thea discusses the costume design for Barbarella and Keegan offers to introduce Reb to the professor from the Practical Medieval Weaponry Seminar he took during his stint as a history major. I eat my tacos in blissful silence, desperately trying to ignore the way Keegan's leg presses against mine.

The weather in Austin is mercurial AF this time of year. So even though I was freezing Saturday night in my house, it's edging on too warm as I sit here in the sun next to Keegan. I refused to think about how I was perfectly fine before Keegan sat down, siphoning all blame firmly into the 'mercurial weather' category. That's the only explanation for how hot my skin feels. For how aware I am of Keegan's proximity. Why else would I be so aware of the denim of his jeans through the silk of my dress?

It can't have anything to do with the way he kissed me yesterday. It can't because I refuse to let that get into my head.

Even if I do space out a little bit during the boob armor discussion. It's because I don't game and don't care about boob armor. Not because that kiss is playing over and over in my mind. Certainly not because I'm imagining a more private, more horizontal version of it.

"Hey, earth to Meg." Keegan stretches his arm over the back of my chair and gives a tug to a lock of my hair.

"What?"

"You spaced out," he chides, tugging on my hair again.

"Boob armor is boring," I say before popping a half-broken chip into my mouth.

"Exactly!" Reb declares. "And the gaming community needs to evolve."

Thea smiles. One of those sneaky smiles she gives that makes me think she knows exactly what's going on in my head. "Dear, we've moved past that part of the discussion. Keegan was asking about your makeover."

"Oh."

"Wait." Keegan holds up a hand, looking from me to Thea and Reb and then back again. "I thought you were just talking about clothes. Now it's a makeover?"

I quickly fill Keegan in on the details he missed, explaining about Teresa being out and how I'll have to do the presentation. When I get to the part about Marion Davies and needing a persona and a makeover, Keegan's huge smile of congratulations falls away. His hand, which had been playing with my hair, drops to my shoulder and taps out an annoyed beat.

"Why do you need a makeover for that?"

"It will give her confidence," Thea explains.

"That's bullshit." He twists to look at me, but doesn't remove his hand. "You're gorgeous. You don't need different clothes or makeup. You're perfect."

I gape for a second, and then laugh out loud.

I elbow him in the side. "Right. Perfect. That's a good one."

"I'm serious, Meg."

My breath catches, because he's pinning me with one of those intense looks of his. Like I'm the only person in the room he wants to look at. Like he really does think I'm gorgeous.

"You're smart and dedicated and work twice as hard as anyone else on your team. You shouldn't need to change anything about yourself to do a job you're qualified for and already doing. Especially not the way you look."

I release that breath I've been holding, because of course, he didn't really mean that he thought I was gorgeous. He's talking about my work ethic. He's just being a good friend.

"But I'm not doing all the work I could be doing," I counter. "If I want to lead my own team, I have to be able to do presentations. If getting a makeover means I can do them, then I'm willing to try."

I say this with way more conviction that I actually feel. Honestly, I'm still not sold on the makeover thing. But now I feel like I have to defend the idea, because Keegan is pushing me to justify it.

"That's bullshit," he pushes back, then looks at Reb. "Come on, you agree with me, right? She's amazing at her job. She shouldn't have to change the way she dresses or wears her hair for them to appreciate her."

"Of course she shouldn't," she agrees, nodding, and then holds up a hand, palm out. "But this is the real world. She shouldn't *have* to change those things. But realistically?" She shrugs and waggles her hand. "If it'll help, then shouldn't she use every tool in her toolbox?"

"Again. That's bullshit." His tone is harder now and his hand has dropped from my shoulder to the back of my chair. "No one would tell a man how to dress for his job."

Everything about this conversation is stressing me out.

First off, I hate fighting with anyone, but I especially hate fighting with Keegan. And, yeah, I know. This isn't a fight. It's a disagreement, and it's not even me disagreeing with him. Still, it feels like he's disappointed in me.

That layered on top of all this jittery awareness that I don't know what to do with? Gah. It's killing me.

To break the tension, I give a laugh that ends up sounding more like a derisive snort, but whatever, I try.

Everyone turns to look at me.

So I shrug and state the obvious. "Of course no o-one w-w-would tell a man how to dress for his job. But society has been policing the way women dress since the dawn of time."

"Exactly!" Reb exclaims.

Keegan is full-on glowering now, but I don't give him a chance to comment.

Instead, I say, "But that's not the point here."

"Wait, it isn't?" Reb asks.

"No. First off, no one is telling me I have to change how I dress to do my job. Secondly, all jobs have a uniform. For some jobs, dictated by company policy, for others it's unwritten. A McDonald's employee can't show up in a ball gown because they have a uniform that's provided to them." I shift my chair, putting a little more space between Keegan and me, ostensibly so that I can gesture toward him. "This is your uniform. Jeans or cargo pants and some vintage concert tee. If you showed up one day in a tux, it would interfere with your ability to do y-your job."

He scoffs. "No, it wouldn't. No one notices how I look."

I laugh at how oblivious he is.

"What?" he asks in what seems like genuine confusion.

I pat him on the cheek like he's a baby. "It's adorable when you pretend you're not stupidly good looking."

He swats away my hand.

Reb gives him an exaggerated once over, then props her chin in her palm and flutters her eyelashes at him, like a cartoon character. "I think it's sweet that he's modest."

He grins at her. "Come on, Reb, you know you're way too smart for a lowly barkeep like me."

Then, as if on cue, he turns on the smolder, and I actually see her breath catch. She flushes, sitting back in her chair as if alarmed at being the focus of his attention. Yeah. I get that.

And that's the thing about Keegan. Being the focus of his attention is a heady, intense experience. It's like staring into the sun. There's a compelling, irresistible urge to do it, but at what cost?

Sometimes, when we hang out, I feel the after-image of the force of his personality for hours. Laying beside him on the floor on Saturday was like that. I felt it for days. That's got to be why I had that fantasy about him on Monday, right?

It wasn't a real fantasy. It was just the aftermath of getting hit by his smolder.

"My point is," I interrupt, putting Reb out of her misery.

"Keegan, people do notice how you dress. Could you do your job all dressed up in a fancy suit? Probably. But it would disrupt things. People would notice and comment."

By which I mean anyone who is even remotely attracted to men would fall all over themselves to get his attention. Even more than they normally do.

There's a reason why he had to use me as a Selah-shield.

"As fascinating as this discussion is, darlings, I think you're all missing the point." Thea pauses dramatically, sipping her cocktail until she has our attention. "This isn't about how Meg dresses for work. This is about her creating a persona, so that she can imagine herself as a different person. Someone who can give her presentation without stuttering."

Since Keegan is still giving her the side eye, she goes into more detail. By the time she's done explaining about Marion Davies, he seems somewhat mollified.

Eventually, he even says, "If I can't convince you this is a shit idea, you should ask my mom for help."

"W-w-what?"

Before I can even get the question out, he's whipped out his phone and is texting her. "This makeover thing. My mom lives for this shit."

"Y-y-you're mother?"

Reb stabs a chip into the guacamole. "Isn't she a former Miss Texas?"

He's nodding as he taps away. "Yep. Miss Texas, nineteen eighty-nine." I see his phone vibrate in his hand while he's still typing, and he looks up. "She's in."

"But your parents don't like me."

"My parents haven't had a chance to get to know you. My mom has wanted to spend time with you for years."

"I find that hard to believe," I grumble before taking another sip of my drink. Crunching ice doesn't help as much this time.

He quirks an eyebrow, turning his phone to show the table. "She is, and I quote, 'Beyond thrilled.'"

"But–"

"Beyond thrilled." Reb grins. "That doesn't sound to me like someone who doesn't like you."

I'm tempted to stick out my tongue at Reb. "She was probably being sarcastic."

"She wasn't. Trust me," Keegan says. "My mom would love to help. She does stuff like this all the time for women on the pageant circuit."

"Is she going to make me learn how to twirl a baton?"

"I doubt it. But she does know some of the best personal stylists in the city, and she can help you pick out a dress for Saturday night."

His phone dings again, and he glances down at it. "And she's already made you an appointment for Thursday evening with someone named Felicia at Downtown UpThreads."

Reb snaps her fingers. "I know that place!" When we gape at her, she gives a diffident shrug. "What? They have great vintage Tees."

Thea looks like it's taking all her acting skills to repress an eye roll. "Yes, they're the most exclusive consignment stores in the city. They're very good– and *not* just for vintage T-shirts."

Reb looks defeated, so I say gently, "Please tell me you'll come with me."

"Can I help with hair?" she asks. "I have an appointment with my hair stylist on Thursday afternoon. I could give you the appointment, and he can do something fabulous for you."

"You have a stylist?"

Reb holds out a lock of purple hair as evidence. "Do I look like someone who has the patience to bleach, dye, and tone my own hair? No, I do not. He's the best colorist in town and an all-around genius."

"How much does this all-around-genius charge?"

Reb waves a hand dismissively. "It'll be my treat. Besides, I think I missed your last birthday, didn't I?"

She did. But she was away at a conference, so it's not like I mind. Still, I'm not sure I'm comfortable accepting charity from yet another friend.

"Okay, I'll see your guy. But you have to let me pay."

"This place isn't that expensive. I promise. Besides, think of all the times you've dragged me out to lunch when I was too distracted with work to eat. I owe you. I'd be wasting away in front of my monitor, trapped in a never ending debate about boob armor if it wasn't for you."

Thea gives a sage nod, then adds, "For this gala and your presentation next week, you deserve to look like a star."

I let the idea of accepting charity battle it out against my need for a self-confidence boost, then nod. "Okay. I'll take the appointment."

"And you'll let me pay?"

"We can reconvene this debate on Thursday, okay?"

I need to go into this presentation feeling like a whole new person. And I want to look amazing at the gala. Not because I expect the gala to change anything about my friendship with Keegan, but because I want him to be proud to be seen with me.

Thea's gaze gleams with anticipation. "Excellent.

Thursday afternoon, we'll get you a fabulous new haircut, a glamorous dress for the gala, and something for your presentation on Friday. Something to show off your marvelous figure," she says with a cluck of her tongue.

"My clothes are professionally appropriate," I try to argue.

"Nonsense. Life's too short to wear such ugly clothing. Besides, you need a costume to help you get into character."

I eye her warily. "Why do I suspect this 'costume' will involve a lot of skimpy clothes I normally wouldn't be caught dead in?"

Thea quirks one elegantly penciled-in eyebrow. "This presentation. You're giving it to men, correct?"

"Yes."

"Men are hard-wired to respond to short skirts and low-cut dresses. Why not use that to your advantage?"

I'm pretty sure my stridently feminist mother could have come up with some excellent reasons why not, as well as my History of Feminism professor.

I nudge Keegan, cuing him to back me up, but he just says, "I'm a man, Meg. I don't think you want my opinion on this."

I gape, shooting over a glare. "What is *that* supposed to mean?"

He shrugs, and his arm brushes mine a bit in a way I'm definitely *not* reacting to physically. So I tell myself. But then Keegan does that thing. That look where he briefly, so quickly you wouldn't see it unless you were looking, which I am, looks me over. His gaze darts from my face down to my chest, lower even, then back up. His eyes—they're a little more hooded, and his mouth is in a crooked grin when he says, "There isn't a red-blooded man in this room who would turn down seeing you in a low cut dress, Meg."

And I'm literally struck speechless.

nine

THERE ISN'T *a red-blooded man in this room who would turn down seeing you in a low cut dress, Meg.*

Keegan just said that … that men want to see me in a low cut dress. Implying that *he* would want to see me in a dress like that. But that doesn't make sense. I narrow my eyes, suspicious that he's just teasing. Just being Keegan about it. "Nice try. W-we're not in a room."

He smirks. "Good point. But I stand by it. So that means there's not a red-blooded man in this city who wouldn't want to see you in a—"

I sock him in the arm. "Just stop. You're making it weird."

He laughs, rubbing the spot on his arm even though there's no way I actually hurt him.

Before he can say anything else, Thea steps in, "See? Men appreciate a beautiful woman—and they *buy* from beautiful women, Meg. It's a quick way to do well with your talk. Don the armor of our kind."

Unnerved by everything about this conversation—and that's on top of being unnerved by Keegan's proximity—I

94

pick up my drink and down the half that's left. "I thought we were better than this as a sex. As a gender. I thought you were a feminist!" I hiss at Thea.

"Do you not think Dolly Parton is a feminist?"

Damn it all to hell.

Keegan piles on. "And Ms. Piggy." He presses his knee against mine again. "You said it yourself. She's a feminist icon, and she can wear the shit out of a low cut dress."

Reb raises her glass in a toast. "To Dolly Parton and Ms. Piggy! I bet no one would dare suggest either of them wear boob armor."

Keegan looks like he can barely contain his laughter.

Since the idea of Keegan appreciating me in a low cut dress is still a little too fresh in my mind, I steer the conversation back. "I feel like using my body to manipulate men at work is a morally gray area."

"Morally gray, hmm?" Thea arches an eyebrow. "Is that the shade of all the clothes in your wardrobe?"

"What? No! I have clothes that aren't gray!"

Thea makes a humming noise that implies she doesn't believe me.

"I have a pair of purple Haunted Mansion themed pjs and a pink hoodie with the words 'I aim to misbehave,' scrawled on it," I argue. I also own a lovely taupe sweater my mom bought me for Christmas. It's too tight, and I never wear it, but it's definitely not gray. It's more beige. Though I'm not sure that detail would work in my favor in present company. "W-whatever," I say, smoothing a hand down my dress, which, for the record, is closer to black than gray.

"You have a gorgeous figure, my dear," Thea coos at me. "With the right push-up bra, you will be unforgettable."

"Push-up bras are uncomfortable."

"Not if they fit you properly," she countered. "Push-up bras are the greatest human engineering accomplishment outside of NASA. Frankly, I'm appalled you haven't been using your body to a better advantage before now."

"Back me up here, Reb. I need to look professional."

"I have the build of a pre-teen Tinker Bell. If I had your curves, I'd show them off."

I frown. Funny, I've always felt as if the type of figure Thea is so impressed with doesn't really fit my personality. I have generous curves—the kind that makes it hard to dress without looking like Jessica Rabbit.

I've never really been comfortable with my curves.

My body has always felt like it's too much.

Too curvy. Too lush. The few times in my life I've dressed to show off my curves, they've garnered me more male attention than I'm comfortable with.

I grew up thinking that beautiful meant lean and petite. So while I intellectually understand plenty of men find my curves appealing, I don't feel it—if anything, showing my curves has always made me feel like a piece of meat.

It's not that male attention is bad, it's just that I'm never sure how to handle it. Men have certain expectations when they see a woman with outrageous curves. They expect me to be flirty and charming. They expect sex-kitten personalities in sex-goddess bodies.

I'm just not ... that.

Men are inevitably disappointed.

In my experience, guys either want Daphne or Velma. They don't want Velma in Daphne's body.

And that was back in college, when I was still trying to dress to attract guys, before I adopted my current "potato sack" wardrobe and put on the extra pounds that inevitably come with working long hours at a desk.

It's not that I'm ashamed of my body. It serves me just fine. And, I know lots of men like curves on a woman. It's not my curves that men don't like. It's just ... me they don't like. The brain inside the body.

Encouraged by my silence, Thea blithely continues, "Of course, you still need to pick your persona. If you could be anyone in the world, who would it be?"

In that instant, Sasha leaps off Thea's lap, swishing her tail dramatically.

Sasha meets my gaze, practically hypnotizing me with her elegant blue eyes, before giving an indignant sounding huff and looking away as if she's dismissed me completely.

"I'll think about it," I hedge, still not sure this is the right path for me.

"Oh!" Reb suddenly looks up from her phone, where she's been scrolling away. "You should be British!"

"What?" I ask.

Reb turns her phone out. "It says here sometimes silly accents help. It's how Emily Blunt got into acting. Ergo, your persona should be British." She snaps her fingers and does an impression pulled straight from Harry Potter. "Wotcher Harry!"

I give her a slow blink. "Do you dye your hair because you're trying to be Tonks?"

She glares at me. "Look, Rowling disappointed us all, but the books are about more than just the author. So you can pry my Tonks fandom from my cold dead hands."

I hold up my hands, palms out. "Just asking."

Thea rolls her eyes and says, "Girls, please! Are we done here, or do I need to order another prickly pear margarita?"

Reb shrugs. "All I'm saying is in a world where you can be anyone, why not be Emily Blunt? Plus, she's married to Hot Jim."

"Who?"

"Jim from The Office. But super hot! What's his name?" She snaps her fingers several times in a row, repeating the phrase. "What's his name? What's his name?"

"John Krasinski?"

"Yes!"

"I think you might have had too many margaritas," I say gently, still not sure where she's going with this.

She leans forwards and plants her hands on the table. "Of course, I've had too many margaritas! Tinker Bell and I are totally lightweights. It's simple biology. But my point is still valid. If Emily Blunt can score hot Jim from The Office, then you, as a British person, could score your hot office guy."

I glance over at Keegan, because I can practically feel the tension rolling off of him. "I think she means—"

"Yeah. I got it. Your hot boss that you have a crush on." Keegan gives me a steely-eyed once over. "Just don't forget you've got a date with me first."

I laugh nervously, not at all sure how I'm supposed to respond to that. Because going with Keegan to this fundraiser isn't a date. Not a date-date. Right?

That's what he called it just now, but that's just because he doesn't like Reid. Right?

There's no way he's actually upset about my crush on Reid. Is there?

More confused than ever, I let out a huff of breath, then raise my glass to take another drink of my margarita, only to find it empty. I'd order another one, but then Reb would too and she doesn't need another. Who knows how the boob armor discussions would go then?

Except when I look back at her, she's got a little smirk

on her mouth that makes me wonder if she was lying about being a lightweight.

Back at the office after lunch, I'm still struggling to concentrate. I should be thinking about the project and my upcoming makeover, but all I can think about is Keegan's comment about Saturday being a date.

Also, why was he at Hung Out to Dry today? Why did we have to run into him at all?

Yes, he's my best friend, and I'm always delighted to see him. But even with best friends, sometimes you need a little moderation. Especially when that best friend is unfortunately hot, and you once had a crush on them. Despite what they say, you can have too much of a good thing.

And when that good thing involves weird lying-on-the-floor-together tension, a sneak attack fake kiss, an unsolicited fantasy, and unexpected knee contact ... well then that's too much.

Or maybe I'm just the biggest dork ever, and I haven't gotten out enough since breaking up with Ollie, and I probably just need to do something to take the edge off tonight when I get home. Yeah. It's probably that second one.

Except that now, with everything that's happened this week, I can't do anything to 'take the edge off,' because it won't feel like I'm just taking the edge off. It will feel like I'm fantasizing about Keegan while I take the edge off. And that's not cool. That's definitely crossing a line.

Like a huge, clearly delineated, uncrossable line. That I will not cross.

Shit, I already said that.

When four o'clock rolls around and I haven't done more

than answer some emails and tweaked some social media posts for one of my long-standing accounts, I slip away to one of the meditation rooms.

Instead of meditating, I pull up Marion Davies's movie *Marrianne*. I watch some clips. I mull. I research. I watch an interview with James Earl Jones talking about his own journey.

By the end of the day, I don't feel any closer to a solution. And, frankly, after listening to James Earl Jones speak, I feel a bit stupid. Maybe we all do when faced with the thoughts and ideas of someone that brilliant.

I'm still mulling over my options, lost in my own thoughts, as I pack up my tote bag and head home, only to find myself alone in the elevator with Reid.

How I managed to step into the elevator with one of the most good-looking men in the western hemisphere without tripping over my feet is beyond me. But I'm extremely grateful for my good luck on that front.

He smiles at me as the doors shut. His black hair is so lustrous the overhead lights cast a little shiny reflection off it, and his eyes sparkle with warmth as he smiles directly at me. Hot Jim ain't got nothing on him.

My belly is somewhere on the floor when he nods at the bank of buttons in front of him. "What floor?"

I open my mouth. My brain fizzles as I meet his intense, dark gaze.

He quirks an eyebrow, and I snap my mouth closed, swallow, and try again.

I'm parked on the first floor in the garage beneath the building. G-1. Simple enough.

Yet I know without even opening my mouth that I'm going to trip over that damn *wa* sound at the beginning of one.

I snap my mouth closed, trapping inside a scream of annoyance. Instead of speaking, I step closer to Reid, edging past him to push the button myself.

The elevator is big enough that he could step back, but he doesn't. Instead, he reaches out at the same moment to push the same button, and for a second, our hands brush. Our fingers tangle.

I jerk my hand away, stepping back as the elevator lurches into motion.

"My bad!"

For some reason, those words come easily.

Of course they do. Because the only thing that is possibly more embarrassing than a stutter is overusing 90s lingo.

Reid chuckles.

It's a gentle sound.

My gaze jerks up to see him looking down. His head is ducked, his hands are in his pockets, and his smile seems ... rueful?

He looks up from under a fringe of dark lashes. "I'm the one who should apologize."

"For,—" The *wa* sound trips me up again, but this time, without the time pressure, I choke it out. "—w-what?"

His gaze meets mine. "I'm sorry I make you nervous. Matt keeps telling me I need to be less intimidating."

I blink, unsure how to respond. Unsure how to process the idea that Reid is apologizing to me. That Reid seems to have doubts and insecurities of his own.

A moment later, the elevator opens, and we both step out. Reid stops by a car near the elevator, parked in one of the primo reserved spots.

As he clicks open his door, he says, "Can't wait to see your presentation on Friday."

What? He ... what? Reid Forester looks forward to something I do? Reid Forester knows who I *am*? I want to reply with something witty and clever, like I'd seen Marion do all afternoon in those clips where she faked the confidence and masked her stutter. But did I have it in me?

I nod mutely and hurry off to my car.

The last thing I needed today was to fail to make small talk with my boss, who I may or may not be tremendously embarrassing to in approximately eighty-one hours, by devolving into a wordless heap.

As if our interaction in the elevator wasn't already awkward, me trying harder and failing would be humiliating.

By the time I get inside, my hands are trembling. I'm not entirely sure if it's nerves from my encounter with Reid or if it's a hit of adrenaline from this sudden burst of clarity I have.

Either way, I dial Thea's number. When she picks up, I blurt, "Sasha."

"Excuse me, Meg? What was that?"

"I figured out who I want my new persona to be. I want to be Sasha."

"The cat who lives at the bar?"

"Yes. I want to be Sasha the cat." Because who better to emulate than this beautiful creature who has zero fucks to give about anyone else? "Think about it. I'm tired of being weak and mousey. Everybody loves Sasha, but she doesn't give a damn about anyone. She's cool, confident, and in control of every situation."

Thea chuckles. "I believe you're right. Sasha just might be the perfect persona for you."

I desperately want to believe it will really be this simple.

If I can imagine I am Sasha, with all her confidence and

style, for just a few hours, for just one day, then I can over-come this fear of giving presentations. I won't be a burden to my team. I won't have to worry about losing my job. I won't blend into the background everywhere I go, like a timid mouse. Everyone at work will realize that my good ideas and hard work are ... well, mine.

And then maybe, if I end up in the elevator with my dream guy, I'll actually be able to speak to him.

ten

I SPEND all of Wednesday working with Tad to digitize and spruce up the pitch. We both keep our eyes on our phones, waiting for messages from Teresa. The last we heard from her was late Monday, when she let us know they were keeping her son overnight. He'd most likely have surgery in the morning.

We don't hear from Teresa after that, which puts Tad and me on edge. It's a sign of how distracted Teresa must be. Two years ago, she had walking pneumonia and still texted us so often from home that Matt threatened to take her off the company phone plan.

Despite our distraction, Tad and I get the presentation ready enough to show it to Matt by late afternoon. He gushes, which I expected, because he can be over the top with his praise. Still, I know the work is good work.

Right before Tad and I leave for the day, we get a message from Teresa letting us know Noah made it through surgery and is doing fine, but that she'll be out all of next week. Tad and I exchange a serious look as we both text back that we've got the presentation covered.

I try to take comfort in the fact that Tad seems confident that I can do this. Of course, I seem confident, too. It's just that I know I'm faking it.

By the time I make it home, I have three voice messages from Thea arranging our plans for my makeover tomorrow. I have over a dozen texts from Keegan's mom, as well as a rant from Reb that starts with the address of the salon and ends with a tirade about what kind of lingerie would be appropriate for a female assassin.

I also have texts from Keegan. I answer those first, keeping my tone light and breezy. He's texted me multiple times this week to confirm our plans for the weekend, and though I've answered them all, I can tell I'm being weird even if he hasn't called me on it.

This gala is looming over me. I know our date isn't a *romantic* date, but all the prep work leading up to it makes it feel momentous. I could text in a hurricane, and it still wouldn't feel breezy enough to balance out this ... I don't even know what to call these flurries in my belly.

I spend the evening sketching while the original Star Wars trilogy plays in the background. Every time Vader is on screen, I close my eyes and imagine him having a stutter.

At bedtime, I try to get into a romance novel from my favorite author, Kat Baxter, who writes these fun, amazing insta-love romances.

Tonight, they aren't working for me. I love the idea that some hot, growly alpha hero could take one look at a curvy, nerdy girl like me and fall head over heels. Normally, that fantasy is totally my jam, but tonight, it feels like entering a danger zone to entertain those kinds of fantasies.

While he's not usually growly, he's definitely hot. The first time we met, I asked him if he was related to Kurt Cobain. After that, I could barely stand to meet his gaze.

The first six weeks of our relationship involved a lot—even for me—of stammering, flushed cheeks, and hiding behind whatever tall object was nearest when I ran into him.

We might never have become friends if there hadn't been an incident involving a dying rat and me getting locked out of my room wearing only a towel. Keegan came to my rescue, loaning me a pair of sweatpants. And he let me stay in his room overnight while the rat finished dying in my room. Yes, that's how bad the co-op was. Once a month, the super put out rat poison, and then it was like the set of a Shakespearian tragedy for rodents.

The next morning, Keegan picked the lock to my room and disposed of the rat's corpse. And we've been friends ever since.

So is he hot? Yes. Does he have all kinds of mad, manly skills that make my girly parts swoon? Also, yes. Did I imagine myself in love with him for a while? Sadly, also yes.

Is he the source of all of my hard-earned wisdom regarding how hot-guys-don't-fall-for-me?

The less said about that topic, the better.

Suffice it to say, I don't have any illusions that this makeover Thea is planning will snag any man's attention. I learned a long time ago how to compartmentalize my fantasy life from my real life.

I keep swiping, looking for something to read that's a little less relatable, and a lot more *atypically* spicy.

A few hours—and galaxies—later, I'm nodding off midway through an alien romance that stretches even *my* penchant for creativity.

And when I fall asleep, I have a ... disturbing dream, for lack of a better word.

I wake up grumpy, because I haven't had a dream like that about Keegan in years. I thought ... no, I knew ... I'd gotten over that fantasy. Keegan isn't some guy I don't know. He's my best friend. A real person, not some fictional creation of my mind.

Despite that, I can't keep my mind from wandering.

The dream had been an unsettling combination of the real events from the past several days mixed with pure, erotic fantasy. Like all dreams, it's a senseless jumble of images until it's not. Keegan and I are lying side by side on the floor. Except instead of getting up and putting away the vacuum, I kiss him. And then he's above me, grinding his hips against mine as he kisses me, one hard leg between mine. Then he's kissing a path down my neck.

Then suddenly, we're not on the floor, but in his kitchen. I'm seated on the counter and he's still kissing his way down my body.

By the time I woke up, my body was a trembling mass of nerves and tension. I was more turned on from a dream about Keegan than from any actual experience I'd ever had with Ollie. I don't know what that says about my relationship with Ollie or about my imagination.

All I know is that this has to stop.

If it's crossing a line to fantasize about your boss, then fantasizing about your best friend is the equivalent of jumping into a formula one race car and speeding over the line at a hundred miles an hour.

Or however fast formula one race cars go. I'm not a car-speed expert.

Whatever. The point is, it's not cool to have dirty dreams about your best friend. It's weird, and I thought I was past it. Which means I'm already in a pissy mood when I pick up Thea for my appointment to get my hair done.

By the time we make it to the salon and I'm ensconced in the chair, things are not any better. Reb breezes into the salon with Thea, who's lugging a caddy of lattes, just as I'm questioning every decision in my life that led me to this point.

The salon Reb goes to is a ridiculously expensive, undoubtedly exclusive hair salon in central Austin. The stylishly dressed receptionist took one look at me and asked for a down payment before she would even let me in.

Reb huffs in indignation and asks them to check the card on file. Thankfully, Thea prevents an all-out brawl. She's brought fancy lattes for everyone, including the stylist and the receptionist, and smooths over everything.

Once I'm in the salon chair, Reb's stylist, a guy named Rafe, consults with Thea and Reb about what to do with my hair. I quell my nerves at the potential price tag by reminding myself I firmly believe people deserve a living wage. Given the person-power involved in my makeover, it should be expensive—ethically speaking.

The result is I'm being treated like royalty. Specifically, that girl from *The Princess Diaries*, who desperately needed a makeover, but still. Everyone seems to have a different opinion about what should be done with my hair. Thea is in favor of a platinum bob reminiscent of Marilyn Monroe. Reb suggests shoulder-length cut and streaks dyed the colors of a peacock—no big surprise there. Rafe makes a chuckling sound of disapproval as he shifts my hair between his fingers and declares I need babylights and a Brazilian Blowout, which will make me look sophisticated.

I don't know what a Brazilian blowout is, but it sounds dirty enough that I don't dare Google it, since my phone is a company phone and therefore Forester+Blake can legally review my search history.

This is probably why Tad has a work phone and a personal phone. I bet he spends at least some of those "naps" in the meditation rooms watching porn on his phone. I only have the one phone, because a) I'm too cheap to pay for a second phone, and b) I rarely need to google things Forester+Blake might find offensive. Maybe I should buy one of those burner phones from the gas station for occasions just like this. I wonder if anyone else at work has a burner phone to watch porn on. Or maybe no one else …

Rafe snaps his fingers beside my ear, bringing me back into the moment. When I meet his gaze in the mirror, he leans over and says in a husky voice, "In the end, my dear, only you can decide."

His tone implies that the fate of the nation depends on my choice. Or possibly the fate of Middle Earth if I imagine him with a long graying beard. Clearly he's determined to give me "The Haircut of Destiny."

The salon employees all nod, as though in awe of Rafe's wisdom. Thank God Thea steps in and sums up my options.

"What do you think? A sexy blonde, artsy peacock streaks, or a few face-framing babylights with a Brazilian blowout for a more sophisticated edge?"

Trying not to feel overwhelmed by my options, I blow out a breath. "Okay, so my choices are: sexy, artsy, or s-s-s-sophisticated."

"I pick sexy."

Sexy is the obvious choice, right? After all, my idea is sexy. This character I'm creating—Sasha—she is sexy.

I'm not, but she is. When Sasha walks into Monday's meeting, she needs to exude that confidence, that va-va-voom sexiness of Jessica Rabbit. If I'm going to be Sasha, then I need a sexy haircut to pull it off.

But just how blonde are we talking here? Platinum blonde doesn't feel right to me. I don't really feel like a blonde, and I definitely don't feel like a platinum blonde.

"Could we do honey blonde? That's still sexy, right? Like Cameron Diaz blonde?"

Reb frowns. "Who is Cameron Diaz?"

I look at her in shock. "Oh, my god! Cameron Diaz. From *There's Something About Mary*? And *The Holiday*? How do you not know who Cameron Diaz is?"

She glares at me. "Shut up. I don't make fun of you when you don't know who Lord British is. Or Captain Crunch."

"I know what Cap'n Crunch is."

"Not the cereal," she hisses at me.

"Okay, okay." I try not to roll my eyes. "What is Captain Crunch?"

"Not what. Who!" Reb's eyes glint with a fanatical excitement. "Captain Crunch was one of the original phone phreaks. Like a proto-hacker. The man himself, John Draper, is considered problematic, but haven't all famous men from the seventies disappointed us over and over again?"

I feel a little like maybe this conversation is treading a little close to Reb's perennially disappointing father, but decide it's better not to jab a finger directly into the bullet wound that's her relationship with her dad.

Thankfully, Thea interrupts before I need to respond.

"Girls," Thea chides. "Is this really the time?"

Even Rafe looks annoyed. Which, given what he's being paid per hour, I don't think is fair.

Reb points an accusing finger at me. "She started it."

Rafe clears his throat. "Luckily, I have heard of Cameron Diaz. And yes, I can do that." He runs his fingers once more through my hair and gives a satisfied nod. "And you will finally be magnificent."

Once again, he is using his theatrical "Haircut of Destiny" voice. This will be the one haircut to rule them all.

But who am I to criticize? I create imagined drama all the time to get my work done. I can hardly blame the guy if he does the same.

"Okay, let's do this," I say with what I hope is conviction and excitement. "I'm ready for my 'Haircut of Destiny'."

Thea, Rafe, and Reb all stare at me blankly.

I blink. Then realize I said that out loud.

Cool. Yep.

I wave a hand dismissively, like they're the weird ones. "That's w-what I named it in my head. Because that's what it feels like. You know, like a big deal. And since Rafe keeps using his sexy wizard voice, I thought ..." I let my voice trail off as I realize that their blank looks aren't getting less blank.

I clear my throat, smile brightly, and pretend I haven't been babbling. "What next?"

Things move quickly after that. Or rather, the people around me move quickly. I mostly just sit there, answering important questions like, "How is the temperature?" and "Can I refill your champagne?"

Yes, this salon is that kind of place. A place that serves champagne in the middle of the afternoon. And, yes, that's how nervous I am. I am drink-champagne-before-five nervous. Which is saying something, since I normally only drink champagne on New Year's Eve.

Other than sipping champagne, my job is to sit still. Early on, Thea spills the beans about why I'm getting the makeover. Before I know it, everyone in the salon is emotionally invested. Reb has been documenting the transformation and sending pictures to Felicia, the stylist who will meet us at Downtown UpThreads. She also pulls up some documentary about hackers from what she calls the "Golden Age of Hackers," but thirty minutes in, Rafe declares he can't work under these circumstances and insists I switch to watching makeup tutorials.

Reb pulls some up for me. I'm skeptical, since she's the one who didn't know who Cameron Diaz is, but the videos teach me a few things. I doubt I'll be able to replicate any of these techniques, but I'm willing to try.

Four hours later, I look like a whole new person, but I'm too hungry to care. I demand Thea and Reb feed me tacos before we go shopping. Dorothea has known me long enough to know that I never joke about needing a taco, so instead of heading straight over to Downtown UpThreads, we swing by my favorite taco joint. Two tacos later, I feel emotionally prepared for the wardrobe makeover. Emotionally, but perhaps not financially.

Downtown UpThreads is just south of the river in a neighborhood with a trendy, funky vibe. It's nestled between a tattoo parlor and a record store. The fact that I didn't know record stores were a thing again is probably a sign I'm not cool enough to shop here.

Based on the look I get when I walk in, the clerk behind the counter clearly agrees, but Thea announces that Felicia is expecting us. The clerk sniffs doubtfully, but heads to the back to find Felicia.

Thankfully, since Downtown UpThreads is a consignment store, I can afford to shop here. Unfortunately, I usually shop at thrift stores. And not the trendy ones, either. We're talking Goodwill and Savers. So even heavily discounted, everything still seems overpriced to me.

When I say this, Thea just waves away my objections.

"Of course, these things are more expensive than your

normal potato sacks. If you want a decent wardrobe, pay for it."

"My wardrobe has been just fine until now."

Thea laughs, like I made a joke.

"I'm serious."

"Nonsense. You are a competent adult woman with a professional career. You have ambition. Dress like it."

I don't know, maybe Thea is a mind reader, because before I can whine some more, she clasps my arm, leans forward, and says, "Suck it up."

"I thought y-you said phrases like 'suck it up' are an indication that my generation can't properly communicate?"

She sniffs and—despite being several inches shorter than me—looks down her nose at me. "Since you are acting like a petulant child, I thought I would treat you like one."

Despite the tacos, I am clearly feeling a bit pissy.

Before I can defend myself, Felicia comes out of the back. I instantly know it's her, because Loretta, Keegan's mom, is right behind her.

I freeze, like a raccoon crossing the road at night, unsure if I have time to bolt or if I can scare off a car just by hissing at it.

Yes, I'm probably being dramatic, but (despite what Keegan said the other day) I've always assumed Keegan's parents have never liked me much. I think they blame me for the fact that he owns a bar instead of joining the family business.

She stops in her tracks, places a hand over her heart and sighs. "Meg, you look gorgeous."

I'm shocked into immobility as she crosses the room and wraps me in a boney-armed hug.

Wait? She's hugging me? Like we're old friends?

What is happening? What strange new world did I accidentally pass into, and why didn't Rod Sterling warn me I was entering the Twilight Zone?

And also, she thinks *I* look gorgeous?

Did I mention that before she married into the McQuades, Loretta was one of the famed Kilgore Rangerettes? And she was a flight attendant for a private jet. A Rangerette, a flight attendant, *and* Miss Texas?

It's like she won the glamor Triple Crown.

She's still thin and gorgeous. I'm sure she's had work done, but she probably paid so much for it, you can't tell.

Don't get me wrong, I'm not judging her for getting work done. I'm just impressed she's nearing sixty and looks like she's thirty-two.

She pulls back from the hug to give me another once-over.

"I love the sexy blowout and face framing! Just gorgeous."

She reaches up and her fingers flit briefly near a lock of hair that's draped over my shoulder before her hand drops away. There's something in her gaze that makes my throat feel too tight. Something that's almost …

Well, I'd say it's almost maternal if I didn't know better.

But I do know better.

Besides, I've never inspired maternal pride. Not even in my own mother, who usually just shakes her head and asks why I have to be so willful.

So whatever I think I see in Loretta's gaze, I'm sure it's not remotely fond.

Impulsively, I pull out one of the linen handkerchiefs I carry and thrust it at her.

She looks from the handkerchief to me and back again, frowning.

"You're having an allergy attack," I blurt. "It's p-probably from the oak pollen."

She stares at me for a moment and then laughs, taking the handkerchief and running it through her fingers before lightly dabbing her eyes. "Of course. It's the oak pollen. It's terrible this time of year."

I glance back at Reb to see her laughing.

"Let's get into the private room in the back," Felicia says. "And get you a glass of wine."

Coward that I am, I follow her without a second look back.

eleven

FELICIA LEADS us into a room that's laid out like the ones you see in those bridal shows with one area curtained off and several cushy chairs. There's a rack on one side already laden with clothes. It's overflowing with silks, satins, and chiffons.

"What'll you have?" She asks, heading toward a tray.

"Oh, I don't need w-w-wine," I say.

"Loretta and I have already picked some things out for you to try," she says, gesturing to what must be two dozen outfits, dresses, and gowns, hand still hovering near the bar cart along the far wall.

Thea claps her hands when she sees them. "What fun! You'll be like her fairy godmother!"

Loretta gives her a conspiratorial wink. "I know, right?"

"I don't know that I'd say 'fairy godmother'," I say, putting air quotes around the word. "Fairy godmother implies a lack of agency on my part. Do I really need a—"

"Yes," all three women say before I can finish the sentence.

I make a noise that sounds more suspicious than I mean it to.

Felicia tips her head, looking at me cautiously. "Why do you keep pushing back on this? Most women would be thrilled to have a few smart, savvy friends give her a makeover."

I look at each of them. I don't point out the most obvious problem with Felicia's statement. Why am I pushing back?

Skepticism, yes, but maybe a little resentment as well.

Eventually, I shrug, thinking of the way Keegan came to my defense the other day at lunch, of how nice it was to hear him tell me that I don't need to change anything. That I look good the way I am. "I guess I just didn't think the way I looked was so bad before."

Loretta and Felicia both make vague noises clearly meant to placate my ego; only Thea gives serious thought to my comment. She clucks her tongue sympathetically, before saying, "My dear, there was nothing wrong with the way you looked—"

"You called my clothes potato sacks. M-m-multiple times."

"Fine." She huffs. "But there's nothing wrong with wearing a potato sack if that's what you want to wear. If you are at peace with every aspect of your life, by all means, wear whatever you want. But if you are not happy with the track you're on, you must change something. Clothes and hair are easy to change, so why not start there?"

"Because I like the way I looked before."

"No, my dear," Thea says. "You were comfortable the way you looked before. You never thought about your appearance or your clothes long enough to like or dislike them."

I open my mouth to protest, but snap it shut again when I realize she's right.

"There is nothing wrong with the way you dressed before, but it's not the way Sasha would dress."

"Sasha?" Loretta asks.

I give myself a mental slap on the forehead for forgetting that they don't know all the details of this weird plan. Thea quickly explains about my stutter, the presentation, and the reason I'm creating this persona. I stand there in silence, cringing the whole time, because, let's face it, the fact that I need to go to these ends to make a presentation sounds pathetic.

When Thea finishes the explanation, Felicia makes cooing, sympathetic sounds, but Loretta just studies me, her expression thoughtful.

"I guess that explains why you've always been so quiet around me and Johnny."

It takes me a moment to realize Johnny is Jonathon McQuade, Keegan's father. Aka, the single most intimidating man I've ever met.

Despite all my Ms. Piggy-inspired karate-chopping of pillows the other night, Jonathon McQuade scares the pee out of me.

"It gets w-w-worse when I'm nervous."

"Hmmm." She gives me a hard look before saying, "I think you need to look for a more supportive work environment."

"I don't think—"

"But if you don't want to speak to HR," she continues briskly. "And you think this makeover will help, then we have some amazing looks for you to try on. And you don't need to be scared or nervous, because we are going to find a wardrobe you'll fall in love with and look fabulous in. When we're done with you, you're going to slay all day."

"Between the four of us, we have excellent taste."

I look over the gaggle of women forming a semicircle around me, each of them with wildly different styles, and each of them stunning or compelling or attractive in their own way. Each of them secure in their image.

A lightbulb clicks on in my mind, illuminating the dots I've never even seen before, much less connected. They all have cohesive looks. Reb, with her multicolored hair, vintage tees, and gorgeous collection of artisan jewelry, has set an expectation for everyone who knows her. Thea commands a room the moment she enters—personality dominating, of course—but that personality is in every line of the silk blouse she's wearing. It has an asymmetrical, oversized collar and artfully drapes wider around her shoulder on one side.

Loretta's polished sophistication would make presidential wives jealous. That's when I realize what they all have that I don't.

Branding.

Hells bells, that's all clothing and hair and makeup is— it's your own personal *brand*. And I'm a brand expert without giving an ounce of my own sense of self in anything I'm wearing.

"Meg?" Loretta asks, snapping me back to reality. As if my whole perspective of clothing and how I dress wasn't just turned on its head. "Are you ready, honey?"

Her eyes are so much like Keegan's Caribbean-blue eyes. Keegan clearly gets his blond hair from his dad, because her hair is a rich sable, smooth and sophisticated, with only a little of the volume Texas hair is known for. She is a stunningly beautiful woman. It's more than that, though. More than the genetic lottery she clearly won. She's not just beautiful. She's stylish and put together.

She looks like a real adult in a way I've never quite mastered.

The presentation aside, I want her help. I don't want to be her. Clearly. That would be creepy.

But I want to borrow a little of her confidence and charm. A little of her polish. So that when I'm at the gala with Keegan on Saturday night, I look like I fit in with his world.

Finally, I blow out a breath.

"Okay. But maybe I should have one of those drinks after all."

The older woman beams at me as Felicia begins to uncork a bottle of wine. "Sounds like a plan to me."

It isn't until I take a sip that I realize she called me honey. And then I realize it didn't feel contrived.

Three hours later, I have ten new work outfits picked out. Each has been styled by Loretta and Felicia to include shoes and accessories, so getting dressed in the morning will be no harder than it was when I was wearing nearly identical black shift dresses every day. The new clothes are bagged and ready for me to hand over my credit card. It's more money than I've ever spent on clothes at once. Maybe I should be freaking out. Probably.

On the other hand, Loretta assures me that these new outfits are timeless, quality items I can wear for years. And, after all, they are secondhand. Less than I would pay for retail.

Once all the work clothes are tucked away behind the

counter, Felicia leads us to a room in the back with chairs and a pedestal, the kind of room you see in Say Yes to the Dress. I am wrapped in a fluffy robe that Felicia provided, so I wouldn't have to change in and out of my own clothes every other minute.

An assistant scurries out with yet another bottle of champagne as Felicia claps her hands together and declares, "Now for the fun part!"

Um ... say what now?

This is the fun part?

The part where I'm faced with picking out a dress that will make me look fabulous and like I fit into Keegan's world?

To me, that seems less fun and more stressful, but I'm willing to give it a try.

"Okay," I say with forced enthusiasm. "Let me see the options."

The assistant stops pouring champagne and wheels over a clothing rack with three options. They're all gorgeous, but I'm immediately drawn to one: a floral silk floor-length dress with tiny straps crisscrossing the back and a slit that would make my legs look even longer.

The second I touch the fabric, I know this is the dress for me. The silk flows through my fingers like liquid. The abstract floral pattern of dappled pinks is both modern and feminine.

There's a faint chuckle from behind me. I turn to see Loretta beaming at me.

"That's the one Keegan liked best, too."

"It's gorgeous," I admit, sounding oddly breathless.

"It's a new company." Felicia takes the dress from the rack and gestures me toward the dressing room. "They focus on sustainable fabrics and fair trade business practices."

It's only once I'm alone in the dressing room that I notice there's no price tag.

When I mention this as I'm slipping out of the robe, it's Loretta who responds.

"Keegan told me to talk you into letting him pay," she says with coy amusement.

I sigh. "I can't let him buy me lavish gifts."

"First off, it's a single dress. Therefore, it's only one gift, not gifts plural. And secondly, whyever not? He picked out this dress because he knew you would love it, and he wanted to see you in it. Think of this as something you're doing for him."

I tug back the curtain to look at Loretta. "I just ..."

"At least try it on," she pleads, laying on the puppy dog eyes. "He made me promise I would get you to try it on."

Why is it that it was easier to say no to Keegan than it is to say no to Loretta?

"Okay." I'll try it on.

It takes a hot minute to get into the dress, just because of the way it's cut, and I need Felicia's help with the various straps and ties that hold it in place. It has a deep vee neckline, a halter that ties in back and side cutouts that peekaboo at the small of my waist.

The silk hugs my curves and reveals more skin than I'm used to, but once I'm standing on that pedestal, I feel like a goddess.

The idea of Keegan seeing me in this dress sends a jolt of anticipation through me.

The idea that he picked it out? That it's what he wants to see me wearing?

Somehow, that's scary and exciting all at the same time.

Too bad he won't actually get to see me in it. If it's the dress he picked out for me, I'm sure it's way out of my budget.

With a sigh of resignation, I step down off the dias. "It's gorgeous. But I can't afford it."

Loretta takes my hands in hers. "You should let him do this. Please."

Gah. That please nearly breaks me. How can I explain to her why I can't? I get it. I understand that this might be a drop in the bucket for him financially, but it's still a huge chunk of change to me. I can't overlook the significance to me.

Even though I know Loretta would never understand.

"I just can't."

As if she senses my discomfort, Felicia hurries forward with another dress option.

"Don't worry. I've got something that will still be perfect."

It's not one of the three gorgeous dresses, but at least the price tag is on it and I know it's something I can afford.

By the time I leave. I have more new clothes than I've ever purchased in one sitting. In addition to several new outfits for work, the self-proclaimed fairy godmothers picked out all the accessories for my gala dress, so that getting dressed will be effortless.

I won't have to make a single decision on that front. Plus, I'll look fantastic, because Loretta and Felicia clearly know how I should dress to fit in with this crowd. And because Reb and Thea are here, the outfit has just enough sass and flare that it still feels like it's something I would wear.

The dress Felicia picked out is a green jersey maxi dress with spaghetti straps. The fabric is soft and flowy, so it highlights my curves. It's sexy but understated. Practical enough that I'll be able to wear it again. I can even wear my favorite sandals with it.

Thea, the sneak, brought along several pieces from her collection of vintage jewelry, which we all *ooh* and *aah* over. Felicia makes her promise to bring the items to her to bid on if she ever decides to sell any of her pieces. In the end, I let Loretta pick out the jewelry, since I figure she knows best.

She picks out a set of earrings, bracelet, and necklace. It's not what I would have picked, but when I see the result, I know it's perfect. I feel like the coolest version of myself I've ever been.

After checking out, Reb and Thea make plans to come over and help me get ready on Saturday. Maybe I imagine it, but Loretta almost looks sad that the evening of epic shopping is over. So, on impulse, I give her a hug and remind her I'll see her Saturday night.

It's not until I'm at home alone, my champagne buzz gone and all my new clothes hung up and organized in my closet that I start to think about lunch the other day at Hung Out to Dry. Was Keegan acting weird about the makeover?

Maybe?

A little?

I mean, if I didn't know better, I'd say some of those comments he made about Reid seemed almost … jealous.

But surely that's not the case. Why would he be jealous of Reid?

It can't be that. No, it must be that he's just feeling protective. After all, it hasn't been that long since Ollie and I broke up. Undoubtedly, he doesn't want to see me get hurt.

I'm rewatching season one of The Good Place when I shoot him a text:

> Thanks for loaning me your mom today. She was awesome. Totally deserves her title as the Queenmaker.

> Thanks for inviting her. She had a blast

I pause, mulling over how different today was than I thought it would be. I expected having her there to be a bother. I expected judgment from her. On some level, I guess I thought she was there to keep me in line and make sure I wouldn't embarrass the McQuades this weekend. In retrospect, I don't think it was that. I got the feeling that she genuinely just wanted to be included.

> But seriously, she was so helpful. 🧓

> And now I will look totally fabulous at work from now on.

There is a long pause and lots of dancing ellipsis before he replies.

> You always look great.

I stare at the text for a moment, because that feels ... off, somehow. Like he's annoyed. Like I've annoyed him.

I want to talk to him, to have some reassurance that things will go back to normal, but I also don't want to text impulsively. I'd rather say nothing at all than say the wrong thing. Do I play it casual and pretend nothing is wrong or do I just come out and ask him?

I go for a joke.

> Who died and left Aristotle in charge of ethics?

As soon as I hit send, I'm hit with a wave of nerves.

I'm being a coward. Maybe I should just own up to the weirdness?

There's a long pause, during which ellipses trickle across my screen, stop for a while, and then start up again. The knot in my belly gets tighter. Or bigger. Or something. When I can't take it anymore, I ask,

> Are we okay?

> Yeah. Of course.

> Are you watching The Good Place? Shouldn't you be preparing for your presentation?

> Um, obviously. 🙄

> You need to get to work. 😐

> But it's the best show ever 🥺

We text for a few minutes before he reminds me again that I should be working and wishes me good luck tomorrow.

I set my phone aside, feeling somewhat mollified. After all, our friendship started when I was locked out of my room in only a towel. We've been in weirder situations than this and made it through.

After binging the rest of season one of The Good Place while finalizing my renderings for the designs for the presentation, I eat cheese and crackers in bed while I review my presentation. In the end, I fall asleep knowing that this time tomorrow, one way or another, this will all be over with and my life can return to normal.

twelve

I GET UP EARLY Friday to ensure I'll have plenty of time to recreate the look that we picked out for me to give my presentation in.

I pick out my favorite of the three outfits I came home with, a navy suit with a short skirt and a double-breasted blazer with a plunging neckline, which Felicia swears is appropriate to wear with only a bright green V-tank. The outfit shows off way more leg and cleavage than I'd normally be comfortable with, but the look is somehow both professional and sexy. Between it and my newly tousled blonde waves, I look like a badass.

I think I do a decent job on the hair and makeup. Reb sends me several encouraging texts and demands to see a selfie of the final product.

I snap a couple of shots when I'm dressed, and she declares my appearance "Tight."

I'm still not sure any of this will actually work until I'm at work in the break room and I run into Tad, who is making his morning coffee at the espresso bar. He's chatting with some guy from Account Services as he waits for the machine to do its thing. He glances in my direction, then does a noticeable double take.

At first, I nearly balk at his reaction. I'm still not comfortable "in character," but it's too late to back out now. With that thought propelling me forward, I weave through the tables toward my co-worker. Tad glances to either side —to make sure I really was waving at him—then straightens, puffing out his chest as he smiles at me.

That's when it hits me. Tad didn't even recognize me at first. I waved and crossed the room to talk to him, and I watched as he put the pieces together. Confusion, then surprise, then amazement all settling into the lines of his face, one by one. By the time I reached him, he was smiling at me like he'd never seen me before.

And I guess he hadn't. Not like this, anyway.

I reach around him for a coffee mug. "Hi, Tad."

"Hi ..."

His eyes go wide and then he squints at me, blinking rapidly. "Jesus, Meg. What'd you do to yourself?"

I shove my own mug under the espresso machine's spout and push a few buttons. "A friend gave me a makeover. She thought it'd give me more confidence at the pitch today. Do y-you think it'll help?" I ask playfully, but when I glance over at Tad, he's still gaping at me. "Tad, close y-your mouth. It's rude to stare."

The machine sputters out the last of my foam, and I snag my mug, relieved to escape Tad's scrutiny. Unfortunately, Tad follows me back to the trio of desks where we sit.

"Meg, I'm sorry. You just look really different."

Trying to hide how flustered I feel, I sigh, as if exasperated by the delay.

"I hope you mean that in a good way?" I say it, but it comes out like a question.

But before I could second guess, he says, "You look stunning, Meg."

"R-really?" I ask, and I realize I really care about his response.

He nods. "Sorry for my reaction. I just—I guess I wasn't expecting a Christina Hendricks lookalike, but Jesus—if this doesn't make the presentation go well," he gestures to my outfit. "Nothing will."

I feel myself blushing.

Great. Because it's my outfit and not my ideas that are now the selling point.

This is not going as I'd hoped. Thea had sworn that this makeover would give me confidence. Instead, I feel like a freak.

And unprofessional at that. I'd said as much to her! But all my protestations had fallen on gleefully deaf ears.

"*Honey,*" she'd said. "*With a body like this, you don't need to look professional.*"

And if the way Tad's staring at me is any sign, Thea had been right.

I pause, my fingers hovering over my keyboard. If Thea was right about that, what else might she be right about?

I squeeze my eyes closed and try to picture Sasha the cat. Her cool, silvery beauty. Her absolute confidence that everyone loves her. Her "you know you want to touch me, but don't you dare try it" attitude.

If Sasha can convey all that with a single glare from her ice-blue eyes, then surely I—with my college education and years of writing experience—can manage a simple sentence or two that will put Tad in his place.

I cross one leg over the other, prop my elbows far back

on the arms of my chair, and spin around to face Tad. I'm acutely aware that my skirt rides up higher on my thigh than I'm used to. And equally aware that my posture displays my breasts to their best advantage.

I've never used my body to get what I wanted, but Sasha would.

"Tad, be a doll and double-check the graphics? We can't afford to slip up on this. And we need to be in the conference room in ten minutes."

Be a doll? Did I actually just say that? I hold my breath, waiting for him to laugh at me.

Instead, Tad nods—the smile he sends me is a little dopey. "I'll get right on it."

I watch him leave, feeling baffled. Should I be thrilled or horrified? Is it really that easy? Could men really be won over with faux confidence and a low-cut blouse?

That's when it hits me. Just now, I hadn't stuttered when talking to Tad. My throat hadn't closed. My words hadn't log-jammed. Score one for Sasha the cat.

Now I just have to fake Sasha's confidence and allure for the meeting with Butler.

And trust that I can pull it off again.

Thirty minutes later, when Matt walks into the conference room with the representatives from Butler, I don't give myself even a moment to consider that I might fail at this. That I might stutter or flounder.

Butler sent over a trio of people for the pitch meeting, two women and a man. Often, meetings like this are done over video conference, but Butler's corporate headquarters are right outside of Houston, only a couple of hours away.

Matt handles the introductions and the small talk. I let him, because it's what he's great at and because I have my own "lines" memorized. I've refined and reworked my pitch to avoid words and sound combinations that tend to trip me up. I may be playing a role, but it's a role of my own creation, and there's no need to make this harder on myself than it has to be.

When Matt hands the presentation over to me, Tad cues up the graphics, and I stroll to the front of the room, already talking. "We've all seen countless ads that sell cleaning products to moms. Nearly every vacuum ad out there shows some variation of spilled juice, tracked dirt, or clinging pet hair. Our ad targets a different woman."

I pause and glance at the screen behind me, letting the images do the selling for me.

I've been drawing since I was eleven. Okay, yeah, I know all kids draw. But, I've been working my ass off at this since I was a tween. I know I'm good. And I've been working in advertising for nearly a decade. After that much time, you get a feeling for when the idea is right. You just know.

This is my creativity—my mojo—at its absolute best. Another fantasy turned into a brilliant ad copy.

Tad and I have refined the images, but the basic concept is the same.

A pair of champagne flutes discarded on the fireplace mantel. A faceless couple slow-dancing, their bare feet shuffling across the plush carpet. Pan back to a shot of them lying on the floor, her hair mussed, his hands braced on either side of her face as he leans down to kiss her. Her knees are bent, her thighs cradling him. Her toes curl into the carpet as her hips rock up to meet him. Pan away from the couple, past the forgotten champagne flutes, to the Butler Steam Vac peeking out of a linen closet's slightly ajar door. Then the tagline appears.

"Because sometimes you want your carpet to be *really* clean."

With that final line frozen on the screen, I turn back to the people from Butler. "Given the current shift in demographic trends, we want to target not just mothers relentlessly cleaning up everyone else's mess. We don't want cleanliness to be associated with monotonous, endless chores. Everyone wants a clean house, sure. But we want Butler to be associated with something *else* we all want. Something relatable and a skosh cheeky. We believe our ad does just that."

Based on the smiles of the two women, they agree. The man from Butler isn't sold on the idea as easily. I continue the presentation while Tad flips through the additional slides, showing off the statistics that prove our point. By the time we reach the last slide, I know we've got them.

Matt leads them off to talk contracts, leaving Tad and me to pack up. The second the conference room door closes behind Matt and the folks from Butler, Tad jumps to his feet and gives me a high five so strong it nearly knocks me over.

Maybe it's the heels, but honestly, I think it's his excitement.

"Damn!" he exclaims. "You knocked that out of the park!"

"*We* knocked it out of the park. I couldn't have done it without you."

Tad blinks, clearly surprised by my praise. Then a smile spreads over his face. "Thanks."

The guy is practically beaming as he gets back to work. It's crazy how such a tiny drop of praise made such a huge difference in his attitude. Teresa doles out praise like the company is going to deduct it from her paycheck. Teresa loved basking in praise, but rarely wanted to share the spotlight. That was just her style. And it might even be Sasha's style, but it's not mine.

Regardless of whether I get a promotion immediately after this, I'm going to remember this. Someday, I will lead my own team. When I do, I'm going to use praise and cooperation to motivate my team.

When we make it back to our cluster of desks, I fully expect him to knock off early for lunch. Instead, he pulls up the work for another account and dives back in. I shoot a text to Thea and Reb, letting them know how the presentation went, and then I do the same.

I kick off my shoes beneath my desk and pull my feet up, tucking them beneath my legs. The movement is familiar. I pull up Spotify and put on my favorite ambient music playlist, deciding to plug into my earbuds and ride the high of success toward the next task waving for attention on my Trello board.

But the moody flow of synthesizer doesn't soothe the tinge of disappointment that's settling in.

We did it. Sasha did it.

I did it.

The deal is made. Contracts signed. Dollars incoming. But somehow I still feel ... exactly the same.

Tad works through lunch, but then takes off early for a dentist appointment. I sit at my desk and eat the fruit and yogurt I brought from home, trying to plow through some of the work I let slide during the big push for the Butler presentation. Plus, since Teresa is still out, the workload seems endless.

In the late afternoon, I get a text from Keegan asking how the presentation went. I cringe reading it because I should have texted him when I texted Thea and Reb.

Why didn't I?

Honestly, I don't know. Or maybe I do know, and I just don't want to think about it.

And, yeah, when we texted yesterday, he said we were okay. But are we?

Because this doesn't feel okay. It still feels awkward and horrible and like we'll never be on solid ground again.

Since I have all the chill of a coked up Chihuahua, I text him back immediately.

It went fine.

As soon as I hit send, I cringe. What is wrong with me? Fine?

It was the greatest success of my career. I should be thrilled. I *am* thrilled! So why did I downplay it?

I'm still staring at my phone, debating whether I should text him anything else when I get a text from Thea, asking if I want to meet up for cocktails to celebrate. I text her back quickly to let her off the hook and explain that I'm celebrating with people from work.

I might feel guilty about the lie if I thought she actually wanted to meet up. On Friday nights Thea has meetings via zoom with friends in Barcelona to practice her Spanish, so I know she offered to celebrate with me more out of loyalty than anything else.

Is it pathetic that my eighty-three-year-old friend has a more active social life than I do? Yes, it probably is. But at least I acknowledge it and don't take advantage of her offers when they're made purely on principle.

The reality is that no one from Forester+Blake made plans to celebrate. If Teresa wasn't home with a sick kiddo, she might have wrangled after-work drinks for the three of us, but without her to steer the celebration ship, Tad has already left for the day. Even if I'd thought to invite him for a celebration drink, what would he and I have had to talk about?

Besides, after such an undeniable success, I should feel great. Fantastic even.

Instead, I feel … Unsettled.

Like I had this big goal, met it, and now am not sure where to head next. Or maybe I'm just not sure what it means for me, for *Meg*, to have met the goal.

Is this why people get a funk after climbing Everest?

Not that doing a presentation about vacuums is anything near the grit and work needed to climb Everest, but you know. It's the same vibe. Finishing a big goal and being in a funk when you finally do it.

I briefly consider the possibility that my funk is related to Reid's absence from the pitch meeting. Though that just seems … childish and unprofessional.

Just because he told me in the elevator that he couldn't wait to see what I came up with, that doesn't mean he meant it. It's a big company, and I'm sure he doesn't have time to attend all the pitch meetings. Even for the ones as big as a company like Butler.

The presentation was a success. That's the important part. I landed the contract. I did good for Forester+Blake.

This is what I wanted, right?

thirteen

A FEW HOURS LATER, as I'm getting ready to leave, a message pops up on the company's messaging software from Matt.

> Good job, kiddo.

> Thanks

> Butler was so impressed they reached out to us about handling all of their accounts. Not just for the steam vac, but for all Butler appliances.

> What? That's amazing!

> They want to see a proposal by Monday afternoon. Think you can put something together?

Heart pounding, I look around the bullpen. Tad is already gone for the weekend and he's notorious for checking out when he clocks out. Teresa is still home with Noah, as she should be.

Maybe I could draw on a couple people from other teams, but most of them are gone too.

I don't know how feasible it is to pull this off.

They do realize it's Friday afternoon, right?

I know, I know. I tried to push back, but they're in a rush. I've got faith in you, kiddo.

Faith? That seems like a compliment, but is it really? Wouldn't resources or time be better than faith?

Still, it's not like I can say no to this. If landing the Butler Steam Vac account was big for Forester+Blake, then this would be huge.

Before I can respond to Matt to let him know that I'll have ideas for him to review by Monday morning, the software dings to let me know that he's logged out. A moment later, I see him walking out of the executive suite toward the elevators.

I stand, wanting to catch him before he leaves, but he's got his phone to his ear. When he sees me, he gives me a nod, pointing with his free hand toward his phone. He winks at me and flashes a big thumbs up.

I smile back, but it feels more like a grimace. He's leaning into his faith in me a little hard.

Yeah, his trust in me sounds great in theory, but what if I can't deliver? Then what?

I message Tad, both in the company software and on his phone, but he's logged out and his notifications are silenced. Just great. To make matters worse, by the time I'm done messaging Tad, I see a message from Teresa. It starts with a message she forwarded from Matt.

MATT

> The work from your team today looked amazing. Butler wants an additional presentation on Monday. There are notes with details for what they're expecting in the team folder.

TERESA

> Thanks for stepping in for me today. Sounds like it went great. Noah should be well enough by Monday that I can come in and do the presentation to corporate. If you can have a rough draft for me to review by Monday morning, that would be great. Thx.

I scowl as I reread her message and hop over to the team folder to the notes Matt sent. By the time I'm back in messages, Teresa has logged out. Which is to be expected since she's got a sick kiddo. Still, I don't love that everyone is expecting me to do the bulk of the work.

How am I supposed to attend the gala and work up a whole new proposal for all of Butler Appliances?

Keegan isn't picking me up until six-thirty. Reb and Thea aren't coming over to help me get ready until 4:00. I'll just have to work all morning and all day on Sunday. It'll be worth it. After all, it is an amazing opportunity.

I should be thrilled. I *am* thrilled. Surely, this weird feeling in my gut is just stress. Or maybe I'm hungry. That's probably it.

By the time I'm nearly ready to leave, I still haven't eaten, so I grab a sandwich from the deli that's on the ground floor of the Prescott Towers, the building that houses Forester+Blake.

The Prescott Towers are two thirty-story buildings in the heart of downtown Austin. The north tower houses a bunch of businesses, in addition to Forester+Blake. The south tower houses The Prescott Hotel and overlooks Lady Bird Lake as it snakes through downtown. The Towers share a ground-level lobby and atrium, complete with a handful of cafes and shops.

The hotel's top floor has a five-star restaurant, with a gorgeous outdoor seating area. The roof of the north tower has an outdoor patio as well that gets rented out for weddings, parties, and other events. And luckily for me, it's usually empty on a Monday night.

Usually you need a special key card to access the rooftop patio, but when I first started working at Forester+Blake, one of the older employees showed me how to access the roof from the stairwell via a door with a sticky deadbolt. Now, when I'm feeling like this—too keyed up to go home and too on edge to work—I come up to the rooftop to just be outside for a while.

Tonight, I can't make myself go home to eat my sandwich alone in front of the TV. After the stress of presenting to the team from Butler and the intensity of the weekend, that just seems pathetic. So instead, I bring my sandwich and iced tea up to the rooftop.

Only the last gray streaks of dusk linger in the west as I make my way across the rooftop to the northeast corner and the best view of the Capitol. There's a long-abandoned wrought-iron table and chairs up here that are the only evidence anyone else comes up here to enjoy the view.

I've just settled in with my sandwich when my phone rings. I stare at it for a second in shock, because no one but Thea ever calls me and I know she's in her Barcelona zoom right now.

It's not Thea calling. It's Keegan.

I have a moment of panic before answering. Do I try to

play it like everything is normal or do I come clean about how awkward I've been feeling?

I come clean.

"Hey, I'm so glad you called. I've been feeling weird about things. But I just want things to be normal between us again. You know?"

The words spill out of me in a rapid jumble.

One which is followed by ... crickets.

No. Not exactly crickets.

I can hear the noise from the bar in the background and him telling someone where the band can park. Did he butt dial me?

Then I hear a door shut and the ambient noise fades like he just shut himself in his office. "Sorry about that. Never fails. The second I pick up my phone, twenty people need something from me."

I laugh, because yeah, that sounds about right. It's been a long time since I was at Hung Out to Dry on a Friday evening, but even this early everyone needs his attention. Mostly I'm just relieved he didn't hear me being a weirdo.

"No worries. W-what's up?"

Though, now that I've said no worries, I am a little worried. Like I said, he never calls me.

"I just wanted to call and check on you." I can hear his concern through the line. "Your text seemed ... Off."

By off, I assume he means overly enthusiastic.

Unless he's talking about the texts last night, when I was just straight up weird.

"Are you okay?" he asks, when I don't respond, his words coming out in a bit of a rush. "You said it went well today, but I know how important it was to you. And if you need a shoulder to cry on, I'm here. Or there. If you need me, I can come to you." Through the phone I hear someone pounding on the office door and he yells, "Jesus Christ, I will be done in a minute. Whatever it is can wait."

I can picture it all so clearly, it makes me laugh. Somehow, even though we're miles apart, it feels like we're back in college. When we first became friends, during the time between the towel incident and moving from the co-op to the apartment, Keegan would call me every night to make sure I'd made it back to my room okay. Yes, that's how sketchy the co-op was. Whether I was coming home late from studying or walking down the wall from his room to mine, he wanted me to call him as soon as I locked the door.

Most nights, the last thing I did before falling asleep was talk to him on the phone. Even though nearly a decade has passed, this reminds me of that. And somehow it's comforting.

"I'm fine. Really."

"Tell me how it went."

"It went really well. They loved the presentation. We got the account."

"That is amazing! Congratulations! When can I see it?"

"W-what?" My voice comes out high-pitched with panic.

Why would he want to see my pitch? And why this pitch in particular? The pitch that's based on a fantasy about him?

"I want to see what you came up with," he says. His own tone is not at all high pitched or weird.

Of course, he probably won't even realize it's about him. And it's not really about him, anyway. So it's okay. I can show him the pitch. Or … Now, just hear me out here … or I can lie and weasel my way out of it.

I lie like the rug I am.

"I don't think I can show it to anyone yet. Because …"

Shit. I should have planned out a lie instead of just jumping in! "I think there might be an NDA or something."

"Wouldn't you know if you'd signed an NDA?"

"Yep. It seems like I would, doesn't it?"

Gah! Could my lies be any more transparent and stupid?

No. They could not.

I'm just not ready for Keegan to see the ad I created based on the fantasy of him kissing me.

I mean, yeah, someday he might see it when it goes live. Someday in the future, when that fantasy feels less fresh. I can live with that. But for now, I want to keep the fantasy as far away from the person who inspired it as possible.

Thankfully, he lets me get away with the horrible, awkward lie.

He and I talk for a few more minutes, and I mention the follow-up meeting on Monday. I play down how much work it will be, because I don't want him to worry about it overlapping with the gala.

Talking to Keegan is comfortable and soothing. I don't mention the meh feeling I have about the presentation or my disappointment at Reid's absence. After all, it was silly for me to expect the CEO to be at the pitch meeting in the first place. Why did I even assume he would be there? Just because of an offhand comment he made in the elevator? He was probably just making conversation.

By the time I'm done talking to Keegan, I feel better about everything. Which is why it's so important that I have him in my life. He grounds me in a way no one else does. He gets me. Our friendship is one of the most important relationships in my life. I can't forget that.

I nearly lost his friendship once by letting Ollie drive a wedge between us. I can't let something like that happen again. Even if that wedge is my own imagination.

BY THE TIME I hang up with Keegan, I've drunk most of my iced tea, but I haven't even touched my sandwich. I'm considering just bringing it home with me when a noise from behind startles me.

I stand and whirl around, hand pressed to my chest, only to see someone else walking out onto the rooftop via the same sticky door I used. For an instant, the person is framed by the open doorway and backlit by the light in the stairwell. All I see is that it's a man.

And isn't it just my luck that today—right after the biggest triumph of my career—is the day I'll run into a serial killer.

Statistically speaking, I'm pretty sure the odds of that are low, but it would be just my luck.

(This, by the way, is the downside of having such an active imagination.)

But then, a moment later, the man pauses, having obviously just spotted me, and says, "Sorry. I didn't mean to startle you. I didn't think anyone else would be up here."

My breath catches.

Because it's not a serial killer. It's Reid Forester.

My unfortunately hot boss who I may or may not have a crush on even though I definitely should not be crushing on him. (At this point, I'm feeling a bit muddled about which of the unattainable men I'm striving to not be attracted to at any given moment.)

And of course now my heart is pounding for another reason entirely. It's one thing to have the occasional sexy fantasy about your hot boss when you rarely see him and almost never talk to him at all. It's another thing entirely to run into him all alone on a rooftop at dusk.

"I'm glad you're not a serial killer."

I want it to sound like a joke, but his steps slow as if he's afraid he genuinely scared me.

Reid, who manages to look amazing in the harsh office lighting, somehow looks even better in the dim ambient light of nearby office buildings. Despite that, my stomach doesn't do that flip-floppy thing it usually does.

Before I can decide what to do, though, Reid walks over to me and holds out his hand.

"Hi. I'm Reid."

His words dash any hopes that I have of forming an intelligent sentence.

He doesn't recognize me.

My boss—my unfortunately hot, younger boss— doesn't recognize me at all.

The realization is unsettling and oddly freeing at the same time.

If he'd realized I was Meg, the same woman that he sat across the conference table from no less than four days ago, I would at least have a roadmap for how to act. Since he doesn't recognize me, I'm in uncharted territory.

He's still standing there with his hand out, so I do the sensible thing. I shake his hand.

The other day when I shook his hand in the conference room in the round of pre-meeting greetings, his handshake was brusque and efficient. Business-y.

This handshake is totally different. His touch is warm, gentle, and lingering. If it's possible for a handshake to flirt, his does.

Disconcerted, I pull my hand back.

"And you are ...?"

He leaves the question hanging in the air.

Well, dang it. This is awkward.

Then he gives me a slow and sensual once over. Suddenly my heart is pounding with panic, because—holy shit—he's giving me let-me-pick-you-up eyes.

My boss is giving me let-me-pick-you-up eyes.

My boss!

What do I do? WhatdoIdowhatdoIdowhatdoIdo????

I never get let-me-pick-you-up eyes from guys. Like, ever.

Once, Keegan and I did one of those speed dating things. I didn't even get let-me-pick-you-up eyes from any of those guys, even though I was literally there to be picked up.

So getting a look like that from anyone would be weird. Getting a look like that from Reid, who is normally so reserved and standoffish at work, who would never in a million years look at one of his employees like that? This is off-the-charts weird. This is there-be-dragons weird.

What should I do?

If I introduce myself as Meg and tell him I work for him, that will be awkward, right?

I'm awkward enough as it is. I don't need additional awkwardness in the office.

But what's the alternative? Run away?

That is illogical as well. Obviously.

So I clear my throat and say the first thing that pops into my head.

"I'm Sasha."

I say the name without really thinking it through.

Yes, it's a lie, but it doesn't feel like a lie. Right now, at this moment, I feel like the sassy, fashionable woman who drinks G&T's and doesn't let anyone body shame her.

I'm dressed like Sasha. I acted like Sasha for most of the day. I feel like Sasha. I feel like someone who isn't Meg Demeo. Someone who isn't worried about losing her best friend.

Unfortunately, when I introduce myself as Sasha, Reid takes a step closer and gives me a slow, sensual once over. It is the look he gives me in my fantasies. But suddenly, I'm not at all sure how I feel about that.

Reid flashes me a charming smile and gestures to the chair I have been about to sit in. "Did you come up here to be alone, Sasha? Or for the view?"

My mind sputters for only an instant of uncertainty before I say, "Maybe it's both."

Still holding my gaze, he gives a sigh that sounds overly dramatic. "If it's both, then I should probably offer to leave. So that you can enjoy the view alone."

Alone? As in alone with my thoughts and my misery and my determination not to cry? No, thank you.

"Shouldn't I be the one to offer to leave? After all, I already had my chance to watch the sunset."

He quirks an eyebrow. "That would assume that I wouldn't prefer your company."

The implication hangs heavy in the air. He wants me to stay.

Which probably means I should leave. That would be the prudent thing to do. Except ...

He doesn't recognize me. And he's giving me let-me-pick-you-up eyes. When does this kind of thing happen to me? Never. That's the answer. This kind of thing never happens to me.

Of course, I'm not going to let him pick me up.

He's my boss, but doesn't know he's my boss. And the moment when I could have reminded him of that has come and gone. Sex with your hot, young boss is a fantastic fantasy, but ... jeez-us, talk about a morally gray area!

Morally gray! It's not just a color palette anymore!

OMG. I think I'm going off the rails here.

Get it together Meg! *Sasha*—whoever the heck you are!

My point is this: right now I'm still very confused about the whole Keegan kissing me the other night issue. That kiss, which should have been nothing more than an innocent favor for a friend, rattled me. And, yeah, I've been telling myself that it only affected me so much because it was unexpected, but does it actually matter why it rattled me?

All of a sudden, after years of ruthlessly squashing any non-friendship feelings for Keegan, those feelings are back. And it's very confusing. Especially given that we have our not-really-a-date tomorrow night.

Given all of that, wouldn't it be better—smarter, in fact—to indulge in a little harmless flirting with my boss?

Isn't that the lesser of two evils? The paler of two morally gray choices?

Thankfully, Reid doesn't seem to notice how long it takes me to do all this moral calculus.

I step to the side and gesture to the table. "Do you want to sit?"

He exhales, giving me the impression that he was holding his breath. Like this moment was as tense for him as it was for me.

He glances pointedly at my ice tea and sandwich. "I don't want to keep you from eating."

I unwrap the sandwich and, on impulse, offer. "Do you want some?"

"I can't eat half your dinner."

"It's a huge sandwich. I won't be able to finish it, anyway."

He eyes the paper. "From the deli downstairs?"

"Yep. Their New York Italian."

He makes the faintest noise of approval. The sandwich is already sliced in half and double wrapped, making it easy to peel apart the two pages of butcher paper and divide up the sandwich.

Clearly still on the fence, he asks, "Hot or sweet peppers?"

"Duh. Both."

That must be the answer he wants, because he pulls one of the butcher paper "plates" towards him and picks up the sandwich.

We simultaneously take a bite, and we both groan. I'm still chewing when he says around his bite. "This is the perfect sandwich."

It really is. "I don't know how they do it. Sandwich geniuses."

After that, we eat in silence for a few moments,

wallowing in the bliss that is the perfect combination of crusty bread, fatty deli meats, and piquet peppers.

It shouldn't be comfortable or relaxing—sharing this random meal with my boss—and yet it is.

My boss that I lied to. Let's not forget that.

I wasn't joking when I said the sandwich would have been too much for me alone, and after a few bites, I'm already slowing down. I'm not even able to finish my half. I set aside the last bite or two and wipe off my hands.

I look out over the skyline and sigh. "I didn't expect anyone else to be here."

"How did you get up here?"

I start guiltily. "One of the security guards who used to work here showed me how. Apparently, the latch is sticky enough that sometimes it doesn't close all the way."

He nods. "Same. My dad showed it to me."

"Oh, I just assumed your badge lets you up."

"My badge?" he asks.

I still, realizing my gaff. I introduced myself to him as if I were a stranger, which means I shouldn't know he's an executive. I shrug evasively. "You probably work in the building, right?"

He gives me a speculative once over. "Which implies you don't. Are you a guest at the hotel?"

This would be the perfect chance to come clean. But I just don't want to. Even though I don't feel that spark of attraction, it's still gratifying to have Reid looking at me like this. Like I'm an intriguing stranger he wants to know better.

Still, I can't keep lying to him. So I stand. "I should go."

He stands too. "I wish you wouldn't."

"Why?"

"Call me crazy," he says, closing the distance between

us. "I know we just met, but I feel like there's some sort of connection between us. Like we were meant to meet tonight on this rooftop."

It's all I can do to not burst out laughing. A connection between us? That's ironic.

"I think you need better lines."

I keep my tone gentle and free of sarcasm.

"It's not a line," he says, his tone earnest as he steps closer, stopping so close to me I can smell the lingering scent of his cologne.

And it's not woodsy at all. There's a hint of citrus and bergamot. He doesn't smell like adventure and home all at the same time.

There's nothing comforting or delicious about his smell. It's just there. A thing I notice without enjoying.

Unaware of my thoughts, Reid says, "There's something about you."

This time I do laugh. But it surprises me because it doesn't sound like a fit of hysterical laughter. It sounds like a sexy tinkle of flirtation. He smiles in response, ducking his head ruefully, for a moment, looking every inch of my fantasy guy.

Badly done, Meg. Badly, done.

He takes another step closer to me. "Can I have your number?"

"That's not a good idea."

That's the understatement of the century.

"Then let me buy you a drink."

"From where?" I look around the empty rooftop with a chuckle, expecting that to be the end of it.

But he doesn't let it go. He nods in the direction of the stairwell. "There's a bar on the ground level. And two or three more in the hotel next door."

For the briefest moment, I'm tempted. My inner Meg-from-a-week-ago is practically screaming at me for what I'm about to do ... that Meg is practically a different person. Because the Meg after Saturday? The Meg who's looking forward to her not-a-date like it's senior prom with the prom king? She's the one who has to answer. And I hope like hell I'm not going to regret this.

At least, if I let him down gently now, there might be a possibility of snagging that drink later, for when I finally get over this horrible, stupid crush on Keegan. And hey ... it can't hurt to be friends with your boss, right?

How the hell do I even begin to answer that question? I could blow him off. Or I could be honest. And maybe if I am, I'll actually get to know Reid a little. Maybe if I'm honest, this won't be as weird later.

"No," I say simply, closing the door to a future ... anything.

I hate what it means for me, for my heart, that I can't imagine going on a date with Reid. Not now and not in the future, even if nothing happens between me and Keegan.

Still, when I think about everything going on between me and Keegan. About how he kissed me the other day outside his condo. About how perfect and right it felt to be in his arms, even though he's supposed to be my best friend and I'm not supposed to think about being in his arms at all.

We aren't an item. I know that. I'm not a total imbecile. But, damn it all to hell, I have feelings for my best friend. Non-platonic feelings. And even though he doesn't feel the same way, I couldn't possibly start something with anyone else while feeling so confused about Keegan.

Especially not with my *boss,* who doesn't even know who I really am.

"I should go," I say again, and this time I sound like I mean it.

I turn and leave, practically running for the stairs.

But what am I running from? The awkwardness of my boss flirting with me? Or the fact that I wish it was Keegan?

fifteen

THE NEXT AFTERNOON, Reb and Thea show up at my house to help me get ready for the gala. I'm still flustered and confused about the conversation with Reid last night on the rooftop, despite my stalwart attempts to put the entire thing out of my head and get work done all morning. Stalwart, but fruitless attempts.

Despite the lack of progress on the new presentation I have to get ready for Monday, I'm determined to have fun at the gala. A fun, relaxing, and (most importantly) platonic evening with my best friend is exactly what I need. After all, I have all day Sunday to work.

Once the girls arrive, Thea takes over organizing my new work clothes in my walk-in closet. Even though I assure her I hung them up when I got home on Thursday, she wants to verify that my organization is up to her standards. I have a sneaking suspicion she is going to hide some of my "morally gray" outfits, or possibly even chuck them altogether.

Reb connects to the Bluetooth speaker in my bathroom and pulls up a playlist on Spotify. It's one that Keegan made for me when we first started hanging out and realized we both love post-punk eighties music. A few minutes later, Siouxsie and the Banshees are playing and Thea is telling us about the time she met Morrissey.

Once I'm dressed and freshly caffeinated, Thea helps with my hair. But Reb and Thea are exactly zero help when it comes to helping with my makeup. Thea's a permanent makeup aficionado—complete with tattooed eyeliner, lash extensions, and bi-annual lip blushing. While Reb either wears no makeup and looks like she's twelve or wears a ton of makeup and looks like she's twelve, but going through an emo stage. With Reb, there is no in between. Still, they stay with me, offering helpful tips, and by the time I've done my makeup, I feel good about it.

No matter how often I tell myself that tonight is just one friend doing a favor for another friend, it still feels like a date.

Probably because I haven't gone on an actual date in what feels like years. And, if I'm honest with myself, I've never been on a date like this.

When Keegan shows up at my door, I wish I had spent a little more time preparing myself. As if the past few hours, somehow, weren't enough to live up to how utterly stunning Keegan looks right now.

Intellectually, I know he's rich; therefore, I can assume he knows how to dress for a gala. But the thing about being his best friend for all these years? Our relationship is casual. I've seen him in swim trunks, ripped jeans and ratty, old T-shirts. I've seen him sweat-stained and covered in mud. But I've never seen him in a suit.

I was not prepared for the sight of him in a suit.

One summer, after all his offers to bring me to Hawaii, I consented to a trip to South Padre. That week, the sight of

Keegan in board shorts nearly killed me. I feigned a crippling fear of sun cancer and bought him a swim shirt with SPF 50 just to protect me from the sight of his abs.

If I thought those board shorts were bad, this is so much worse. The dove gray suit looks like it was made just for him. Of course, it probably was. When you roll in McQuade level circles, bespoke suits are expected.

The suit is linen, the shirt underneath a pale shade of teal.

The aquamarine of his shirt makes the blue flecks pop, so his eyes are even more potent than usual. And if that combination wasn't deadly enough, he's clean-shaven, something I've never seen before.

The suit. The clean shave. The perfect shirt ... all of it looks so ... intentional.

This isn't an old concert tee he threw on for an evening of lounging on my sofa and eating take out. He put thought into this. As if it were a real date. The idea is so unsettling, I almost don't know how to handle it.

But that doesn't mean it's about me. Of course, he put thought into tonight. He's representing his family. He may pretend not to care about his family connections, but I know he'd never purposefully embarrass them.

Of course, there's also the possibility that he's actually considering this job with his father. That he wants it. That he's trying to earn it.

The thought makes me want to cry because it feels like we're crossing some momentous threshold, and I'm not sure what our relationship looks like on the other side.

Yeah, that kind of thinking isn't helpful. Besides, I'm one-hundred percent the person who makes a huge deal out of nothing and then feels silly afterwards. So, I shove all that anxiety deep and try to focus on this moment.

Though I almost miss the flicker of disappointment in his gaze.

"What?" I ask automatically. "What's wrong?"

He looks me up and down, taking in my simple green maxi dress. "You didn't like the dress I picked out for you, I guess."

"It was gorgeous, just out of my price range." I say, hoping honesty will help wash away the disappointment in his tone.

He smirks. "Right. I should have known you were never going to let me pay."

I swallow, stung. Feeling his disappointment as deeply as my own, though, I try to shrug it off.

I give his arm a playful punch and say in my lamest, teasing voice. "You know I can't be a moocher."

He rolls his eyes. "Yeah. I guess not."

There's a bit of distance to his voice and resignation as well, and I can't help but feel that in some tiny way my independence on this ruined something. Like I've hurt his feelings.

"Keegan, I—"

"You look great, though." He cuts me off, his tone suddenly too cheerful.

"Y-you don't look so bad yourself." I say. It comes out breathy, and I stumble over my words.

I'm usually so relaxed around Keegan I either don't stutter or I don't notice it when I do.

He must realize that my stutter now makes me feel unexpectedly nervous around him, because he reaches out and nudges my chin. "Come on, Glasses. Don't freeze up on me now. I love the sexy new hairstyle." Then he blinks, takes a step back, blinks again, and says "Whoa. No glasses."

"Contacts."

"I thought you hated contacts."

"Normally, but my eye doctor had been encouraging me to try this new brand. They're formulated for dry eyes, so they shouldn't bother me. It seemed like as good a time as any to try them."

He gives me a long look, like there's something he wants to say but doesn't. Then he takes my arm in his and guides me out of the house. Shutting the door behind me. "I guess it's a good night to try new things."

Before I can ask what he means by that, he takes my keys from my hand and locks the door. The gesture is oddly old-fashioned and reminds me of the old Doris Day romcoms I've watched with Thea.

Keegan leads me down my front path to the road, but I stop when there's a black town car there instead of his Jeep.

"Did you rent that?"

Before he can answer, a driver gets out, scurries around on my side, and opens the door for me.

Keegan chuckles. "I don't want to worry about driving later."

Keegan holds my hand as I climb into the car. Another one of those unexpectedly polite gestures that I'm not used to.

A moment later, he climbs in on the other side and the driver takes off. It's not a stretch limo, but it definitely has more room than a standard town car, and there's a partition between the front seat and the back.

Once we're settled in the car, Keegan takes my hand in his. I don't know what gives me away. Maybe there's a faint tremor in my hand, or maybe he just knows me that well. As soon as my hand is in his, he senses how nervous I am.

He gives my hand a squeeze and asks, "Why are you nervous?"

"I don't know," I admit. "I guess I've just never been on a date like this."

"A date like this?" he teases. "I've known you for a decade. You've been on dates before."

"No, silly." I punch him playfully on the arm. "A date like this. Fancy, dressed up, the guy in a suit, a hired driver."

"What?" He feigns shock. "Ollie never treated you like this?"

Yeah, Ollie was my boyfriend in college and for a couple of years after. Keegan never liked him, so I'm sure he thinks his derision is fair. Still, I dated the guy for nearly four years, so I feel obliged to defend him.

"We were poor college students. So, no, there were no galas."

"What was that asinine thing he used to say?"

"That he respected my earning potential too much to conform to outdated conventions established by the patriarchy."

"That's a lot of words just to say he didn't want to pay for dinner."

Keegan and I had this argument a lot when I was dating Ollie. When I was twenty, I admired Ollie's progressive stance on feminist issues. Besides, I was used to making my own way in the world. My parents' relationship had taught me early on that a woman shouldn't, and can't, depend on a man to support her. Financially or emotionally.

In hindsight, I wish Ollie had tried a little harder. He could have respected my earning potential *and* spoiled me every once in a while—like I did for him.

"I still think the guy is just a dick."

I shrug. "Probably. But on the bright side, he's someone else's problem now."

"What about prom? Did you go to prom?"

"Yes," I hedge. Prom did not turn out great for me.

I glance over at Keegan and realize he's grinning, a teasing glint in his eyes.

"I feel like maybe you remember my prom story."

He tips his head and makes a humming noise like he's digging deep into his memories. "This is the story that ends with your date making out with your best friend?"

"So, you do remember?" He's grinning now, and his teasing makes me feel better about the memory. "It's hard to hold a grudge about prom, when they're still together and married with two kids. I guess it really was true love."

"Still, shitty move for your best friend."

My hand is still in Keegan's, and I realize, suddenly, that I'm not nervous anymore. All of this teasing, which might've seemed harsh coming from anyone else, was his way of helping me relax.

I give his hand a squeeze. "I like to think I upgraded on the best friend front."

He pulls me closer, wrapping his arm over my shoulder, tucking me to his side. Just like that, any lingering apprehension I have about tonight fades as I'm surrounded by the familiar scent of him. Woodsy and spicy and everything comforting and wonderful in my life.

"Do you want to tell me why you're really nervous?"

I feel his breath in my hair as he asks the question. Did I? Not really. It was ... complex. So complex. And if I said the wrong thing, it could set this night off on the wrong foot.

"You look so professional." I'm waffling, but it's the best I could come up with.

It sounds like an accusation when I say it out loud.

"Wow," he says sardonically. "You really are observant."

I elbow him in the ribs. "You know what I mean. You never shave."

He's devastatingly hot with a scruff on his jaw, rocking that lazy, surfer dude vibe. But this look? Jaw completely smooth? It's unsettling in ways I can't quite explain it to myself. He somehow looks younger and more intense.

"We lived together for three years. You really mean to tell me you never noticed when I shaved?"

"No, I mean that you never shaved. Not like this."

"Okay, so you don't like the clean-shaven look. Noted."

"Don't get me wrong—I do like it!" I correct him.

"I'm just surprised, that's all. I didn't realize tonight was such a big deal."

"You didn't?"

His voice sounds husky, and once again I feel his breath in my hair, and it feels like he's practically kissing the top of my head. Heat unspools in my belly, and it takes all my willpower to shut that shit down. I don't need to be thinking about how it feels to be this close to him. I lean toward the window, putting some distance between us, and twist to face him, trying to read his expression in the flickering street lights as they pass overhead.

"You're dressed like a professional. Like a businessman. It means you're serious about this job offer from your dad."

I feel his gaze on my face, like he's studying me as intensely as I'm studying him. After a second, he blinks and lets out a huff that could be laughter or frustration. "Yeah, I guess that's what it means."

Before I can say anything else, the car is slowing, and we've reached the Lady Bird Johnson Wildflower Center, where the gala is being held.

The Wildflower Center occupies nearly three-hundred

acres in Southwest Austin and straddles the Edwards Aquifer and the Blackland Prairie, two of the more environmentally fragile areas in Texas. Lady Bird herself and the Wildflower Center are intrinsic to, if not wholly responsible for, Austin's modern sustainability movement. The center has nine acres of maintained gardens highlighting native plants. They host workshops and educational events. The buildings look like a modern Texas barn built among the remains of a limestone hacienda.

Personally, I always thought that if Texas had a crumbling castle, this is what it would look like.

There's a big open courtyard, flanked on one side by a stone cistern and by the great hall on the other. The great hall has floor to ceiling windows that show off stunning views of the Blackland Prairie savanna.

The Wildflower Center is one of my favorite places in Austin, and I've been there countless times for lectures and educational events. Once I even took a stargazing seminar here. But I've never seen it like this. The fairy lights crisscross the courtyard, making the entire place feel like an ethereal springtime getaway, effortlessly blending glamor with its eco-friendly practicality. If Tinker Bell and her pals threw Cinderella's ball, this is what it would have looked like.

Keegan stops to check in at the front table. I stand to the side, waiting while the attendant links his credit card to a special QR code he scans to bid on auction items.

Then she turns to me. "If you'd like, I can get you a separate code."

"Of course." I fish out a credit card, knowing full well I won't be bidding on anything—given that my new wardrobe maxed out my discretionary spending money for the next eighteen months.

Before I can hand over a credit card for her to link my bidder number, Keeagan says. "She'll be bidding on my account."

"Excellent." The woman beams, tapping away on her digital pad, and then hands me a fob with the code on it. "Here you go, ma'am." She smiles cheekily as she hands me a glossy flier. "Here's a listing of some of the more exclusive items. Be sure to spend lots of his money."

Keegan steers me away from the table as I tuck the fob safely in my purse. "Don't worry," I whisper. "I will not be bidding on anything."

He slows and looks at me. "Why not?"

"I'm not going to spend your money."

He rolls his eyes and chuckles. "I wish you would. It's for a good cause. Please bid on whatever you want."

Knowing I will not be spending his money, I still glance down at the flier. Then chuckle. "Dove hunting in Argentina?" I read off the first item on the list. "Who would bid on that?"

He leans close to look down at the flier over my shoulder, then reaches his arm around me to point at an item. "That one seems more your speed."

The way he's standing, just behind me, looking over my left shoulder, pointing with his right hand, I am practically cradled in his arms. Enveloped by him.

I feel nervous and jittery, but completely safe and protected at the same time.

I have to force myself to look at the item he's pointing to. "A week at an eco-friendly resort off the coast of Belize, including a private tour of a turtle rescue facility."

"Haven't you always wanted to go to Belize?" His breath brushes my ear as he asks.

I shiver. "Yes," I murmur, though I'm suddenly not sure

if I'm answering his question or just generally agreeing to having him this close.

"Then you should bid on it. I insist."

Everything about this moment is just too much. Too much of everything I've wanted and can't let myself have. Being cradled in his arms. Being pampered by him. Being protected by him. Being spoiled by him.

It's a fantasy come to life. But that's all it is. A fantasy. An illusion created by the romantic setting and the intimacy of this date-that's-not-a-date.

It's no more real than the fairy lights are actually sparkling fairies.

I can't let myself get caught up in that fantasy. Doing so would put our friendship at risk.

I step away from him. "Okay, I'll bid on it."

He gives me a shrewd look. "Promise?"

"Of course," I say as breezily as I can when my heart is pounding. I don't tell him that I'll just place the lowest bid possible.

After a second of studying me, he turns us both toward the entrance. As we walk, Keegan's hand shifts from hovering at the small of my back to straight up resting on the curve of my hip. It never occurred to me that there was a difference between the two things. But there is.

A second ago, he was merely walking beside me. His hand on my back felt polite. Believably fake date appropriate. This feels ... like something else entirely.

I can feel the impression of each of his fingers on my hip, and the spot where his thumb brushes lightly up and down. Plus, his hand on my hip pulls me closer to his side. I am all but wedged under his shoulder, pressed to his side, enveloped in the steady heat of him.

Everything about this feels natural and yet so different

from every other time he's touched me that there's some-thing illicit about it. Something darkly forbidden and dangerously habit-forming. Something I could get used to. Something that could break my heart when it goes away.

It's a difference of mere inches, but these inches feel like miles.

They feel like the difference between me remembering that this is a fake date with my best friend and me pretending this is a real date with a man I once had a serious crush on.

Except I don't have a crush on Keegan any more. I have genuine feelings for him. I have love for him.

That love has always been strictly platonic, but it's still love.

And if that line between platonic love and romantic love blurs, I will be in serious trouble here.

sixteen

AS KEEGAN LEADS me further into the gala, a knot of anxiety forms in my belly.

And it's not there for any of the reasons I thought I'd feel dread in a moment like this. It's not because I'm afraid I won't fit in or I'm not dressed right. It's not even because I'm afraid of stuttering and embarrassing myself or Keegan. Those are all the things I thought I would be worrying about in the days leading up to tonight. Ironically, those aren't the things I'm worried about now.

Instead, it's because I'm too comfortable. Being here with Keegan, his hand on my hip, his breath in my hair ... all of it. It all feels too good. Too right. Too dangerously addictive.

"Do you want to start out looking at the auction items?" he says as he guides me across the cobblestone. "Do you see anything in the pamphlet you want to bid on?"

I scoff, fanning myself with the pamphlet. "You mean, in addition to y-you buying me an all-inclusive Belizean getaway?"

He just smiles. "Let's get you a glass of wine and see if anything strikes your fancy."

We pass under the stone archway into the courtyard. Servers are wandering around with trays of hors d'oeuvres. A local musician is playing an acoustic guitar in the corner. He must know Keegan, because he smiles, giving us a nod. It's not crowded, but Keegan is staying close.

We stop at the edge of the courtyard, where the walkways weave down across the terraces to the gardens. A server stops to offer us glasses of wine and Keegan snatches a glass for each of us. Another moment that feels way too date-like.

I've got to rip the bandaid off on this before I get too lulled into the romance of this date.

"What's the game plan here?" I take a fortifying gulp of wine. "Who do we need to talk to? W-who do we need to meet and impress?"

"Calm down there. We just walked in."

Well, yeah. We just walked in. But already I'm blown away by how charming and romantic the setting is. And that's on top of being blown away by how great he looks.

So basically, I'm in danger of being blown all the way to Oklahoma. And I don't want to live in Oklahoma. The commute would be unbearable.

All of which means I need to get my emotions and my imagination under control before they get ideas. Dangerous ideas about how amazing it would be if this *was* an actual date.

But it's not a date. It's a fake date. The date may be fake, but we do have a real goal here. Keegan clearly wants to impress whoever it is that his father wants him to meet.

"Well, sure. We just got here. So that means it's the perfect time to devise our game plan."

"Our game plan?"

"Yes. Our strategy. I mean, w-we're here for a specific reason, right? This isn't just our normal Saturday night hang out. We need to set s-some goals." Keegan looks at me like I'm crazy, so I swat him on the arm. "I'm serious. Your dad wanted you to come here, right?"

"Yes, but I wasn't aware that we needed a plan of attack for the evening." He hides a teasing smile behind a sip from his glass.

"Well, we do." I tilt my chip up at him, and somehow feel like a petulant toddler. Keegan might not need a plan, but if I'm going to get through this evening mostly unscathed by the emotional and physical warfare that is being on a not-a-date with Keegan, I need something to focus on. Something besides the feel of his hand, steady and warm on my back.

"So, who did your dad want you to meet?"

Keegan makes an exaggerated shocked expression. "Since when are you and my dad on the same side of any argument?"

"I'm not saying I'm on his side. But, you know ... know your enemy and all that jazz."

"Settle down there, Sun Tzu."

"I'm serious."

"You're adorable."

I swat his arm again and give him take-me-seriously-damn-it eyes.

Keegan takes a sip and then uses that hand to gesture to an older couple walking out into the gardens beyond the courtyard. "Those are the Langleys."

"Am I supposed to know who the Langleys are?"

"Shush. I'm setting the stage here."

"Right. Langleys. Older couple." The woman has her

hand resting on his arm as they wander through the garden. "Clearly plant lovers."

"Exactly. Plants. Trees. Clean water. They're the real deal in conservation. They own about 1000 acres of land just west of Austin."

"Nice." I pull up a mental map of that part of Austin and try to picture a spot where there's that kind of undeveloped land. "That must be in the Edwards aquifer recharging zone. I bet that's why they're so eco aware."

"Exactly. My dad has been talking to them on and off for years, trying to get them on board with developing that land. They've always shut him down."

"But suddenly they're interested?" I ask. "And that's why he's bringing you on board?"

"Smart girl." Keegan gives me a smile of approval. "With land getting more and more valuable around Austin, it's harder for them to say no. Plus, they're getting older. If they die before it goes into development, their kids can do whatever they want with it. They want to get the deal on the books while they still have some say and how it's developed."

"Think I like these people."

"Don't sound so surprised. Not all rich people are assholes." Keegan takes a sip of wine without quite meeting my gaze.

For the first time it occurs to me that all of my rich-people-are-assholes comments over the years might hurt his feelings. It also occurs to me that I might be wrong. After all, Keegan is rich, and he's not an asshole. The Langley's clearly aren't. And after all that Keegan's mother has done for me lately, I certainly can't keep thinking of her that way. As for his father, well, the jury is still out on him, but I find it hard to believe that both

Loretta and Keegan would put up with him if he was a total jerk.

I give his arm a squeeze, hoping to convey my diehard support, regardless of any sweeping judgmental comments I've made in the past.

"To sum up, your dad wants to cut a deal with the Langleys, so he's trotting you out, since you have a reputation as a badass eco-warrior. He's hoping that if he can get you on board, you'll get them on board, and then it'll be one big happy family. Do I have that right?"

"So far, yes." He and I are still standing there, sipping wine, watching his parents as they enter the gala. "There's more?"

"There's always more." Another couple comes up and starts talking to Keegan's parents. "That is Bruce Barajas."

"And he is?"

"Potential investor."

"Of course he is." I should've guessed that based on appearance alone.

Everything about this man screams Texas oil money. He's dressed in pressed wranglers, cowboy boots, a crisply ironed white oxford shirt, and a cowboy hat.

It might be wrong to make assumptions about him based solely on his appearance, but I've lived in Texas my whole life. And I'm in advertising. Advertising is all about extrapolating who a person is and what they want based on just a few details. So here's what I'd extrapolate about Bruce Barajas based solely on what I know so far:

"So, he's Texas oil money. Either out of Houston or Midland. Which means he thinks this whole sustainability movement is a fad, but I'm guessing your dad wants to convince him to invest in the project, anyway." I tear my gaze away from where Bruce and the McQuades are chatting. "Am I right?"

Keegan is beaming at me like he'd give me a gold star if he had one handy. "Close enough."

"Which brings me back to: what's the game plan? Are we here to convince the Langleys that your father can be trusted with their precious project or to convince Bruce that there's money to be made in developing a project while still respecting the land it's built on?"

I study Keegan as I say this, so I see the exaggerated, almost comical wince he gives.

I blow out a breath. "It's both, isn't it?"

"Yep. It's both." His grin is beleaguered, and it makes me so grateful I'm here by his side. "Whose ass should we kiss first?"

I take another drink of wine and survey the victims. "Well, the Langleys are going to be easy. Bruce will be the harder sell."

"Let's get the easy one out of the way."

Keegan gives a courtesy nod to his parents before taking my hand in his and leading me down the steps of the terrace to the gardens below. We stop just long enough for him to snag us fresh glasses of wine.

As we reach the gardens, the woman turns, and I see her clearly for the first time.

Oh, this really is going to be the easy part.

She glances at me and breaks into a grin. "Meg, I didn't know you would be here."

Before I can respond, the older woman bustles over to me and throws her arms around me in a big hug.

She pulls back to give me a once over. "You look gorgeous."

I glance over at Keegan to see him staring open-mouthed and dumbstruck. "You … know each other?"

"Clara is the volunteer coordinator for Dig Deep," I explain.

"Of course she is." Keegan slants me a look. "And since you volunteer, you know each other."

Clara looks from me to Keegan and back again, her expression curious. Clearly she's wondering why we were talking about her.

"Clara, this is my good friend Keegan."

Even as I say the word friend, I feel the fingers of his hand tightening on my hip, tugging me just a little closer to him as he holds out a hand to Clara.

"Keegan McQuade," he says as he shakes her hand.

She is busy giving me a knowing smirk—like she's amused by my use of the word friend. Her husband steps forward, shaking Keegan's hand and introducing himself.

And he clearly connects the dots between Keegan's last name and McQuade Development.

The conversation flows easily from there. Clara slides in subtle questions that imply she doesn't believe Keegan and I are just friends, which I field with details about our history—both for her benefit and for my own, since I definitely need the reminder that this is not romantic. I'm less a date and more of an emotional support dog.

Clara's husband, Steve, asks Keegan a lot of questions about McQuade Development, all of which Keegan fields easily. I do my part to sing Keegan's praise whenever I can. Which is easy enough to do. The Langley's are old-school Austin hippies, so it's easy to win them over with the story of how Keegan transformed Hung Out to Dry from a campus dive bar into a thriving cornerstone of sustainability in the local restaurant industry.

Time passes, and I never need to trot out my Sasha persona because the Langleys are just too easy to talk to. Then they see someone else they know and make their excuses, leaving Keegan and me alone in the crowd.

He turns to me, his gaze playfully sharp. "I bet you think you're pretty smart, huh?"

I mock curtsy. "You're welcome."

He takes my hand and leads me to a standing table, snagging a couple of appetizers and more wine on the way.

"Aren't you always saying that I know everyone who's anyone in Austin? And then you just so happen to know people I need to meet, and you don't even give me a heads up?"

I hold up my hands in surrender. "In my defense, I didn't remember Clara's last name, and I didn't recognize her until she turned around."

Keegan makes a suspicious humming sound. "Likely story."

We munch on appetizers in companionable silence for a few minutes, and I try to tell myself that everything is going exactly as planned, but my unease from earlier in the evening is still burrowing into the back of my mind.

I don't have time to think about it too long though, because soon Keegan's parents approach, dragging Bruce with them.

Keegan's dad makes the introductions. The men do the hearty handshake, good old boy routine. Bruce shakes my hand, in a way that's brusque and indifferent. It doesn't bother me because it's easy for people to overlook me and sometimes it gives me an advantage.

As he shakes hands with Keegan, he says, "The kid who owns the bar, right?"

Keegan nods. "Correct. Hung Out to Dry down near campus."

Since Keegan isn't likely to toot his own horn, I chime in. "Hung Out to Dry has flourished under his management. It's gone from a local dive to a mainstay of the area and he's created a model of sustainable business in Austin."

Bruce gives a dismissive chuckle and claps Keegan on the shoulder. "Well sure, the eco-nut angle is admirable, but selling drinks to college students is like shooting fish in a barrel. Am I right?"

I grit my teeth.

Oh, he did not just belittle Keegan's entire career! And 'eco-nut angle?' Is he kidding me with that bullshit?

Keegan chuckles in response, taking the jab on the chin.

So, I follow Keegan's lead.

After all, we're here to schmooze, not pick fights.

Still … there's no way I'm putting up with that behavior. I just have to find a way to politely put this man in his place. And that is something I am very good at doing.

The conversation shifts away from Keegan's bar, and I can hear Johnny trying to shift the topic back to the project the McQuades are trying to pitch. I let him handle that and focus on sizing up Bruce.

I wish I'd thought to ask Keegan who we're supposed to shmooze before now, because then I could have researched him online beforehand. First rule of advertising is always understand your market.

In lieu of that, I'll have to figure him out based on what I see and what he says. Obviously, he has money to invest or the McQuades wouldn't be bothering. And again, my gut says oil money. Old money in Texas comes from oil, banking, or land development, often some combination of all three. There's lots of new, high-tech money in Texas, particularly in Austin, but that's just not the vibe I get from Bruce.

His clothes are crisp and pristine, but his cowboy boots are worn, scuffed, and heavily creased. These aren't the boots a poseur wears for show. They're a working man's boots. And his hands support my theory. They're big and rough. Several of his fingers jut at odd angles like they were broken and set at home.

This isn't a man who earned his money working in an office, so he's not out of Houston, but probably West Texas—either ranching or farming, with oil payouts from mineral rights. Which, ironically, makes selling the green angle easier because he's making money off the oil industry and likely isn't emotionally invested in it.

Which means I just need to show him how profitable the *eco-nut angle* can be.

I summon my inner Sasha—and also give her a new job title: Sasha, VP of Marketing Keegan's Awesomeness. And then I lie in wait.

When the conversation turns to the price point of the more expensive sustainable features in the project, I say, "You know, I think I read an article recently in the *Harvard Business Review* that millennials are willing to pay ten percent more for a sustainable product. And that while most sustainable building projects cost more upfront, they are more profitable in the long run."

Keegan gives my hip a little squeeze that feels like the seal of approval.

Loretta smiles broadly. "Is that so?"

"I can send you the links if you'd like."

"Certainly."

I can feel Bruce's gaze on me, assessing, but I keep talking to Loretta like this is a secret just between the two of us. "But the fascinating thing is how those numbers shift with the demographics. Older consumers will pay eight percent more, Millennials ten percent, and early research indicates that Gen Z will pay even more. And since Millennials and Gen Z trend towards smaller homes and minimalism, you have a smaller footprint per unit. They'll also be willing to pay extra for access to those green spaces that are built into the design of the community."

Bruce clears his throat and I turn toward him, slowly, blinking innocently. "Why don't you share those links with me, too?"

"I can airdrop them right now if your phone is compatible."

He gives me a slow blink and then chuckles as he pulls out his wallet and then hands me a business card. "I'm too old school for airdrop, but here's my email address."

I snap a picture of his card with my phone before handing the card back. When he frowns as he takes it, I grin. "More eco-friendly this way."

He chuckles, looking a little chagrined. "I guess you kids take this stuff seriously."

"Yep. And you should too, if you're marketing to millennials and younger."

"Remind me what position you hold at McQuade Development." He gives me an assessing look, as if he's actually seeing me for the first time. Since I'm not used to being in the spotlight, it's a little unsettling. Until I remind myself that it's not me he's seeing. It's Sasha. And this kind of thing comes naturally to her.

"I don't work for McQuade Development. I'm in advertising."

He turns to Johnny. "Doesn't McQuade need people in advertising?"

It's Keegan who answers, giving me a little squeeze. "Oh, we're always trying to recruit talent like this."

I gape at him in surprise. "Say what now?"

Bruce gestures to Johnny with his drink. "You should hire this young lady and put her to work on the project. If she can sell me on the idea, she'll be an asset."

"Of course she will," Keegan says softly.

Johnny and Bruce keep talking, the conversation shifting away from the green aspect of the project that I'm familiar with, and on to the financial part of the deal. Which is a win, because Bruce is talking with more enthusiasm now, as though my input actually helped convince him.

I should be overjoyed, right? Sasha kicked ass!

Except ... for starters, Keegan is still holding me close to his side, which is disconcerting in its own way. And it makes me all too aware of how comfortable it feels to be tucked against his side.

But there's something else troubling me as well: what Keegan just said. *We're always trying to recruit ...*

Like he's already part of the company. Like him going to work for his father is a done deal.

I'm being silly, of course. This was the whole point of coming tonight, right? For Keegan to test the waters. But it's still disconcerting that Keegan—*my* Keegan, the affable, laid-back guy who lounges on my sofa and tolerates my boxed wine—melts seamlessly away to reveal a man I don't even know. A man who uses terms like 'cap rate' and 'modified gross' like he was born to talk like this.

That's when it hits me. Keegan isn't just holding his own in this conversation like he was born to it.

He *was* born to it.

The guy I know, the guy I hang out with on a weekly

basis, the guy who's been my best friend for a decade, isn't the real Keegan. That's college Keegan.

This guy right here is the man Keegan was always meant to be.

He's confident and competent. He's good at this.

I don't fault him for it. I can't.

He's charming and subtle and practically a genius.

I don't know why I'm surprised. I've always known Keegan is crazy smart, despite his efforts to downplay it. I've always known his ability to charm and disarm is next level.

But this? Seeing it in person?

It's stunning.

And not in a good way.

In a hit-up-side-the-head with an anvil Wile E. Coyote kind of way.

In a someone-just-cut-a-best-friend-sized-hole-in-my-chest kind of way.

I take a few deep breaths, fanning myself again with the flier about the auction. Keegan notices, and pauses in the discussion to whisper, "Do you need another drink? It is warm out here."

Do I need another drink? Not necessarily, but I welcome the distraction it provides when Keegan flags down a server and another glass appears in my hand.

Briefly apart from the conversation, Keegan grins down at me. "You were amazing."

The pride in his voice heals the best-friend-sized-hole in my chest. Just a little bit. "Thank you."

It helps too that he's not touching me anymore. A few steps away from the conversational knot, he doesn't have a reason to keep his hand on my hip to steer me clear of topics I should avoid.

"Harvard Business Review, huh?"

"I have to read something to help me fall asleep at night."

He's about to reply when something catches his eye over my shoulder. Lips pressed together, he angles us back toward his parents just in time for me to see Selah approach the group.

She's wearing an asymmetrical, cut out dress that displays sizable chunks of cleavage as well as her ridiculously tiny waist. It's the kind of thing I would look ridiculous in, but because of her height and willowy frame, she looks like modern art. Her platinum hair is ironed to sleek perfection. If she's feeling the effects of the heat, it doesn't show at all.

If I were less kind, I'd say it's because cold-blooded animals don't sweat.

But I know that's just me being petty because she's gorgeous, and I shouldn't let my own insecurities affect how I view other women. So, I smile as she joins the group.

Bruce pauses to put his hand on her shoulder, suddenly beaming. "Keegan, I believe you know my favorite niece, Selah."

Wait. What?

She's Bruce's niece?

"Yeah, we're neighbors."

Wrapping her hand around Keegan's arm like he's her property, she gives him a kiss, barely missing the corner of his mouth, as she trills, "It's such a small world, right?"

Keegan gives a smirk. "Yeah, I think we knew that already, though. Weren't you the one who introduced my parents to your uncle?"

"Oh, that's right." She twitters, as she turns to Loretta and Johnny. "I've known y'all for so long, I forgot." She releases her death grip on Keegan's arm long enough to give Loretta and Johnny hugs and air kisses. "It was when we were on the trip to the Bahamas, wasn't it?"

It's the way she looks at Keegan as she asks that clues me in.

I would have missed it if I hadn't been watching her so closely because I was waiting to see if she even acknowledged my presence. For the record, she doesn't. But I don't even have a chance to be insulted by that, because that subtle undercurrent to her question just about knocks me off my feet.

When we were on that trip ...

And she glanced at Keegan for confirmation as she says the word *we*.

Suddenly, my understanding about everything that's happened this week shifts. The way Selah is always hanging around Keegan's place. The way he kissed me to throw her off. The fact that he wanted me here with him tonight. He wanted me here enough that he tried to doll me up in that outrageous dress he picked out for me. And seemed disappointed that I didn't let him buy it for me. Or was that just so that I would look presentable enough that Selah would see me as a viable threat?

None of this is about the job at McQuade Development at all.

His dad has wanted him to work for the family company for years, so the job is his if he wants it. He never had to prove to his dad that he's worthy of it. Furthermore, it's obvious from this entire conversation that him taking the job is all but a fait accompli. This wasn't actually about accepting the job with his dad. No, this was something wholly different.

He knew that if Bruce was here, Selah would be as well. And he needed me here for *that*.

If she was just a pesky neighbor, it wouldn't be a big deal, but she's clearly more than that.

She's a former ... something.

Keegan doesn't really do relationships. But trips to exotic locations are totally in his wheelhouse. Which means that, at some point in the past, he hooked up with Selah and they went to the Bahamas together. Which is where his parents met Bruce. Which is why he needs to not piss off Selah if McQuade Development is going to get in bed with Bruce.

Well, fuck.

Just when I think it couldn't get any worse, Selah gives another trill of laughter.

"No, it wasn't the Bahamas trip. I'm such an airhead sometimes. It was St. Maarten."

Even though she hasn't yet acknowledged me, her gaze flits smugly to mine as she says this.

It's like she read my mind. Because you might bring a hookup on one Caribbean vacation, but not two.

Two Caribbean vacations is definitely girlfriend territory.

Excuse me, sir. Can I upgrade my *well, fuck* to a *double fuck*?

As in, Keegan fucking McQuade and his stupid Caribbean blue eyes have fucked up my emotions and my heart. He *lied* to me.

seventeen

DESPITE MY VIVID IMAGINATION, general flights of fancy, and ability to get lost in my mind, I don't think of myself as an overly dramatic person.

I don't pick fights. I don't throw temper tantrums. I don't indulge in emotional outbursts. I don't cry in public.

Honestly, I don't remember the last time I cried at all.

There was this one documentary about how storks mate for life. Yeah. I cried during that. Don't judge me. There was this one stork who'd lost his mate and … well, I'm not dead inside. Anyone would have cried during that.

My point is this: despite my normally stoic nature, as soon as I realize Selah and Keegan aren't just neighbors, they're exes, I need some space. So, I whisper something about finding a restroom and excuse myself. And he doesn't even notice. All of which makes me feel like …

I just *feel*, okay?

It isn't a lie-lie. He didn't tell me an untruth. But he also didn't tell me the *whole* truth. He didn't tell me who Selah was to him so that I could be better prepared. He didn't tell me she's an ex, not just a girl with a crush. And he damn sure didn't tell me that she's Bruce's niece.

I feel all kinds of very complicated emotions I am not prepared to deal with. Certainly not in public. Definitely not anywhere within range of that human jellyfish Selah (i.e. all clinging tentacles and poisonous sting).

So I do what strong women have been doing for hundreds of years.

I order a drink at the bar.

Thankfully, there's not a line, so I smile gamely at the bartender. He's young and hot and the flirty smile he gives me tells me he probably earns big tips at events like this.

"What do you recommend?" I ask the flirty bartender.

It's what Sasha would do. If a hot bartender gave her a flirty smile, she wouldn't assume it was for tips. She would assume it was genuine. So I try to channel that energy. Let's face it, right now, I don't want to be frumpy Meg who's been duped by her best friend. I want to be someone else.

Every other time I tried to be Sasha, it was because I thought I should act like someone else. This is the first time I've actually wanted to be someone else.

The bartender smiles back, leaning in. "There's a signature cocktail for the event. It's called the Bluebonnet. It's got butterfly pea syrup, tequila, Paula's Texas Orange, and a twist of lemon."

"That sounds amazing!" I don't even have to fake my excitement. "I'll take that!"

His grin widens as he jumps into action, slicing a lemon and then pulling out shakers and carafes and an expensive-looking bottle of tequila. "One Bluebonnet, coming up."

"It's not like something that's premade?"

He shrugs as he works. "Yeah, but I'm going to make yours fresh because I want to see the look on your face."

"Okay, that sounds ominous."

"Just wait." He pours. He shakes. He pours and shakes some more. And then he slides a tall glass of bright blue liquid across the bar between us.

"That's beautiful!"

"Just wait."

"For what?" I ask, looking from the drink to him.

He nods back toward the drink, indicating I should watch. Then he drops several lemon slices on top and pours in the Paula's Orange. The second the acid hits the liquid, the drink turns purple.

I clap my hands to my mouth, trapping my gasp. "That's amazing."

He props his elbows on the bar and grins. "Right? The perfect drink for a charity about transforming unused spaces into something beautiful, right?"

I stare at the drink, hesitant to pick up something so lovely. Something that suddenly seems fraught with meaning. "It's almost too pretty to drink."

"Nah." He flips his towel over his shoulder and steps back. "It's the same drink it was a minute ago, but that's the butterfly pea syrup. It takes something that's already gorgeous and makes it stand out."

Nodding, I pick up the drink and ask, "What do I owe you?"

"The signature cocktail is included." He winks. "Just be sure to place some bids, okay?"

I nod, still smiling, drop a tip in his jar, and then head over to the stairs that lead up to the roof.

In the summer there's not enough shade on the roof, but last winter—when it was cool enough to be on the roof without risking heat stroke—I took a stargazing seminar up there.

I head up to check out the view and give myself a pep talk. It's two flights up, and I'm thankful that I'm not huffing by the time I reach the patio. The whole way up, I repeat mantras to myself.

Keegan is a great guy, but he is not my great guy. I tell myself.

We are not on a date. This is a wing-woman situation, and you've done your job by getting Keegan the contacts he needs.

As I'm climbing the last set of the steps, I look over the crowd mingling below. Keegan is still entrenched in the conversation with his parents and Bruce, and he's laughing at something someone says.

A bittersweet sadness grips me. *He did it.*

And so did I. Because I did—I'm here. I had a conversation that I didn't fumble through. And I actually feel beautiful. I nailed the presentation yesterday. Objectively, it went better than I dreamed it would. And tonight has been ... a revelation. Yeah.

Let's go with that.

Knowledge is always a good thing, even if it means realizing my best friend is someone different than I thought.

There is no one better to be than myself. I reach the top of the steps. There's a pergola dripping with Carolina jessamine, a scattering of tables, and some discreet mood lighting.

Tonight is going to be an amazing night. I just need a little time alone to regroup.

And maybe to, I don't know, download Bumble or Tinder or that one app that's based on MBTI and pairs you with people who are compatible. Someone compatible would be nice. I just need to distract myself from the fact that whatever I'm feeling for Keegan is too close to that crush I had all those years ago.

The organizers obviously thought people might venture up here, but so far, I'm the only one.

I sigh with relief, thankful to be away from the crowd.

Except when I do, a man I hadn't noticed before pushes away from the pergola column he was leaning against.

When he turns to face me, my breath catches.

It's Reid Forester.

Holy shit.

Reid Forester.

Dressed in a frickin' tux. Looking dapper and handsome and like every fantasy I've ever had of him. But somehow, although he looks stupidly gorgeous, my stomach doesn't do that flip-floppy thing it usually does.

"I didn't mean to startle you. I'm sorry."

Suddenly, my heart is pounding. Mostly because he scared the shit out of me when I thought I was all alone, but also because—holy shit—what are the odds that I would run into Reid on another rooftop?

It's one thing to have the occasional sexy fantasy about your hot boss when you rarely see him and almost never talk to him at all. It's another thing entirely now that I seem to be running into him on every rooftop in town.

What the hell am I supposed to do here?

He didn't recognize me the other night, but that doesn't mean he won't today. So I just stand there mutely—my mouth probably gaping like I'm a fish—wondering what I'm supposed to say in this situation.

"Y-you didn't."

I say, lamely. He raises a brow and smirks, wordlessly calling me on my lie.

Damn. Why did I even say that?

Should I offer to leave, letting him have the space to himself?

After all, he was here first.

Or should I strike up casual conversation about things around the office?

I'm tempted to bring up how well the Butler presentation went, but that seems like bragging. I can feign confidence as Sasha, but I'm not ready to brag about my work performance to my boss.

Before I can decide what to do, though, Reid walks over to me. The light on the roof is dim, but I feel him studying me as he walks closer. After a second, he says, "Meg, right? From Teresa's team?"

I blow out a breath, relieved that I don't have to decide about whether to lie to him.

Except then, his gaze narrows slightly, and he asks, "Or is it Sasha?"

"Um ..." Oh, shit! Ohshitohshitohshitohshit! "I ... um ..." Oh, shit!!!

After a second of my fumbling, he chuckles. "Sorry. That was mean of me. I shouldn't have put you on the spot like that."

Heat burning my cheeks, I press my palms to my face. Head still reeling, I half-moan, half-say, "You recognized me? Last night?"

"Yeah." He chuckles again. "Not until after you left, though, if it makes you feel any better."

Peering at him from over my fingertips, I shake my head. "I don't think there's anything about this situation that can make me feel better." I sink into the chair from a nearby table and bury my head in my hands. "I flirted with my boss last night and didn't tell him who I was."

I hear the scrape of the chair opposite me, realizing he's joined me.

Probably to fire me.

Yep. My days at Forester+Blake are definitely limited.

"Or your boss flirted with you, and you hid your identity so that it would be less awkward for him."

I inch my fingers down and look at him again. "That's a generous way of looking at it."

His lips quirk. "Maybe we both need some generosity right now."

Okay, maybe he isn't going to fire me.

Maybe.

Since he's still looking at me, almost like he's waiting for me to say something, I nod. Then, on impulse, I channel a little bit of Sasha and make a joke to lighten the mood. "I have to ask, do y-you spend all your weekends lurking on rooftops like Batman?"

He holds my gaze for another beat, laughs. "I could ask the same of you."

"Good point." I hope he doesn't think I'm stalking him. I should say something so he knows I'm totally normal and not a crazed stalker.

"You caught me." I lower my voice. "I am the Batman."

For exactly one second, I feel cool.

And then I ruin it. "Wait, is it Batman or the Batman? Or should I be Batgirl, since I'm a w-woman?"

He laughs. "I could answer the Batman-vs.-The-Batman question, but then you'd realize what a colossal nerd I am and I'm trying to preserve my dignity."

"Wait! You're a comic book nerd? No way!"

Lips twitching, he waggles his eyebrows. "If you out me at work, I'll deny everything."

Then, unexpectedly, he ducks his head, looking a little bashful. "I came up here because I'm horribly overdressed."

I blink in surprise. "What? No. You look amazing."

I cut myself off before I can slobber over him like a Goldendoodle with zero chill.

He grins, clearly more amused by my lack of chill than I am. "Thanks, but my assistant didn't read the invitation well enough and told me the event was black tie." He lets his voice trail off, shrugging his shoulders as if to say, c'est la vie. "So here I am in the stupid tux at an outdoor event in the spring."

He tugs at his collar and pulls a face. I try, unsuccessfully, to smother my laughter. When I don't quite manage it, I bite down on my lip.

"It does look a bit hot," I admit, then hastily add. "You know. Temperature wise. For the season."

Dear God, I hope he didn't think I meant he looked hot. In addition to looking amazing, which I already admitted.

Jesus. Why am I even allowed to speak out loud? Maybe it was better when I stuttered?

"Y-you could go down to the main room where they're holding the silent auction. At least there it's air-conditioned."

"But I'd have to socialize with all the people who are dressed appropriately." He shakes his head. "I don't think I can stand their pitying looks."

Not fooled by his hang-dog expression, I tease him.

"I guess you'll just have to live up here forever, then."

I make to turn, but he reaches for my arm. "Or you could stay here and keep me company."

He does that eye contact thing again. The one that unsettles me so.

How much did I drink, anyway? Because suddenly I feel lightheaded. As if the two flights of stairs were actually two hundred and the air is thinner this high up.

"I can't stay up here all night," I say breathlessly. "Eventually I have go back down to find my—"

I cut myself off before I say the word date.

Why? I don't know.

Maybe it's because it's Keegan, and it's not a date. Not really.

Maybe it's because this is Reid, and he's been my dream guy for so long. And he knows I'm an employee, but he's still talking to me like I'm a person, not an employee. No, not a person. A woman.

Or maybe it's because it's what Sasha would do.

Sasha wouldn't feel obligated to stay with the man who brought her, certainly not if he didn't even notice when she walked away.

"I have to admit ..." He meets my gaze over his drink, and I nod to indicate he should continue. "That sticky door latch? What would you say if I told you I lied about that?"

I shake my head. "I don't follow."

He pulls an exaggerated wince. "I really do have badge access."

"W-why'd you lie?"

"No idea." He shrugs. "I guess I didn't want to admit to having C-suite perks. I liked seeming like an ordinary guy."

I give him a once over, taking in his outrageous good looks and his freakin' tux. As if he could pass for ordinary. "How very *Prince and Pauper* of you."

"It sounds ridiculous when you put it like that."

"That's because it is ridiculous." I channel Reb and pull up my worst British accent. "Oh, hello, fine sir. Please ignore my bespoke tux while I pretend to slum it with you commoners."

He scrubs a hand down his face. "Please tell me I don't sound like that."

I look at him with overly-wide eyes and deadpan, "You would never."

"In my defense, the badge access thing isn't because I'm the CEO. Forester+Blake has been in the building long enough that access to the roof is in our company contract."

I gape. "So, what? All our badges give us clearance to the rooftop?"

He nods.

"So I've been sneaking up there, subject to the whims of a sticky latch, when I could actually just use my badge?"

"Afraid so."

"Um ... then w-why aren't we having parties up there all the time?"

"I guess I enjoyed keeping it to myself."

"Greedy bastard," I mutter, propping a hand on my hip in outrage.

He laughs and counters. "Unruly subordinate."

The easy repartee surprises me. I shouldn't be this comfortable with my boss. Not even my actual boss. My boss's boss.

I glance over at him to find his gaze on my face, his expression ...

I don't know what to think about how he's looking at me. My heart rate kicks up, but not in a good way. Not in an excited way.

It's more like my brain and my heart have suddenly realized that my mouth is getting us into trouble. Suddenly nervous, I blurt, "I should go."

Reid stands, too. "Don't."

I still, hands clenching in front of me, and meet his gaze.

My breath catches. What am I doing here?

If I stay, this is dangerous, reckless territory.

The angel on my right shoulder tells me I need to leave. She's urging me to get the hell out of here before I make a mistake. But the voice on my left? The little devil who, in my mind's eye, is Sasha wearing a little red devil-horns headband and speaking with a Zsa Zsa Gabor accent, says, "Why leave? So you can run back to that man who rejected you?"

I look over at Reid. He's beautiful. And smart. And, apparently, he's both funny and emotionally intelligent enough to communicate his desires. And he wants me to *stay*.

"I'm sorry," I whisper. "I really can't."

I make it less than a step before Reid stops me with a hand on my arm.

"Wait," he whispers.

I turn back to face him. His hand is still on my arm, warm on my skin.

His touch isn't demanding. I don't feel manhandled or controlled. If I pull away from him, he'll let me go. So why don't I?

He pulls me to him with a gentle tug, his free hand moving up to cup my cheek. His gaze meets mine, the question in his eyes obvious. He doesn't ask permission to kiss me. Not out loud, at least. But I see the question in his gaze. I have time to stop him before his mouth lowers to mine, but I don't.

Reid's lips are warm on mine as his hand drops to my hip, pulling me closer.

As kisses go, it's not unpleasant. It's not bad. It's not offensive or invasive.

But it's not magical either. It's just a kiss. Just one body part touching another.

I feel no zing of awareness. No spark of desire. No urge to deepen the kiss. No want.

I pull away from him, breaking off the kiss. Stunned by what I've done by letting him kiss me. For a moment, I just stand there, staring at him.

Then, I turn and flee.

eighteen

I SLIP down the stairs and make it nearly to the patio when I pause, pressing my hand to my chest, as if I can force my heart rate to slow by squeezing my heart. Then, trying to look like I wasn't just flirting with my boss on the roof, I round the corner and go down the last few steps.

I stop short when I see Keegan is standing by one of the open bar stations, ordering a drink ... with Selah plastered to his side.

She's got a hand wrapped around his arm in a way that presses her exposed cleavage to his arm. As I watch, she leans even closer and whispers something in his ear. Because she's tall and willowy, she doesn't even have to rise up on her toes to do it. Her lips are right at ear level. Like some trickster god designed her specifically to torture me with the image of her whispering in his ear. Probably planning more trips to the exotic places in the Caribbean.

That's probably where she got so tan. I bet she's the kind of person who does yoga on the beach while she's on vacation instead of drinking cheap rum cocktails like a normal person.

Of course, the only time I've ever laid on a beach was back in college when I drove down to South Padre for a weekend and all I could afford was cheap rum cocktails. So what do I know?

But none of this petty nonsense is actually productive, so I cut off my train of thought before I can spiral any deeper. Besides, he clearly wanted me here to serve as a buffer. Me getting all pissy and butt hurt because I wanted it to be more isn't exactly helpful.

So I gird my emotional loins and walk straight up to them. "Hey, Keegan. I found you!"

I make it sound like I'd merely wandered off instead of fled to regroup emotionally.

Keegan glances at me without quite meeting my gaze. Selah gives me a feline smile. "Oh, hey, you're back from your little jaunt up to the roof. Did you enjoy the view?"

What exactly does she mean by that? Did she see me up there with Reid? Or am I just being overly sensitive and feeling guilty? And why isn't Keegan looking at me?

Should I be a little honest or totally honest?

"Yeah, I ran into a friend from w-work."

Keegan finally meets my gaze. "A friend from work?"

He says the word friend like he knows it was Reid and he's asking if the "friend" is more than a friend. Which is pretty ballsy of him, given the whole Selah situation.

Some petty small part of me wishes I could taunt him with the idea that Reid is more than a friend or might someday be more than a friend. But I'm not that petty, and if I realized anything tonight, it's that I don't want Reid to be more than a friend.

So I'm able to say, with complete and unreserved honesty. "Yep. Just a friend. We've got a big presentation due on Monday, and the breeze up there was great."

"Oh? Is that why you went up there?" Selah asks, with the air of a person annoyed at being excluded from the conversation. "Was it too hot for you down here?"

What is that supposed to mean?

Is that a dig at my weight? Is she implying that I was hot just because I have the padding of a healthy adult woman and not an underfed supermodel? Or that I couldn't take the pressure of competing against her for Keegan's attention?

I don't know which is worse.

Either way, I don't have the energy or desire to play her verbal reindeer games.

"Keegan, I do feel a little overheated." I make a show of fanning myself with the flier again. "I think I might leave early. I can call a ride share if you plan on staying longer."

"No," he says, his tone resigned. Finally he looks at me, but when his gaze meets mine, there's a flicker of surprise, before his expression settles into something unreadable. "I think we're done here, anyway. I'll get you home."

Selah balks. Clearly, she was hoping I'd leave so she could have Keegan all to herself. She collects herself quickly and coos at him, "Are you sure? There are some amazing vacations up for auction."

"Yes." He moves to put even a centimeter of distance between them.

For a second, she clings even tighter to his arm, before releasing her hold on him with a long stroke down to his hand. Then she kisses him on the cheek ... barely, since her lips almost land on his mouth. "Okay, then. I guess I'll see you around the building."

She doesn't bother to say goodbye to me, even though she was just plastered against my date like he was her life preserver. Then she turns and saunters off without so much as a backwards glance. Which leaves me watching Keegan watch her walk away.

Why is he watching her walk away?

And why does she look that good doing it? Did she take some sort of class on how to be mesmerizing?

Probably. It's probably the kind of thing Loretta teaches when she's coaching to-be beauty queens.

I started this evening feeling pampered and gorgeous. Now I just feel like a hot troll. And not hot in the sexy sense of the word. Hot in the overheated sense of the word.

God, this sucks.

I turn back to Keegan to see that his attention has shifted back to me, and I wish I could read his expression, but I can't.

Does he regret inviting me?

Now that he's seen Selah look so gorgeous and so at ease in this crowd, now that he's reminded of how she fits into his world, he probably wishes he was with her.

Part of me wants to just ask him, but I'm not brave enough. If I ask him, I have to hear his answer.

So instead, I ask an easier question.

"Are you sure you don't want to stay?"

He makes a huffing noise that I might mistake for a chuckle if I didn't know him so well. But to me it sounds like annoyance. "No. We're done here."

We walk toward the entrance. This time, he doesn't put his hand to my back to guide me through the crowd, either because he's busy texting the driver that we're ready to go or because I complained about being hot, I'm not sure.

Either way, I miss the comforting weight of his hand on my skin.

Funny how quickly I got used to having him touch me

like that. How addictive it was being the focus of his attention tonight. How much I miss it already.

I would have thought, after knowing him all this time, that I knew his every expression and mood, but suddenly I can't read him at all. It's like tonight we've entered the upside down world where nothing makes sense anymore.

"Are you done talking to Bruce?" I ask, less because I'm curious and more just to have something to say. When he doesn't answer right away, I blurt, "I thought it went well. Did you think so?"

He slides his phone back into his pocket and then keeps his hands tucked there as well, like a deliberate signal that he's not going to touch me. Lips pressed into a hard line, he says, "It was fine."

"Don't you need to mingle more?" I ask.

He shoots me a look that's at least a little less annoyed than his earlier, uncharacteristic growling.

"No. I think we've had enough of that."

"Okay." I nearly push back on that.

Shouldn't we at least make another round? With any luck, we'll run into the Langley's one last time so we can say goodbye, and I can cement their budding opinion that Keegan is the only guy who can develop their property with the care it deserves.

But before I can suggest this, I glance at Keegan. He looks ... tired. His perennial smirk has flattened into a frown. There's no spark of humor in his eyes. A decade of friendship and this is the first time he's been eager to leave a party..

I want to chalk it up to the strain of dealing with his dad, but is that really it?

His inexplicable moodiness is a puzzle my gut wants to solve, but my brain just isn't up for.

"I wish you'd just tell me what went wrong. Did I embarrass you?"

But he doesn't answer and before I know it, we're out by the circular drive and the car is pulling up in front. We didn't stay long, so we're clearly among the first to leave and there's no wait for our car.

Instead of letting the valet open the door for me, he does it. As he holds open the car door, I turn as I'm about to slide into the car. For a moment, we're standing so close, not side by side like we have been most of the evening, but facing one another. I feel myself getting lost in the storm of his eyes. Getting drawn in.

The magnetic pull of his gaze is something I usually avoid. That's the key to quashing a secret crush on your best friend. One of them, anyway. No prolonged eye contact. Keep it light. Keep it fun. Avoid deep and soulful, longing-inducing gazes.

I don't know why I break my rule now. Maybe it's all the wine I've had—not to mention the Bluebonnet. Or maybe it's because I'm still unsettled by my encounter with Reid. Or maybe it's because I feel like something shifted between us tonight, and I just want to go back to the familiarity of our normal relationship.

Whatever the reason, I break my keep-it-light, no-lingering-gazes rule. I nearly reach out to touch him, but pull back, because stroking his arm feels like something Selah would do. If breaking the no-lingering-eye-contact rule was dangerous, stroking his arm would be even more dangerous. Even if stroking his arm is something Sasha would do, I don't.

Maybe I've broken enough rules tonight.

I settle into the seat as he closes the door and rounds the back of the town car. He climbs in on the other side and shuts the door with what feels like more force than necessary.

We ride back to my house in miserable, stony silence. The car is filled with tension. Not the kind of fun tension that filled the car on the ride to the gala. Not anticipatory, tingly tension. No, this is cold, angry tension and I don't even understand how we got here.

Everything feels so different than it did just a few hours ago, and I don't know how to get back to where we were. I would be fine going back to where we were before today. Before he kissed me. But I can't even figure out how to go back to that.

As soon as the town car stops in front of my house, I fling open the door and jump out.

"I guess I'll see you later."

I slam the door, expecting Keegan to have the driver just leave me there. But he doesn't. He climbs out and shuts his own door. I'm already halfway up the path to my condo when he says, "Meg, slow down."

I barely glance over my shoulder. "Y-you don't have to w-walk me to the door."

"Of course I'm going to walk you to the door."

"It's okay. Really. You can just leave and go back to … Whatever."

Whoever.

I don't say that out loud, but it's what's in my head.

He's clearly unhappy with me right now, and I don't know why. Maybe he wishes he hadn't invited me or that he'd taken Selah instead.

I make it to my door, but my hands are shaking so much I can barely get the key in the lock. It doesn't help that he's right there behind me, watching as I fumble.

God, that feels like a metaphor.

I hate feeling this way, like I'm incompetent and foolish. I hate even more having someone witness it.

Keegan is my best friend, so maybe it should be easier, but somehow it's worse.

I finally get the key in the lock and unlock my door. I would slam the door in his face, but he's faster than I am and catches the door with his hand. "What the hell is wrong with you, Meg?"

I'm already stomping up the stairs to the main level of my condo when I shoot back over my shoulder, "That's rich. What the hell is w-wrong with you?"

I don't know why I'm so angry all of a sudden. I don't lose my temper. Not with anyone, certainly not with Keegan. We have literally never fought.

The idea of us fighting upsets me so much that I just wish he would leave. I want to be alone to sort out all of these weird feelings, but he doesn't leave. He stomps up the stairs behind me, pulling off his jacket and tie as he follows.

"You want to know what's wrong with *me*? You want to know why *I'm* mad? It's because you left me alone. You disappeared for half an hour to go flirt with some random guy on a rooftop."

My mouth drops open.

All the bluster leaves my sails.

I was prepared with a defense about why I disappeared on him. Prepared to feel indignant since he's the one to blame for not telling me about Selah ahead of time. But the moment he mentions flirting with some random dude on a rooftop, I'm stumped. How did he know I was up on the rooftop with Reid? How much did he see? And why do I feel guilty about being there?

I cross my arms over my chest. "I disappeared because I didn't know what else to do. And I didn't disappear with the intention of flirting for some 'random dude' on a rooftop." I bracket the words with air quotes. "I went up on the rooftop to get some air and he happened to be there. And he wasn't some random dude. That was my boss. Once I ran into him, I couldn't very well leave without making conversation."

Now it's Keegan's turn to look shocked. "That was him?" Keegan's voice is suddenly soft. "That's the guy you have a crush on?"

"That was Reid Forester. Yes. But I w-wasn't flirting with him. I didn't run into him on purpose."

"You may not have meant to flirt with him. God knows you never seem to know when you're actually flirting with someone, but he was definitely flirting with you."

I snap my mouth shut, any possible defense stuck in my throat. What the hell is that supposed to mean? I don't know when I'm flirting with people? I don't know which accusation is more shocking: the idea that I somehow unknowingly flirt with people or that Reid was flirting with me and I didn't notice.

On the other hand, didn't I?

I did notice that Reid was giving me pick-me-up eyes, but that doesn't mean I responded to it. Or did I?

If I really didn't want Reid to flirt with me, shouldn't I have told him that I work for him? I'm not interested in Reid. I see that with so much clarity now, but did I see that then? When I was back on the rooftop, still reeling from the realization that Keegan dated Selah, did I know that I wasn't interested in Reid? Did I stay and talk with him merely because his apparent interest soothed my ego?

Maybe, but I know he's not actually interested in me. Anyone could get caught up in the heightened romance of fancy clothes and amazing rooftop views.

"I didn't go up on the rooftop to meet him. I didn't flirt with him. Honestly. We chatted, but it didn't mean anything."

He nods, but the gesture is terse, and his expression hasn't cleared. "Why did you leave?"

"Why do you think? I left because I was upset. Because I didn't know how to handle Selah being there. And I didn't expect—"

"You didn't expect what?" He takes a step closer to me. His arms falling down to his sides.

"You didn't tell the truth." I say the words like an accusation. "She's not just some neighbor who flirts with y-you all the time. Y-you were with her."

Keegan scrubs a hand over his hair and then down his face. "Yes."

I swallow, giving a tight nod. Suddenly feeling more like crying than ever, and I'm not even sure why. It's not like I didn't know that Keegan has dated a lot of women. It's not like I didn't know that he took people on trips, but there's a difference between knowing it, and having to watch one of his exes throw herself at him when he's on a date with me.

Not that this was even a date.

I wrap my arms and press my chest like the action can somehow hold in all the feelings that I don't want to feel. I turn away from him, kicking off my shoes as I walk over to my kitchen cabinet and get out a water glass. It's just an excuse to keep my back to him while I get water from the fridge. "I knew this was a bad idea. Even before Selah showed up."

"What do you mean, this was a bad idea?"

"Dressing myself up like I belong in y-your world doesn't even get me close to the thing. We don't exist in the same w-world, Keegan. It was a bad idea from the start. I just made a fool of myself."

"What are you talking about? You were brilliant. I even said as much. I thought we were having a fantastic time."

"We were, at first." I sigh out loud. "W-what do you want me to say? You w-want me to pretend that it didn't matter to me that Selah was there?" Yeah. That's probably what I should do. Because it shouldn't matter to me that she was there. Or that they were once together. Keegan and I are just friends and therefore it shouldn't matter to me who he's dated in the past. Or taken to the Bahamas or St. Maarten, or anywhere.

"No," he says, surprising me. "I don't want you to pretend that it doesn't matter to you. I want the opposite. I want it to matter to you."

"What?" I don't understand, and I'm whirring through the logic of his statement, finding none. "What does that even mean?"

"What do you think it means? It means I *want* you to care that I was with her. I want you to be jealous. If you and I are on a date and some ex of mine puts her hands all over me, I wish it would piss you off. Just like it pissed me off to find you up on the roof with Reid. And that was before I even knew it wasn't some stranger you were talking to. I want you to care what I do and who I do it with, because then at least I would know you felt something for me."

My mind is churning over his words, trying to make sense of what he's saying. Except his words don't make sense. "I don't understand. W-what do you mean? You want me to be jealous? So this is how you expected tonight to end? With us fighting about Selah?"

He releases a huff of exasperation. "No, trust me. This is not how I expected tonight to end."

"Oh, really? How did you think it was going to end?"

I don't know what I expected his response to be when I threw out that question. Something glib, I guess, because Keegan is a master at keeping things light and playful. And right now, I desperately wish we could get back to the playful, light banter I'm used to between us.

But apparently, my question was the wrong one to get us back in the banter zone. Because as soon as the words are out of my mouth, his expression darkens. For one long moment, he just stares at me, the muscle in his jaw ticking as his gaze moves over my body. There's something so intense in his eyes, something even worse than the anger that I'm not used to seeing. If I didn't know better, I'd think he hated me in this moment.

But I know he doesn't hate me. So why is he looking at me with such ... Such what?

"Fuck it," he mutters. Then he tosses his tie to the ground and stalks over to me, his long legs eating up the space between us.

I take an instinctive step back until I feel my hips bump against the counter behind me. A moment later, he's stopping in front of me, wrapping his hands around my hips. He lifts me, easily, and sets me on the counter, stepping between my legs.

"You want to know how I thought tonight would end?" His hands slide up into my hair, angling my jaw. "Like this. I thought it would end like this."

Before I have a chance to ask what this is, he's kissing me.

nineteen

I BARELY LET myself enjoy the sensation of his lips on mine before I wedge my hands between us and push him back enough to look up at him. "Wait. What? You wanted tonight to end with us kissing?"

He gives me an exasperated look. "Yeah. Obviously. Jesus, Meg, I want to end *every* night with us kissing. And tonight, you look even more amazing than normal. Do you have any idea how hard it's been to keep my hands off of you? Frankly, I—"

I don't give him a chance to finish that thought. I fist his shirt in my hands and tug him close again.

"Then don't keep your hands off me."

"What?" he asks, his annoyance slowly giving way to something else.

"Don't k-keep your hands off me," I repeat, but this time the shock of my demand wears off and nervousness creeps in, having me stumbling over the words.

Keegan's gaze searches mine, and I half expect him to pull back from me. To tell me he was joking. Instead, his hands find my waist, his fingers squeeze me there lightly, as if making sure I'm real, before they run up my ribcage. His other hand finds my thigh, and my skin pebbles under his caress.

"God, I have waited so long to hear you say that," he murmurs. "Do you want me to show you what I imagined doing to you the moment I picked you up? Can I show you how I've wanted to touch and kiss you ever since the day we met and a million times in between?" Keegan's gaze searches my face, and I half expect him to pull back from me. Instead, his focus lasers in on my lips. He leans closer in, his breath whispering across my lips. "So many kisses," he murmurs.

His fingers grip my hips, tugging me closer until he's pressed between my legs.

"Keegan," I whisper. I have no more words. My skin feels two sizes too small and even though I'm dying to ask him a thousand questions about what he just said, I know I will actually die if he doesn't kiss me.

"Fuck, Glasses." He slides one hand behind my neck and then finally lowers his lips to mine. There's nothing tentative or sweet about the kiss. He doesn't ease us into it. No, Keegan devours me in a no-holds-barred-I-can-make-you-come-just-from-a-kiss kiss.

The slide of his tongue against mine is like a live wire to my clit, and I shamelessly rock myself against his thigh.

His mouth leaves mine, only to blaze a heated trail down my jaw to my neck and across my collarbone. I'm pretty sure I'm moaning like a porn star, but I try not to think about it. This is one moment I don't want to fantasize. I want to be wholly here. With him. Enjoying that deliciously wicked thing he's doing with his tongue on the sensitive skin between my neck and my shoulder.

"That day we met," he says, but his mouth keeps licking

and biting at my tender skin. "There you were with these big gorgeous eyes, wearing nothing but a pair of glasses and a towel. I got hard so fast I think I lost some brain cells."

He leans up then. His eyes are molten as he stares at my face.

His fingers fumble at my back to find the zipper of my dress. He tugs it down all the way to the small of my back, skimming his fingers along the bare skin he reveals before bunching the fabric of my dress in his hands, lifting me just enough to pull my dress up and over my head. He tosses it to the floor, leaving me dressed only in my bra and panties.

"So damn perfect," he whispers. He cups both my breasts. His calloused fingers and warm palms weigh my breasts, his gaze moving over my body as if he's thought of this moment again and again.

He strips away the last of my clothing with brusque, frantic hands. Again, I rock myself against him, desperate for more pressure against my clit.

"Jesus, Meg, I can feel how fucking wet you are through my pants."

Maybe that would embarrass me if I couldn't feel how hard he is. And even that is baffling. Keegan wants me? Has *been* wanting me, if he's to be believed.

How is that possible?

As if he can sense the questions racing through my mind, he pulls back and gives me another searing, searching look. "Are we on the same page here? I need to know you want this as much as I do."

It's not a question I feel qualified to answer.

Wanting Keegan is terrifying. It always has been. For so many reasons.

But hasn't the main reason always been that I've been afraid to want him because I assumed he didn't want me? If I'm wrong, if he does want me, then what's holding me back?

"I do. So badly."

The words come out on a breath, little more than a whisper. But it's enough.

Without warning, he plants his shoulder in my stomach and picks me up, fireman style, and marches to my bedroom.

My body bounces when he tosses me onto the bed. He carries me like I weigh nothing, like he's too desperate to get to my bedroom to wait. I lean up on my elbows and watch him undress. He's all masculine energy and grace as he toes off his boots. When he's standing in nothing more than black boxer briefs—ones dotted with the Enterprise—he crawls up the bed, kissing his way up my body, not stopping until he's wedging his shoulders between my legs and parting my lips with his tongue as he slides a finger deep inside me.

Under different circumstances, I might feel self-conscious. I might get too much in my own head, my thoughts and insecurities keeping me too grounded. But not with Keegan.

With him, I can't think of anything but him. His touch drowns out everything else. That, plus the never-ending litany of words. It's like being worshiped by his mouth, by the touch of it on my body, and by the things he says.

Oh, the things he says.

He tells me how much he wants me. How much he's always wanted me. Spelling out detail after detail of every fantasy he's had about me. About us.

How he used to lie awake in the room next to mine when we lived together, imagining all the things he wanted to do with me. To me.

That's how I come the first time with Keegan. With his teeth and tongue pressing against my clit and his words of praise and filthy fantasies burrowing into my soul.

twenty

I DON'T FALL asleep after climaxing. At least I don't think it was sleep. It's more like I pass out. Or lose time. Or have some kind of out-of-body experience.

Which almost makes sense, because surely there wasn't room in my body for all of those sensations and feelings and for me as well.

So, of course, I must have just drifted away for a few minutes.

When I come back to myself, it's to find Keegan above me, holding himself just off my body, his arm muscles bulging. He looks as bemused and as shell-shocked as I feel. I can feel him, hard and hot, nestled against my core. I shift my hips, rocking the slick folds of my pussy along the length of his cock.

He groans, his eyes closing, but he reaches down, clamping a hand on my hip to still me.

He breathes out slowly, eyes still closed as he mutters, almost under his breath. "Please stop."

"Stop?" I ask.

His eyes flicker open, still looking dazed. "Yeah. I'm

211

going to need you to not move for a couple of minutes, otherwise this is going to be over really fucking quick."

I bite down on my lip, trying to buck my hips again, but he holds me still. "I don't mind quick. I don't think I'm in a position to complain about quick considering just how quick I was."

"Maybe." He leans down, kissing me, and I can taste myself on his lips. "But I've waited too long for this to rush now."

I run my hands up his chest, wanting to touch every inch of his body, every perfect muscle he's been hiding from me. Wanting to touch him. To revel in the flex and strain of muscles and flesh.

He abandons my hip to grab both my hands in his, his gaze pinning me. "Wait. I'm serious."

His tone is hard. Intense in a way it usually isn't. Like he's scolding me. Chastising me for breaking some rule I didn't realize he'd made.

"I'm tired of waiting."

He searches my face, his gaze catching and holding mine. Whatever desperate neediness he sees there seems to satisfy him. The single arm he's holding himself up with is trembling now, and he releases my hands to shift his balance. On a sigh, he lowers himself again. Then stills just before his body comes back into contact with mine.

"I need a condom."

"Please tell me you have one."

He nods, briefly rolling off me to grab his pants. I watch as he pulls a condom from his wallet, and although I know it shouldn't be sexy to pause like this, it somehow is.

The way the light highlights the lines and shadows of his body is amazing, and I'm itching to run my fingers over the plains and valleys of his abs. The ridges of his hips and the divots on the sides of his ass. I bite my lip, resisting the urge to crawl over to him and nibble him.

He tears the foil with his teeth then, turns toward me as he rolls the condom over his cock, and fuck if it's not one of the sexiest things I've ever seen—Keegan walking toward me as he holds his cock, his hand trailing up and down its length as one knee lands on the bed is an image I won't forget. Ever.

I lean forward, half sitting as I reach for him, unable to keep my hands from him for a moment longer. My fingers twine around his neck, bringing him in for a kiss as he crawls up me, repositioning us so he's settled between my thighs once more.

He notches himself at my entrance, and then he's kissing me. Lips and tongues, teeth and groans—we kiss as he slides all the way inside me. It's been a while, and he's big and it's tight, and I'm full and it's everything. I'm glad we're kissing, so I can keep my eyes shut as I adjust.

And then he starts to move. I wrap one leg up around his waist, the position opening me up more, so the root of his cock presses to my clit with every thrust. Everything is still so tender, still buzzing, from my first out-of-body climax, that all of this new pressure is almost too much. And then he starts talking again.

"Fuck, Meg. You feel so damn good. So good. So perfect. So fucking right."

My climax slams into me, and I call Keegan's name. It is part plea, part praise.

His own orgasm pulls my name from his lips, and it sounds like so much more than just my name.

twenty-one

I'M NOT great with change.

Back in college, I saw a therapist for a while, mostly because it was covered under the university's health care and because I knew I wouldn't be able to afford it with whatever salary I would start with fresh out of college. Talking to a therapist while it was essentially free seemed like the fiscally responsible thing to do.

When my six weeks were up, I didn't know anything I hadn't known going into it. Namely: I have trust issues relating to my parents' divorce, I resist change, and (to use my mom's phrasing) I'm stubbornly independent. All of that seemed pretty obvious.

And, honestly, none of that seemed bad to me. Doesn't everyone have trust issues of some kind? People without trust issues end up being catfished or sending all their money to "buy" a gold mine in Bolivia or something. And independence (stubborn or not) is a good thing.

My independence meant that, when Ollie and I broke up, I still had my career and my condo and I didn't end up living out of a van. Not that I have a van, but you see my point.

Independence is good.

As for the not-liking-change stuff ... tell me this, who *does* like change?

Still, I wish change didn't make me feel quite so panicky.

I wish that the morning after having sex with Keegan for the first time, I could wake up, warm and content with his arm thrown over my waist, and just enjoy the sensation. I could wallow in the luxury of amazing orgasms and post-coital bliss, instead of waking up with a knot of dread in my belly and a brain full of racing thoughts.

I try to fall back asleep, because getting up before six on a Sunday seems borderline psychotic. I do some deep breathing exercises, but every time I inhale, my skin brushes against Keegan's arm. Because I'm in bed with Keegan. Because I slept with my best friend. And that seems scary and life altering. In reality, I'm paralyzed by that fear, but in my gut all I want to do is hold on to Keegan and never let go.

Keegan has been so much to me, and now it feels like he's my everything. How the hell am I supposed to live up to that for him? It's a stupid fantasy, and I need to start thinking straight. So I shove aside those thoughts and try to do that thing where you imagine warm, relaxing water lapping at your feet. Except my blankets are already too hot. Probably because I'm not used to having another body in bed with me. And the fact that I do and that it's Keegan ...

If I had my phone, I might even have been able to ease myself back to sleep by watching relaxing videos of Flemish Giant rabbits or something. But my phone is downstairs, still my clutch from last night. And I don't think I can get it without waking up Keegan. Because he's in bed with me. Because I slept with my best friend. And ... You can probably see where this is going.

The undeniable, unignorable truth is that last night Keegan and I slept together. And it was amazing. Definitely the best sex of my life. (Mostly because apparently I hadn't known how good sex could be.) But now, in the cold hard light of day ... okay, not day ... in the cold hard semi-light of six thirteen, I don't know how to do a morning after with Keegan.

What does this mean?

How is it going to affect our friendship?

What if I ruined everything?

How is it that he and I lived in the same apartment for three years and I don't know how to act around him in the morning?

All I know is that I can't just lay here, quietly panicking until he wakes up. Because the longer I lay here, the more likely I am to be a crazy, neurotic nutjob by the time he wakes up.

So I quietly slip out of bed and sneak off to the shower to devise a plan. Well, wash my hair and devise a plan.

Clearly, step one of said plan is that I need to carve out some emotional distance between Keegan and I, ASAP. And physical distance wouldn't hurt either.

It's not until I'm out of the shower and drying off that I even remember that I'm supposed to spend the day working on the new presentation for Butler Appliances. And I haven't even thought about work in the past twelve hours.

And that moment, that right there, is the moment the knot of anxiety in my belly blossoms into full-blown panic.

Maybe sleeping with Keegan was a mistake. Maybe it

wasn't. Maybe I've taken a risk and ruined our entire friendship. Or maybe everything will work out okay.

But no matter what happens with him, I've made a bigger mistake. I've let myself get distracted by my relationship with him. This presentation is happening on Monday. The fate of my career hangs in the balance. If I pull this off, Forester+Blake will have a new client, our biggest client, all because of my work.

Snagging a client like Butler Appliance is the kind of thing that can make your career. Blowing it could ruin mine.

The fact that I haven't even thought about the Butler account in the past twelve hours is a sign I'm in way over my head. Risking my friendship with Keegan is bad enough. Risking my career is unthinkable.

But it's okay. I can regroup from here. I just have to work all day and come up with a fabulous idea. That way, I'll have something to present to Matt and Reid in the morning before the big meeting with Butler in the afternoon.

Once I'm out of the shower, I brush my teeth and throw my still damp hair up into a sloppy bun. Yes, my hair is different, but once I twist it into a bun, the lighter color is hardly noticeable.

I throw on one of my normal potato sack dresses. No one else will be in the office on a Sunday, so it doesn't matter how I look. By the time I return to the bedroom, Keegan is awake and sitting up in bed, with his elbows wedged behind him, the sheet pooling at his waist to reveal those impressive muscles I drooled over last night. His gaze rakes over me and he flashes me a crooked smile, one full of fondness and 100% smirk free. He pushes back against the headboard and raises a hand to shove his hair out of his face.

"Good morning." His voice is low and gravelly from sleep, and I'm instantly thrown back to those years we lived together, when I heard that just-woke-up voice of his all the time.

Back then, college Meg would have never imagined that someday grown Meg would ever hear that voice in a morning-after-context. Or that voice groaning her name.

Damn it! This is not helping.

For a moment, I'm struck mute. But I clear my throat and offer a vague, but somehow still awkward.

"Heyyy."

I'm not turned on. I'm not turned on. I'm not turned on.

Keegan holds out a hand, gesturing me back to the bed. "Hey, Glasses."

Fucking hell—I'm turned on. And I don't know that I will ever be able to listen to him say those words again without thinking of last night.

I wonder how that Eternal-Sunshine-Spotless-Mind memory-wiping technology is coming along. I'll have to Google that when I get to the office.

I clear my throat. "I ... I have to go."

"What?"

I clear my throat again and realize I sound like I've come down with tuberculosis.

"I have work today."

"It's Sunday."

"Yes. But I have that big presentation tomorrow. I have so much to do to get ready for it."

He's frowning now, running his fingernails over his bare chest in a way that makes me want to climb back into bed with him. But isn't that the kind of thing that got me into this trouble in the first place?

He glances around, looking confused. "Isn't it early to go to work?"

"Yes. Totally. But I'm so behind." I can't stand to look at him, so I go to my closet and dig out a pair of shoes. I can feel Keegan watching me as I move about the room, but I don't let it distract me from getting ready.

"Come back to bed," he says.

"I can't. I told you already. I have too much work to do."

From the corner of my eye, I see him push himself up to lean against the headboard. It's all I can do not to turn to just look at him. To get lost in the magnetic pull of him.

But it's always been like this, hasn't it?

This is what makes Keegan so dangerous to me.

Without ever meaning to, he can snag and hold all of my attention. He can distract me from my own goals. He has the power to knock me off track. If I was a different person, maybe it wouldn't be so bad. Maybe I'd be able to pick myself up, get back on track, and chug ahead. But that's not who I am. If I get off track, I'd be like one of those trains overloaded with toxic waste. I'd explode into a fiery blaze that destroys everything I've worked so hard for.

After watching me getting dressed for several moments in silence, he sighs. "Okay, I get it. You have work to do. But can you meet me for brunch?"

I still, trepidation tiptoeing up my spine. Keegan isn't a brunch kind of guy. Unless it's his family's infamous Sunday brunch.

I force myself to ask the question I don't know if I want the answer to. "Sunday brunch?"

"Yeah. My parents mentioned it last night. They invited us both. I think they want to talk about the development."

Keegan's parents invited us to brunch? Like we're … what? A proper couple? And they want to talk business?

As if I didn't have enough to panic about this morning!

"I don't have time for brunch." I have to force myself to take a deep breath, because the sentence comes out high pitched and frantic.

He holds up his hands, palms out. "Okay. No brunch. What about breakfast? Just the two of us."

He climbs out of bed and ambles over to me. I purposefully turn my back to him to dig through the drawer, like the no show socks I'm looking for are the difference between life and death. He steps up behind me, brushing a strand of hair off my neck and pressing a kiss to my shoulder. He's naked except for boxer briefs and that's entirely too much yummy naked skin and not enough layers of fabric. It takes all of my restraint not to melt back into his arms.

"I know the manager of Snooze," he murmurs. "It's ten blocks from your office. If I call now, she can have a table waiting for us. We'll be in and out in less than an hour." He chuckles, and I feel the heat of his breath on the back of my neck. "Not that there'll be anyone else there this early on a Sunday."

I grab a pair of socks and dodge out of his embrace to go sit on the bed and put them on. "That's an hour I don't have. Why are you making such a big deal out of this?"

He leans back against my dresser. "I'm not. You are."

"Because you're not listening to me." I let myself look at him, really look at him for the first time this morning. He is, as always, so fucking beautiful it hurts in my chest just to look at him. "This presentation is something I've been working towards my entire career. I—" I cut myself off and correct myself. "It has to be perfect."

He gives me one of those hard, assessing looks of his. The kind I seem to get a lot of lately.

After a second, he swallows and nods. "It has to be perfect, or you have to be perfect?"

"What is that supposed to mean?"

"It's just a presentation. For a job you're amazing at. It's not going to make or break your career."

"It's just a presentation to you. To me, it's everything."

He crosses his arms over his chest. "Everything? It's everything to you?"

"What?" God, he sounds so hurt. I feel like I kicked a puppy.

"Jesus, Meg. We slept together last night. How is your presentation more important than that?"

And I can't look at him anymore because it hurts too much. I can't think about what he's saying. I just ... I just can't.

I push myself to my feet and head for my closet, snagging my shoes. I flee the bedroom, putting the shoes on as I walk down the stairs, nearly tripping as I do so. "I can't have this conversation right now."

He follows me out of the bedroom, grabbing his pants off the floor on his way. I can hear him putting them on as he walks down the stairs. "Then when? When can you have this conversation?"

"I don't know," I tell him, honestly.

Though I somehow can't bring myself to look at him without feeling like a jerk and a coward.

When am I going to be ready to face what happened last night?

I slept with my best friend. I had sex with the one person who should have been off limits. The one person I don't know how to live without. And now, I might have ruined everything.

I reach the main level of my condo. I make it halfway across the room toward the coffeemaker, before turning back around. I don't have time for coffee. More to the point, I can't stay here with Keegan while the coffee brews. I'll make some at the office.

I head toward the stairs, but Keegan is in my way. He must have grabbed a shirt as well as pants, because he's pulled it on. But he hasn't bothered with the buttons yet and it's hanging open over his bare chest. I'm trying so hard not to look at him, I nearly run smack into him.

"If you don't know when you'll be ready to have this conversation, you better figure it out. Because I'm ready now." He reaches out towards me like he wants to grab me by the arms, but instead he takes a step back and runs his hand through his hair in frustration. "What is it you're so afraid of?"

"Seriously?" Okay. He wants to do this now? We'll do it now. "I'm afraid sleeping together ruined everything. I'm afraid it changed things and we can't ever go back. I'm terrified that a year from now, I'll run into you somewhere, and I'll be as desperate for your attention as Selah was last night. That's what I'm afraid of."

"Selah? I told you last night. You don't have any reason to be jealous of Selah. She means nothing to me. We were just friends with an ... agreement."

"God, do you even hear yourself? You were just friends with her. Until you slept together." He just blinks at me, clearly still not seeing it. "I'm not jealous of Selah. I'm afraid of being the *next* Selah."

"You are not ever going to be the next Selah. That's not what's happening here. You and I didn't fuck one night because we were both bored and didn't have anything better to do. And if that's what you think happened here, then we really do have a problem."

"Which is why I can't talk about this right now. I need to—"

This time he does grab my arm. Not hard and not for long. Just until I cut myself off. "This isn't just a fuck buddy situation. This is more than that."

"Look, I know you think that. But your life is in transition right now. You're thinking about stepping away from the bar to go work for your dad. It's natural that you're clinging to our relationship because it's familiar and comfortable."

"That's not what's happening here. You're a person, not an emotional support animal."

"But—"

"I'm not confused. This doesn't have anything to do with my selling the bar or going to work for my dad or anything like that. This is about you and me. I'm in love with you. I've *been* in love with you."

His words knock me back a step.

He's in *love* with me?

He's *been* in love with me?

His words don't just knock me back a step. They knock me all the way back to the corner of the boxing ring. They have me shaking my head to clear it after a sucker punch. And then they have me coming out of the corner swinging.

"Don't lie, Keegan. You don't have to lie about this."

He looks at me like I've slapped him. Like my words shocked him. "I'm not lying, Meg."

I want to believe him. I really do. But that part of me— the part that knows who I am and all that Keegan is— knows that just can't be true. It can't be. Reid's words come back to me, reminding me of the *reality* of my friendship with Keegan, and I argue back. "If you've been in love with me, then why didn't you make a move until last night? Why is this the first time in our decade of friendship that this has come up?"

He just gapes at me for a second and then laughs, incredulity in it. "This isn't the first time it's come up. That first year, I asked you out."

"No, you didn't." I shake my head, take a step back.

"Yeah. I did." He's not laughing anymore.

"Sure. A couple of times. Out of pity or whatever. You were just being friendly. Because I was this weird, pathetic girl you had to rescue."

"No. You were this gorgeous, brilliant girl who had her life all planned out." He takes a step towards me. "I didn't ask you out because I pitied you. I asked you out because I wanted to spend time with you. Because I wanted *you*. But you turned me down. Over and over again."

"No. That's not what ..." I take another step back.

But he follows. "You're the one who made it clear that you just wanted to be friends. You wanted to focus on college. You didn't have time to waste on a boyfriend. So I settled for friendship, because I wanted you in my life. I thought I could be patient. I was ready to wait for you. To wait for you until you were ready for something more. But then you started dating that douchebag, Ollie. Do you have any idea how hard it was to watch you date that guy? That loser who was never good enough for you? But he seemed to be what you wanted. So I pulled back. I tried to move on."

He pauses, seeming like he's waiting for me to say something. But I don't know what to say. I have no words at all. No way to respond, because I can barely process the words he's saying.

When I don't say anything, he shrugs. "And then you broke up with him. You kicked him out. And I thought, okay. I finally have my shot. Only now you've got a crush on some boss of yours. On the boss who doesn't even recognize how much you contribute to the team or pay you what you're worth."

"That's not—"

"Don't defend him. I have zero interest in talking about Reid. Or your job. I just want to know if you're finally ready to give us a chance. You wanted to know why I haven't made my move before now? I have made my move, Meg. I've *been* making my move for the past decade. You just haven't been paying attention. You've pushed me so far into the friendzone that even after we spend the night making love to each other, and I'm telling you right to your face that I want this, I want us to be a couple, you're still grappling for reasons I don't like you. When the truth is, I've loved you for years."

My back is against the counter now, but it might as well be against the wall, because that's how I feel. He's not even touching me. He's not caging me in with his arms or anything, but I feel trapped.

Trapped by his words and the implications behind them.

He's been in love with me all this time? He's been making his move, and I just ignored him?

How is any of that possible?

It's so contrary to my understanding of our friendship. To my understanding of the world and the laws of physics.

Is this what the pope felt like when Galileo tried to

explain Copernican astronomy? Like, suddenly, nothing in the world makes sense anymore?

How am I supposed to fold any of this into my understanding of the universe? Into my understanding of my life?

What am I supposed to do with this information?

Now. At this moment.

I don't know. I don't know how to process any of this.

So I do the only thing I can do. I push back.

"This." I jab a finger in his direction. "This right here is why I didn't want to have this discussion right now."

"What?"

"I can't handle this right now. I don't have time to reframe our entire relationship. I can't process any of this. I have to get ready for the presentation that is happening in less than twenty-four hours. It's the most important presentation I've ever done. Nailing it could mean a promotion. B-blowing it could mean my job. And frankly, the fact that you would even try to have this conversation with me right now is kind of a dick move."

"Jesus, Meg. Last night we made love for the first time and this morning you're running away."

"I'm not running away!" I say, and it's louder, more shrill than I mean to be. I take a breath and make sure my tone, and volume, are level when I say, "I'm going to work. Because my job is important."

"Right." That single word cuts through the air. "It's more important than us. As fucking always."

"Okay, that is really not fair. Yes, my job is important to me. It has to be, because it's all I have. If I lose my job, I could lose everything. Because I can't pay my rent or eat or live if I don't have a job."

"Yeah, it's your job, but they don't pay you enough. They don't value you. If they did, they wouldn't expect you to work all weekend long right after you nailed the presentation that got them this huge new client in the first place."

His words slice, cutting a part of me I didn't know was even susceptible to damage. I push back, defending my choice to take on this job and the responsibility that comes with it.

"You have it all wrong, Keegan. This whole thing over the weekend isn't normal or typical—usually, I have time. P-plenty of time. I wanted this responsibility because I want to climb the ladder." I say it reasonably, like if I can keep my tone even and calm, I can rationalize everything. Like I can make him understand. "I told Matt I'd do it so that I can p-prove I'm capable. That I'm ready to lead my own team."

"Have they offered that?"

"What?"

"To lead your own team– have they offered it?" He arches a brow, and it's enraging to know where he's going with this. That my careful maneuvering is backfiring. "Have they actually said, 'Meg, if you get us this client and present this new concept Monday and the client goes for it, we'll give you your own team.'?"

I scoff and roll my eyes, as if I can make his question come off as ridiculous, even though a quiet part of me knows it's not. "Don't be ridiculous."

That stupid eyebrow arches higher. "Am I being ridiculous?"

No. Not really. "Yes! You know that's not how things are done. Nobody offers deals like that!"

"Yes, Meg, they do. *I* do. My father does. Companies with healthy working environments give their employees metrics that are measurable and achievable, so that people can understand what's needed to climb the ladder, earn raises, etc. That is the bare fucking minimum."

I open my mouth to reply, but it just sort of hangs there as I draw a blank. His anger is surprising. Shocking, even. Part of me knows he's right. Very right. I don't even have a good response. "Well... if I don't work on this today, we could lose the account. And then people get laid off."

"If you get laid off, you can get another job."

"Right. Because great jobs in Austin are just everywhere."

"Yeah. They are."

"They're not."

"For people who are as good as you are, they are."

"What are you going to hire me out of pity? And what, I'll write ad copy for a bar that's already thriving? Or maybe I'll take over managing the bar after you go to work for your dad. Or maybe—"

"You'll come to work for McQuade Development. I've already talked to my dad about it. He's ready to hire you on the Langley project. You heard Bruce last night. You'd be perfect for it. Last night wasn't about convincing my dad I was right for the job. It was about convincing *you* you are."

"What are you even talking about? I can't go work for McQuade Development."

"Why not?"

"Because I just can't."

"Why?"

"Because it's too much. I can't have you as my friend and my boss."

Something in his expression hardens. "You wouldn't be my friend and my employee. We'd be partners."

"No. We wouldn't. Because your dad owns the company. If things don't work out, you'd still have a job, and I wouldn't. And I don't have a trust fund to fall back on. I don't have a safety net."

He gives a huff of exasperation. "Is that what you think? That you don't have a safety net?"

"It's not what I think. It's what I know. I *don't* have a safety net. I don't have a trust fund to catch me if I fall. I don't have my dad waiting in the wings to hire me if my bar doesn't succeed."

"Wow. Is that what you really think of me?"

"I didn't mean—"

He takes another step closer to me. "You *have* a safety net, Meg. *I'm* your safety net. Our decade of friendship is your safety net. When you broke up with Ollie, I was there to catch you when you fell. I have always been there for you. I will always be there for you."

"You can't guarantee that."

"I'm not your father. I'm not going to walk away and never look back. You'll never have to beg me for tuition. I'm not your mom. I'm not going to prefer your sisters because they're easier to deal with or control. I am here for you. I have been here for you. Just like you've been here for me. That's what love is."

I take a second, letting his words flow over me. And I still can't wrap my head around them.

This time, maybe for the first time this morning, I force myself to look at him. To really look at him.

And I just shake my head. "Yeah, that sounds great. But that's not how our friendship works."

"What does that even mean?"

"Our friendship only works because I don't ask anything of you. Everyone wants something from you. That's how it's always been. All those people who come and go in your life. The Selahs of the world. They want something from you. They expect something from you. I don't. That's why I get to stay. That's why you put up with me. Because I never ask you for money or favors. All I expect is your company and your friendship. That's what makes me different."

"God. you have it all wrong. What makes you different is you're *you*. I'm in love with you. I'm not in love with the idea that you don't need me. Frankly, I could handle you needing me a little more. I would welcome that, because then at least it wouldn't feel like I was the only one in this relationship."

He takes a step backwards, towards the door. I don't stop him.

He just stares at me, like he's waiting for me to say something. When I don't, he just shakes his head as he turns and walks away.

He pauses at the top of the stairs, glancing back at me just long enough to add, "And stop calling it a friendship. It's a relationship. A real, adult romantic relationship. At least that's what I'm in. When you're ready to be in it with me, you can come find me."

And then he walks out the door.

twenty-two

I AM PROBABLY TOO upset to drive, but I do anyway. Even Austin can't produce dangerous traffic at this time of day on a Sunday. I keep it together all the way downtown, mostly by refusing to let myself think. It's not until I pull into the parking garage beneath the Prescott towers that I let my mind go.

This is a disaster. Worse than a disaster. I knew this was a bad idea. I knew it. I should never have given free rein to my emotions and urges. But it's not like it's a disaster solely of my own making. I'm not the only one to blame. Keegan holds at least as much responsibility for the situation as I do. Maybe more. After all, I was the one who didn't want change.

After all, I was the reasonable one. I was the one who wanted to keep our relationship exactly where it was. Safe. He's the one who pushed things. And what did he mean, saying he loved me? That he's been in love with me? Is he delusional? Does he think I don't remember what's happened?

Does he think I don't remember what our relationship

231

has been like for the past 10 years? Is he trying to gaslight me? And what about popping all of this on me on the weekend when he knows how much work I have to do? What's the idea with that? It's like he's trying to sabotage my career.

This isn't helpful. I can't just sit in my car all day and mentally rant about Keegan. So I pry myself out of the car. Through sheer force of will, I make it all the way up to the office. By rote, I sit at my desk, stashing my purse in the drawer and my tote at my feet. I boot up my computer and pull out my tablet and stylus. I stare at the blank screen. I wait. And wait.

I wait for my mind to stop churning. For my brain to stop replaying scenes from last night, from this morning. The things Keegan said to me. The way he said them. His claim that he's in *love* with me. That he's *been* in love with me.

Am I really supposed to believe that? *How? How* am I supposed to believe that?

Which is not what I should be thinking about! I glance down to see that I've written the word "how" over and over again. A couple of times in cursive. Once in big block letters with hashed-in shading.

I should be wondering *how* I'm going to get all this work done by tomorrow!

I'm just about to—literally—throw up my hands in exasperation when someone clears their throat behind me.

I spin my chair around to see Reid standing by my desk. He's dressed in gray sweatpants and a T-shirt. There's a faintly damp vee at his neck, and he's holding his earbuds in his hand. He looks effortlessly hot. Competent. Total thirst trap material.

Which should have my tongue lolling out of my mouth

like a cartoon character, but somehow leaves me unaffected.

He must notice me taking in his outfit, because he clears his throat again, sliding his earbuds back into their case. "I was out jogging and thought I'd stop by."

"I was working on the presentation," I say quickly, but also cringe a little inside. Because how long was he standing there watching me writing "how" in different styles?

Then I shove aside my cringe. My process is my process. Right now it sucks, and it's slow, but I can't apologize for that.

"Did you want something?" I ask, hoping to sound collected and Sasha-like.

"Can we talk?"

"I was just—"

"Please."

We're the only two people in the office. If he was someone else, I might feel weird being alone with him on a Sunday in an empty office, but I'm getting zero aggressive vibes from him. So I nod. "Okay."

He slides his hands into the pockets of his sweatpants. "Meg, you know I value you as an employee and—"

I cut him off, standing. "Do you?"

"What?"

"Do you value me?" Suddenly all the things Keegan's been saying about Forester+Blake are tumbling around in my head. "Because if you really value me, why am I the only one here on the weekend working on this project?"

"I ..." Looking very much like this conversation is not going how he expected, he takes a step back, ducking his head.

I've seen him do that a thousand times, that self-effacing, bashful head duck. I used to think it was sexy.

Now, it leaves me cold. Annoyed, even.

Of course, now I also feel ever so slightly like a creeper, because I should not be watching my boss this much.

Don't judge me. The point is: it doesn't seem sexy now. It seems boyish, like he's dodging his responsibility. There's nothing sexy about that.

Of course, just last night, he admitted that he feels overwhelmed by the job. Outclassed by everyone around him. Maybe he seems boyish because he is.

I sigh.

"I'm sorry. That was harsh." I say, his obvious chagrin taking the wind out of my sails. "Last night, you complimented my work, but this morning it feels hollow when I'm the only one here working my ass off on a Sunday."

Not that I'm actually getting work done. But I am really trying and that should count for something, right? I'm here, putting in the hours when I could be with Keegan. Except … Keegan's accusation flits through my head. That I'm putting work in front of us because I'm afraid of talking about us.

I shove that thought aside.

"I'm sorry," I say, trying to reclaim some of the ease of last night.

"You didn't come here to hear labor complaints from an unruly subordinate."

"Actually, I did." He takes a step closer to me. "I mean, I came by, hoping you'd be here."

"I don't understand."

"I kissed you last night, Meg. That's what I wanted to talk to you about. We need to visit HR. Together. Disclose our relationship. Set up guidelines so that I'm not in charge of anything having to do with your career. And you're right. You shouldn't be the only one working on this presentation. We'll push the deadline back so all the work doesn't fall on you."

"HR?" I stumble back another step. "Are you serious?"

"Of course. We kissed, and—"

"Wait a second."

Horror washes over me as I understand the implication of his words. "Do you think I expect special treatment because we kissed last night?"

"No." He does that shoving-his-hand-through-his-hair thing again. "I guess." His gaze searches my face, and I can't tell if he's baffled by me or wondering how to fire me. "I don't know," he says finally. He seems as flummoxed by the question as I am by this entire conversation. "Nothing like this has ever happened to me before. I've done nothing like this before."

He seems genuinely distressed.

"Anything like what?"

"Like this." He gestures to the two of us. "Meg, I like you. I think we would be good together. But I've never dated anyone who worked with me. I don't know how to proceed or if—"

On impulse, I step forward and take his hands in mine. He cuts himself off and just looks at me, something hopeful in his gaze.

Okay, yeah. I see now how this looked. Like I had something to say, rather than I just wanted him to stop talking.

But really, it was just the wanting-him-to-stop-talking thing.

"I'm sorry," I say gently, but without hesitation.

A month ago, I thought Reid was everything I've ever wanted. Now, when I'm presented with the possibility of actually having him, it's not what I want at all. Probably, he was never what I wanted. He was a distraction. A safe way to keep my mind occupied and away from what I really wanted.

His mouth twists into a wry smile. "I suspected that would be your answer. Just out of curiosity, it's not because I'm your boss, is it?"

I shake my head. "No. That's not the problem."

"The guy from the gala?"

"Yes." My cheeks flush as I realize how that sounds. I flirted with Reid on the rooftop and then again at the gala. "We went to the gala as friends. He's my best friend. When you and I ran into each other on the rooftop, I thought that was all we were. I didn't purposely mislead you."

If anything, I purposely misled myself.

Reid's wry smile twists into a smirk with just a hint of self-deprecation to it. "No, I don't suppose you did. That's not your style, is it?"

"I am sorry."

Reid gives a terse nod, then turns and walks back toward the elevator, pulling his earbuds out as he walks.

"You're not staying to do work?" I ask.

"No." He pushes the elevator button and turns back to look at me while he waits for the elevator to arrive. "You were the only reason I came in." A moment later, he steps back into the elevator, holding the door open just long enough to give a wistful smile. "You should head home, too. I'll have the presentation to Butler pushed back. You shouldn't be working on the weekend."

I watch the elevator doors close, not entirely sure what to make of this encounter.

Reid is a good man. More complicated than I imagined

him to be. And he's still not the guy I want. Worse still, I'm not sure anymore that this is the job I want.

I think of how exciting it was last night to talk to the Langleys about the development of their property. Of the challenge of convincing Bruce that the project would work, that sustainable development can be profitable. Do I really want to hawk vacuums when I could be doing work like that?

No.

But do I really want to leave my job at Forester+Blake?

I've worked so hard to get where I am. For so many years. And this job has given me independence that I never could have hoped for growing up. Do I want to surrender all that? Do I want to work with Keegan and also ... what? *Be* with Keegan?

I don't know. I only know that sitting here in the office won't fix anything.

I grab my purse and my tote and head for the elevator. On impulse, I punch the button for the top floor. I'll just ride all the way up and then back down, because the last thing I want is to run into Reid in the lobby.

Despite the fact that my life is collapsing in on itself like an ancient burned out star. Despite the fact that I've messed up everything.

When the elevator doors open, I'm not on the top floor, but a few floors up on Twenty-six, where Reb works.

At least I assume this is her floor, because when the doors open, she's there, waiting. She's wearing a pair of purple overalls with a tank top underneath, and she doesn't have any shoes, though I can see rainbow striped socks sticking out in the bottom of her pant legs. She's facing away from the elevator and hopping up and down.

The collective image is just bizarre enough to snap me out of my stupor.

The door nearly closes and I reach out to hold it open with my hand. "Reb?"

She turns to face me, but doesn't stop hopping.

"Oh, it's you." She gives me a little two-finger salute as she marches onto the elevator. "Fancy seeing you in green pea stew," she says, once again using her fake English accent.

I wouldn't know what to say to this, even if I wasn't having a shitty day. But I am having a shitty day. A day that's making me doubt everything. Making me question my whole life and my future and every decision I've ever made. So I do the only logical thing. I burst into tears.

"Whoa," Reb gasps. "What's wrong?"

I deny the obvious, as if I could speak a new reality into existence. "I'm not crying!"

The elevator lurches back into motion and I feel so discombobulated I have to lean against the wall to support myself. My bag drops to the ground as I bring my hands up to wipe at my eyes.

Reb, wide-eyed with shock, just shakes her head. "Um ..."

"These aren't tears."

"Those really look like tears to me," Reb blurts.

"I'm not crying."

"I'm pretty sure you are crying."

"Yeah, but they're not sad tears."

Reb looks around the elevator, like she's hoping for an escape route. "They don't look like happy tears."

"They're mad tears!"

"Oookay."

The door opens on the top floor to reveal the lobby for

the law office on the top floor. There's a man standing there, shirt sleeves rolled up, a stained mug of coffee in his hand. His hair sticks up at odd angles like he definitely slept in his office overnight. He takes one look at Reb and me and takes a big step back. "I'll wait for the next one."

Reb starts to push the close door button, but I lurch forward, holding the door open. With my other hand, I tug Reb forward and push her out into the law firm lobby. "You should leave, Reb! I don't want anyone to see me like this."

Before the doors can close, she jumps back in. "I'm not leaving you in tears in the elevator."

The guy takes another, even bigger step back. "I'll just —" He gestures vaguely over his shoulder as he walks backwards, gaze darting from me to Reb.

I try again to push her out. "I don't want you here."

Reb ignores me and jabs at the button to close the door. It slides closed, and the elevator lurches into motion again.

"You should just leave me here." I sag against the wall, squeezing my eyes closed. "Save yourself."

"Oh. My. God." Reb snaps, sounding annoyed. "Stop being so dramatic. And tell me why you're crying."

"I'm not crying," I insist again. "I never cry."

"You're crying now," Reb says.

"Obviously!" I wail.

I squeeze my eyes closed, vainly trying to trap the tears inside, as if that can somehow help me keep my emotions inside.

Since my eyes are closed, I don't see what Reb is doing, but suddenly I feel the elevator stop. When I open my eyes, Reb is standing beside the control panel, clearly having just pushed the button to stop the elevator.

"What are you doing?"

"Stopping the elevator, obviously."

"Can you do that?" I ask.

"Yeah." Reb points to the red button on the control panel. "It's right there on the button. Stop Elevator."

"Isn't that for emergencies?"

She shrugs. "You just said you never cry. So if you're crying, clearly it's an emergency."

Before I can respond, a voice comes through the elevator's intercom. "Reb, is that you again?" a male voice asks.

Reb looks up at the corner and waves. "Hi, Steve." She waves, then she points in my direction. "It's an emergency."

I follow her gaze up to what I assume is the security camera. The bizarro-world-ness of this whole scene stems my tears. I raise my hand to wave at Steve on the other side of the camera, because it seems rude not to.

"You can't keep doing this, Reb," he says.

"You do this often?" I ask her.

She doesn't answer, but the disembodied voice of Steve does. "About once a week. She likes to brainstorm in the elevator."

"But this isn't brainstorming." Reb holds up a single finger to emphasize her point. "This is an emergency."

"An actual emergency would be someone having a heart attack, or going into labor, or the elevator stalling on its own. Whatever this is, it is not an emergency."

"Yes it is," Reb says. "She's crying. And Meg never cries." She waggles her hand in a back-me-up-on-this gesture. "Right?"

I shake my head and croak, "I never cry."

"That's still not an emergency," Steve says. "I'm starting the elevator, Reb."

"You are a party pooper," Reb says to the security camera while flashing him the finger with both hands.

The elevator moves again and I ask, "I thought you said you were trying to cuss less?"

Reb looks at me and blinks. "Shooting someone the bird isn't cussing."

"I'm pretty sure it is."

She waves a hand dismissively. "So, do you want to tell me what happened? Now that you're not crying anymore."

I raise a hand to my cheek, surprised to find that I am indeed not crying anymore. Somehow the sheer absurdity of the situation—being trapped in the elevator with Reb and the conversation with Steve—seems to have shocked me out of my despair.

"I don't know that I can talk about it without bursting into tears again," I admit. "And I hate crying in front of other people."

"Everybody hates crying in front of other people."

I glare at her, because, yes, everyone hates crying in public, but she clearly doesn't understand. "No. I really, really hate it. And now I'm crying in front of you. And Steve, apparently. In a minute, we're gonna be in the lobby, and then I'll just be crying in the lobby of my building, like a fool, where anyone can see me."

"It's Sunday. No one is going to be here."

"We're both here," I point out. Reid was here, just a few minutes ago, but I can't tell her that without opening that whole can of worms, so I add, "Steve is here."

As if the elevator seconds my argument, the doors open and there are, indeed, other people in the lobby.

Reb hits the button to close the doors, and then the button for the 26th floor. "Problem solved," she says cheerfully.

"What if the elevator stops on my floor?" Because after

that shit show, the last thing I need is for someone from work to see me crying in the elevator.

Reb tips her head to the side as if she's considering the question and then pushes the call button on the elevator control panel. "Hey, Steve, can you make sure this elevator doesn't stop on the 23rd floor?"

"You know you're not my boss, right?"

"Please?"

Steve's voice comes back to the speaker. "Reb, you are a pain in my ass."

"I know," she says. "Do you need me to bring you some croissants from that bakery down the street?"

"Yes. And macarons."

Reb turns to me and beams. "Problem solved."

"You are genuinely weird," I tell her. What I want to do is yell at her again and make her leave me alone, but that's clearly not going to happen. Also, I'm afraid if I say that, I'll start crying again.

"Thank you." She looks genuinely touched by what she obviously takes as a compliment.

Five minutes later, I'm sitting in Reb's office on a ratty old sofa. An intern appears with mugs of hot tea. I leave mine untouched, sitting with my knees pulled up to my chest, my arms wrapped around my knees, my chin propped on my knees to hide the way it's still trembling, as I glare defiantly at Reb.

Despite our years of friendship, I've never been in Reb's office before. It looks like it was decorated from a Goodwill in the 1980s.

This sofa, for example, is at least forty years old, and there's a spring poking me in the ass that is probably going to give me tetanus. There's a Ms. Pac-Man gaming console in one corner and an enormous bean bag in the center of the room. The only sign that any work gets done in here at all is the whiteboard that spans the entirety of one wall covered in notes and the standing desk in front of it with one of those curved computer monitors that looks like it belongs on a space shuttle.

Reb rolls over a yoga ball and sits down on the other side of the coffee table.

"Okay, talk."

I glare harder. "This sofa is gross. I thought you were supposed to be the lead developer at this company."

"I am."

"Then why haven't they bought you better furniture? I think I got hepatitis just sitting here."

She smirks. "A) you suck at being mean. B) you can't distract me. Now tell me why you're crying."

"I'm not—"

She cuts me off with a wave of her hand. "Yeah, yeah. Not sad tears. Mad tears. I get it. But those were definitely tears and you're definitely upset."

"I'm not upset. I'm just mad. And humiliated. Because I should be able to be mad like a normal person and not get so upset that I'm crying in the elevator like a crazy person."

"Um, I'm pretty sure it's not okay anymore to say things like 'crying like a crazy person'."

"How is that helpful? That's not helpful!"

"So don't think of this as crying in the elevator at work like a crazy person. Think of this as a much needed opportunity to normalize emotional expression in a male-dominated workplace."

"Okay ..."

"Look," she cuts me off with a swipe of her hand. "I am the only woman in an office of forty-three men. These guys need to know that every time I display an emotion, it's not a sign of the apocalypse."

When she puts it like that ... like I'm doing her a favor and not the other way around, I can't say no, can I?

Clearly, I can't, because she makes a speed-it-along gesture as she sips her drink. "So what has you this ... not sad, but angry?"

I'm trying not to cry as I grapple for an answer. If I tell her the real reason I'm upset, I'll definitely start crying again, and I don't want to do that. Of course, I have plenty of non-Keegan related reasons to cry.

So do I blame it on work and try to keep myself together, or do I tell her about Keegan and let the snot-soaked Kleenex fall where they may?

"I think I'm too invested in my career and use it to distract from my lack of personal life."

Reb pauses, her drink halfway to her mouth, and gives me a blank stare. "Um ... definitely too invested." She takes a hasty sip and then adds. "And just to be clear on this, I am the queen of being too invested in my work. So if I think you're too invested, then it's bad."

Her ready agreement makes me defensive. "But maybe working on Sunday is okay. I mean, you're here and–"

Reb cuts me off. "Do not use me being at work on a Sunday as inspiration. I have a horrible work/life balance."

I glance over my shoulder toward the plate glass windows that reveal the bullpen where so many other people are also working on a Sunday.

"No. Don't look at them either. Gaming is a shit industry that over-works and undervalues all of their employees. Besides, all of those fools are here because I'm here on a Sunday, and they're afraid I'll fire them if they go home when I'm still at work. And I'm only here because I think success at work will earn me my father's love."

I sit up straighter in my chair. Who is this person and what has she done with my friend?

"That is very insightful," I say slowly. For someone dressed like an overgrown toddler.

She jabs a finger at me. "Damn straight it is. There are only a few advantages to having a rich, but emotionally unavailable father who marries a 'spiritual journey' coach who is half his age. But one of them is his willingness to pay for a lot of therapy."

"Okay," I draw the word out slowly, because, honestly, this might be the most Reb has ever said to me about her family life. If she's suddenly in the mood to talk about her daddy issues, shouldn't I let her? "How do you feel about that?"

She gives me a flat look and then slowly arches an eyebrow. "Don't do that."

"What?"

"Try to distract from your problems by talking about my problems."

"I wasn't—"

"Yes, you were." Reb gives me a hard look. "Just like you're trying to distract me from what's really wrong by talking about your career. You're hardworking, and you're talented, and your career will be fine."

"But I—"

"Please tell me you're actually crying because you finally had sex with Keegan and it was amazing and earth shattering."

But then she tips her head to the side and seems to consider her words. "But wait, if you did have amazing and earth-shattering sex with Keegan, why are you angry crying about it?"

Suddenly, I can't sit still. I leap to my feet and start pacing. "Because sex ruins everything."

"I'm pretty sure that's not true."

I turn and glare at her.

"Okay, admittedly, I don't have a ton of experience in the area of meaningful relationships, but isn't sex supposed to make everything better?"

"No. Not friendships. Sex ruins friendships. It's a documented fact."

"Really? Documented? I'm going to need you to send me your references on that."

"Okay. I will."

Her gaze narrows. "So what? Like, you've got a list of journal articles curated about scientifically rigorous, double-blind studies about how sex ruins friendships?"

"Actually, I do."

"Without quoting from *When Harry Met Sally*?"

Despite myself, despite still feeling like I'm about to burst into tears, my lips twitch. Damn Reb and her clever, smarty-pants brain.

"Shut up." I flop back into the sofa, careful to avoid the rogue spring, and bury my face in my hands. "Just trust me on this. Keegan and I had sex, and now everything is ruined."

"Is it …"

I still have my face buried in my hands, so I hear rather than see her drawing out the question. I peek at her from between my fingers.

"What?"

"Was the sex bad?" she asks with an exaggerated wince.

"No!"

"Whew." She leans back, but since she's on the yoga ball, it nearly rolls out from under her. "I don't think I could handle the knowledge that Keegan isn't amazing in bed. I am simply not that imaginative."

I roll my eyes at her drama, but don't say anything. I'm not going to discuss with her what sex with Keegan was like. Partly because it's just not something I'm willing to share with anyone. And partly because I can't even think about what happened between us without feeling flushed and nervous and I don't even know what else.

Last night, in the moment, when he was with me, everything felt perfect. Like I was exactly where I was supposed to be. It was only this morning that things started to get messed up in my mind.

"Okay," Reb is saying thoughtfully, "So, if the sex was good, then what's the problem?" She jerks back, as if suddenly struck by an idea. "Did he try to brush this off like it's no big deal? Did he try to pull that friends with benefits bullshit on you, because I swear to god, I will shiv him."

"Not exactly," I hedge, because suddenly telling the rest of the story seems dicey.

"Then what? What did he do that has you this freaked out?"

"He ... he told me he loves me."

Reb gives me a long, slow blink. "Okay. And then what?"

"He wanted to take me to brunch."

"Okay, I'm not sure I see the problem here. I mean, he's your best friend, right? Great sex plus friendship plus love plus brunch should equal the perfect relationship."

"No. It doesn't. And that's the problem right there." I jab a finger at her, half in accusation, half in a eureka moment. "He's my best friend. What happens if this doesn't work out? I've put all of my relationship eggs in one basket. I drop the basket, all the eggs are gone. Then what?"

"Okay, first off, ouch. Keegan is your best friend, not your only friend."

"You know what I mean."

"Maybe. But why wouldn't it work out? Y'all are perfect together."

"It's already not working out. We've already had our first fight."

Reb rolls back, again nearly falling right off her yoga ball. "About what?"

"He was mad that I needed to come into work today instead of going to brunch with him." I go full throttle with my indignation here, because I know I'm in the right. "Can you believe he said that?"

"No, I can't."

"Right?" I demand. "Criticizing me for spending too much time at work is crossing a line."

"No, I meant, I actually can't believe he said that. Normally, he's very supportive, right?"

"Yeah," I admit, a little unsettled that she's not agreeing with me.

"Okay, back it up. Lay it out for me. How did you go from hot crazy sex to him criticizing your work ethic?"

So I do. I talk her through the morning, glossing over my mental freak out, and ending with him accusing me of holding people at arm's length. I finish with, "Can you believe he would say that?"

Reb gives me a cagey look. "What? That you try to control relationships?"

"Yes."

Instead of being immediately and definitively supportive, she tips her head to the side and says, "Hmmm. Let me think for a minute."

"What does that mean?" I demand, horrified. "Why do you have to think about it for a minute?"

"Um ..." She winces. "Don't you think he's kind of ..."

I cross my arms over my chest. "Kind of what?"

She holds her hands out in front of her, like she's trying to calm a spooked horse. "Okay, don't get mad at me and start crying again."

"Kind of what?"

"Don't you think he's kind of right? Just a little?"

"No, I don't think he's right!"

"Okay, look at it from my point of view. You like to be the ..." she seems to struggle for the right word. "The boss in a relationship."

"So, what? I'm a dominatrix?"

"That's not what I meant."

"Then what did you mean?"

"You like to be the person who brings the most to the table."

"What does that even mean?"

"You like to help other people. And you never let anyone help you."

Suddenly, my jaw is trembling again. I clench my teeth trying to stop it, but it doesn't seem to help because my throat is closing and the flood of tears in my eyes is too vast to be blinked away. Just like the flood of emotions is too vast to be shoved back down.

"No." I'm going to choke on my tears. Or drown in them. One way or another, this swell of emotion is going to kill me. "No. He's not right. I can let people help me."

"Well, sure. But do you?"

"Yes. You're helping me right now."

"When I first found you hiding in the elevator, you told me to go away. In fact, you ordered me to go away."

"No, I didn't."

"Um. Yeah, you did. You tried to ditch me with the tired business suit guy. You wouldn't even tell me what was wrong until I told you it would be good for programmers to see a woman crying at work. As soon as I made it seem like it was a favor to me, then you let me help you."

"Are you saying you manipulated me?"

She shrugs, looking both smug and diffident. "Yes. But I think we can both agree I don't have the social or emotional intelligence to have done it on purpose. So you can't be irritated with me about it."

"Maybe." I squeeze my arms tighter around myself and concentrate on not crying. "But I'm definitely going to be annoyed that you're taking Keegan's side in this."

"I'm not taking his side. I'm just pointing out that he might be right. In any given relationship, you like to be the one who's giving more."

"That's just not true!"

"Isn't it? Come on, your best friends, other than Keegan, are an elderly cat lady and a nerdy recluse."

"I'm offended on both of your behalf. Thea is so much more than an elderly cat lady. And you are a badass boss bitch."

Reb rolls her eyes. "Okay, yes. Sure. But I also am a nerdy recluse. And you are like the first female friend outside of work that I've had as an adult."

"What's that got to do with anything?"

She shrugs, looking a little sad. "You're my best friend. One of my only friends."

There's an odd break in her voice that is so at odds with Reb's normally relentless cheerfulness. I hardly know how to respond. "You're my best friend, too!" I insist. When she arches a brow in question, I hastily add on, "Along with Keegan and Thea. And a person can have more than one best friend!"

Her lips twist. "Sure. But my point is, as far as friends go, you're it for me. I need you more than you need me."

"That is ridiculous!"

"But is it?" She gives another shrug. "If our friendship ever ended, where would I even find another friend? I work ridiculous hours. I'm surrounded by people who are intimidated by my talent and work ethic, who also resent me because my father started the company. Everyone I know other than you, Thea, and Keegan work in gaming. They all hate me for one reason or another. Without you, I'm a friendless troll with no social skills."

"That is not true! You are delightful and wonderful and funny and–"

She stands, cutting me off by taking my hands in hers. "It is true. And until now, I've let you do all the heavy lifting in our friendship. And that hasn't been fair of me. I've let you give more, because ..." she rolls her eyes. "Well, probably because I'm lazy. But my point is, I've been selfish. But you've been selfish, too. Because as long as you're doing all the heavy lifting in every relationship you're in, then you believe no one will ever leave you."

"I don't—" I start to protest automatically, but then cut myself off, because suddenly I can't breathe. "That is not true. That is not why we're friends!"

And just like that, I'm crying again.

Reb gives an exaggerated wince and makes that horse-soothing gesture again. "Are these mad tears or sad tears?"

"They're mad tears! You completely underestimate your own value and you make me sound like a horrible person."

Reb takes a cautious step towards me. "Should I hug you or something? I feel like you need a hug."

I glare at her before answering.

"Do not hug me after being so mean," I clam up, uncomfortable with her insight.

She doesn't hug me. She does something more surprising. She wraps her hands around my arms and shakes me. "Stop being so dramatic. You're not a horrible person. You are amazing and loving and kind and, unfortunately, just as broken and emotionally fucked up as the rest of us. That doesn't make you a horrible person, it makes you human. I wasn't mean to you."

"You were a little mean."

"But if I let you walk away from Keegan just because you're terrified that he's all in, then that would be mean of me. And maybe I've been a slacker in the friend department until now, but I'm going to try to be better. Which means I'm going to make you go talk to Keegan."

"What?" I know I'm looking at her like a deer in headlights, but all the run-and-hide instincts are coursing through me when it comes to Keegan. "I can't do that."

Reb shrugs as if it's not a big deal. "Why not? You love him. He loves you. You screwed up, and you need to make it right. Now that your work is postponed, you've got nothing but time and problems, Meg. Put on your big girl panties and fix them."

twenty-three

AFTER REB GIVES me an epic pep talk, way more chamomile tea, and lets me wash my face in her executive washroom, she takes me back down to the lobby and reminds me I have to go talk to Keegan.

"I will."

"Right now."

"I will."

She makes a hurry-it-along gesture. "Okay then, get out your phone and stalk him."

"I don't stalk him."

She arches an eyebrow.

"You're not going to let this go, are you?"

"I am not. You need to go talk to him. And you need to do it now before you chicken out."

"Fine." I turn on my find my friends app so I can figure out where Keegan is. Even after all that's happened, it's still barely nine o'clock. I expect to see his little blinking dot at his condo a few blocks west of here. At least, that's where I hope he went after our big argument. But instead it pings northwest of here, right on the shores of Lake Austin.

Reb leans over my phone and stares at the map with me. Then makes a huffing noise. "He's not at his house?"

"Apparently not. If I had to guess, he's at the family Sunday Brunch."

"Is that where his parents live? I thought Loretta said they live in Tarry Town."

"No. They do. This is worse than that. He's not at brunch at his parent's house."

That would be bad enough, but this is so much worse.

Keegan's dot is a residential neighborhood in Westlake Hills.

I tilt the phone so Reb can see the map better.

"Oh," she says knowingly. Then blows out a whistle. "Right on the water? On Lake Austin? Those mansions sell for nearly ten million dollars. When they go on the market. Which is not often."

"Thanks, Reb. That's very helpful." Does she think I'm not nervous enough?

"I know this kind of thing only because Zillow makes it disturbingly easy to imagine how the other half lives."

I give her the side eye. "Doesn't your father live in that part of town."

"No, his house is up on one of those hills with the stunning views of the lake. It's not actually on the waterfront." She says it as if there's a world of difference between a house on the lake or a house looking over the lake, but when you get in the 7+figure range, I'm not sure there is. "So what's he doing over there?"

"He's probably at the family brunch with his grandfather."

Reb lets out a low whistle. Then nods resolutely. "Okay. My car or yours?"

It takes a second for her words to register. "You're coming with me?"

"Yeah. I'm worried that if I don't, you're going to bolt again."

It's not a long drive from downtown to the neighborhood where Keegan's grandfather lives. After all the most expensive lake front homes are the ones near the downtown. But it is just long enough for my nerves to crank up to high alert.

By the time Reb pulls into the circle driveway outside of a legit mansion, I'm starting to panic.

"This was a bad idea."

Reb just shakes her head. "No, it's a great idea."

"Do you remember that twenty-four hours ago, I was nervous about spending the evening with his father? Can you even imagine how much more intimidating his grandfather is going to be?"

"Sure. But the evening with his father was fine, right? I mean, before you acted like a moron and sabotaged everything."

"Thanks, that's very helpful."

"Look, I get that this is scary. But you're not actually afraid of his grandfather. You're not intimidated by this big fancy house. You're not even afraid that he's going to reject you."

"I don't know. I think I am afraid of that."

"You're not. You're afraid that you're going to get in even deeper than you are now and then one day, down the road, he's going to realize you're not smart enough or pretty enough or rich enough, and then he's going to leave you."

Her words take my breath away. Not in a good, pretty sunset kind of way. But in a horrible punched in the stomach kind of way.

"This is the worst pep talk ever!"

Reb winces. "Yeah. I suck at this. But my point is this: you're afraid that someday he's going to hurt you. But right now, you're hurting him. So you need to fix it."

"God, you're right," I say, hating that it's true.

Before I can lose my courage—again—I climb out of the car. A moment later, I'm ringing the doorbell.

The man who opens the door is a smartly dressed older man, with snowy white hair. I look from his neatly pressed suit to my rumpled potato sack of a dress and die a little inside. God, I am so underdressed for brunch with the McQuades.

Reb, who must have followed me out of the car, plants her hand in the center of my back and pushes me forward. "Go get 'em, tiger."

I swallow and thrust my hand out. "Hi. I'm Meg. Meg Demeo. I'm a friend of Keegan's. It's good to meet you, Mr. McQuade."

The man gives an odd look, his lips quirking up ever so slightly as he shakes my hand. "I'm Jefferson. Mr. McQuade's house manager."

"His what now?"

Reb leans closer and whispers. "It's an old-fashioned valet or butler, but ... new fashioned."

"I know what a house manager is," I hiss back. Bluffing. I mean, I probably could have figured it out. I add more loudly, "I was surprised that he works on Sunday."

The man clears his throat. "Would you like me to take you to Mr. McQuade?"

"Actually, if you could just take me to Keegan, that would be great."

His lips twitch again, and this guy is definitely laughing

at me. "That is, in fact, the Mr. McQuade I was offering to bring you to."

"Oh."

He stands back, gesturing for me to follow him. After closing the door behind me, he says, "Though all three Mr. McQuades are currently together, having brunch on the terrace."

"Fantastic," I mutter through clenched teeth.

"Along with Mrs. McQuade, Ms. Dubois-McQuade, Mr. Dubois, and Mr. Barajas."

Beside me, Reb snorts. "What the King couldn't make it?"

Jefferson ignores her, leading us both through the foyer, past an enormous floating staircase. Beneath the staircase, the foyer spills into a living room larger than most hotel lobbies. The far wall is floor to ceiling windows. Beyond those windows I can see the terrace, and beyond that, a lush green lawn that leads down to the water. On the terrace, there's a long table, around which everyone, except the King, is seated.

My grand romantic gesture isn't exactly playing out the way I had envisioned. I imagined Deborah Kerr and Cary Grant at the end of *An Affair to Remember*. I did not imagine the fanciest brunch west of the Hudson.

This might be the problem with hanging out and watching movies with an aging movie-star and trivia master. She likes the classics. If there are modern day romcoms that involve declarations of love via text, we haven't watched them together.

My steps slow and for a moment, I'm tempted to turn and leave. To put this off until later. No one has seen me yet, other than Jefferson.

Yeah, I could play it safe. I could act cool, like my heart isn't pounding out of my chest. But I don't wanna do that.

In the immortal words of Billy Crystal, "when you realize you want to spend the rest of your life with someone, you want the rest of your life to start right now."

Then, before I have a chance to question my resolve, Jefferson opens the doorway out onto the terrace and leads us out. Everyone on the terrace looks up, but I'm only looking at Keegan.

My heart pounds as I watch him realize I'm there and then slowly push back his chair and stand. Not just because he's hot—after all, he's always been hot. And not because last night he did unspeakably delicious things to my body —although that probably doesn't help matters.

But because the next few minutes will change everything. All morning I've been wallowing in my own doubts. Yes, it's my fault, because this morning, I chickened out.

The only way out is to talk to Keegan. To open my mouth and suck in a big breath of air. Either our relationship has grown lungs, and I'll be able to breathe on land, or I'll die.

Okay, there's a slight chance this metaphor has gotten away from me.

My point is: it's do or die time. I can't just flop around on the shore anymore. I have to breathe.

Shit, I'm back to that stupid metaphor again!

The point is, I'm nervous and I can't even think. Suddenly, my brain feels as clumsy as my words always have. And that never happens!

Keegan, who has been watching me with that intense gaze of his the whole time he's been walking from his spot at the table toward me, finally reaches me. Something in his gaze tells me he's going to pull me into his arms and kiss me.

Which is exactly what I want, right? Or should I, I dunno, talk before I'm enveloped by the inevitable haze that comes with Keegan's kisses?

I hold up my hands to keep him at arm's length. I can't think when he's touching me, much less say what I need to say.

Maybe I should take his willingness to kiss me in public as a good sign, but I can't afford the confusion that will inevitably follow.

After all, the last time he kissed me in front of someone else, it was because he was trying to ward off the advances of his predatory neighbor, Selah. What if this is the same kind of thing?

And if it is, that's exactly the kind of thing a friend with benefits would do to help a friend out, right? I can't let him kiss me again until I know if he forgives me.

Thankfully, he doesn't seem offended by my dodge. Or maybe I'm delusional and he wasn't even going to kiss me.

"Hey, Glasses. Whatcha doin' here?" He takes my hand in his and links our fingers.

"I think we should talk," I blurt. And then keep blurting in a rush, because I feel like I need to get out my thoughts first, or I won't have the courage to do it at all. And also, word vomit is super attractive, right?

I am vaguely aware of Loretta greeting Reb and coaxing her into an empty chair, and of the much older man sitting down at the far end of the table. He is somehow smaller and more fragile than I expected him to be.

He's not the intimidating mountain of a man I've imagined in my mind, but I still don't want to bare my soul in his earshot. So I step closer to Keegan and say softly, "I know this morning I was the one who rushed off to work and didn't want to talk yet, but I was an idiot. You're right. I was just avoiding everything, and now I can't stop feeling like one of those fish with feet instead of fins and lungs that might or might not work on land."

I pause here, because now I really do need to breathe. In a non-metaphorical way.

Keegan blinks, his smile a bit bemused, like he's having trouble following me. "Lungfish?"

"No. The older ones. The first ones." I wave my free hand like I can somehow erase that part of the conversation. "Never mind. The metaphor is cumbersome. My point is, this morning, I was a chicken."

"I thought you were a fish."

"I ... are you making fun of me?"

"Maybe." He smirks, then seems to make a visible attempt to be serious. "You're adorable when you're this flustered."

"I'm trying to have an honest and serious conversation about our relationship."

"Right." He nods, flattening his lips into a scowl that just looks like he's trying not to laugh. "Serious discussion. Continue."

"Look, I know I should probably be cooler or more chill or whatever, but I need to know if I blew it this morning."

He shakes his head, taking another step back. "Is that what you think? That I waited for you for a decade and then I'm going to walk away after one fight? One misunderstanding?"

"Look," I don't answer him, because I'm a little afraid at this point that he's going to escort me out and dump me on the sidewalk. "I know I'm making a mess of this. Just hear me out, okay?"

"Okay."

I look over his shoulder at the family members who are all watching this. Should I try to get him alone first? Part of me is terrified of ripping off the bandaid in front of his family. The voice inside me is begging to have this conversation in private, so that if it goes south, I will be less-mortified. It's like time slows down as my gaze darts between Keegan's deep sea eyes, which are somehow warm despite the cool blue of them.

Go inside! Take him somewhere private!

I recognize that voice. It's the little girl inside—the eight-year-old who begged her dad to come to her dance recital, and who believed him when he said he would. Who cried herself to sleep that night after he never showed up. It's me in a dress while my mom's then-boyfriend pinned on a corsage for my daddy-daughter dance in eighth grade because my dad stood me up—again. It's my voice at college graduation when I elected not to walk because I knew no one would be there.

But the other part of me, the older-than-a-lungfish part that's gaining her voice, sounds older. Calmer. She's not afraid.

He said he wasn't leaving, Meg. He never has. That part of me urges me to believe him—to trust that he's not going to embarrass me. To trust that I'm safe with him. That I can say what I need to say right here.

"Maybe not in front of your entire family?"

I know I should listen to the older voice. The brave one. But I just ... I'm not quite there yet.

He doesn't escort me to the door, but leads me several steps away toward the railing.

"We've known each other for a long time, right?"

"About a decade."

"And you know I'm not good at any of this. I'm not good with romance. Or emotions. Or talking. Or—" I press my hand to my belly, which suddenly feels queasy. "God, are they just going to watch while we talk?"

"You really want to talk about my family?"

"No. But … Okay, I see your point. The thing is … Here's the thing … There's a pretty good chance I'm in love with you. And that I've always been in love with you. And that I've just been in denial for, like, a decade. And if that's true, then surely you see why I'm doing this so very badly. Because the idea of risking our relationship is frankly terrifying."

"Yes," he says simply. Keegan's expression hasn't changed, other than maybe a slight softening around his eyes.

"Yes? Yes, what?"

"Keegan, boy, are you going to pull up a chair for your friend or should we continue without you?" asks a voice from the table.

For a second, Keegan's eyes flicker closed, like he's mentally cursing the timing of that interruption.

"Eat without us." Then he takes my hand in his and drags me off the terrace, through the kitchen and into a butler's pantry, closing the frosted glass doors behind us.

"Yes, what?" I ask.

"Yes, to all of it. The love. The denial. The messing everything up."

He drags me to the back of the pantry, then picks me up and sets me on the counter. He plants his hands on either side of my hips, stepping between my legs, and he looks down at me. "And especially yes to how absolutely terrifying this is. Because when you realize you're in love with your best friend, and you have no idea if she loves you too or if she's falling in love with her asshole of a boss, it's completely fucking terrifying."

I inhale sharply, because I need more details more than I need more air. But I don't get either, because he leans down and kisses me.

He's touching nothing but my lips, but he's surrounding me—his body mere inches from mine. His hands moving to my hips and pulling me closer.

And this kiss feels different from any of the kisses last night.

Yes, all of those kisses were intense. Fraught with sexual tension and need. We had a frantic rush toward something bigger and unstoppable.

This is something else.

This is a desperate, needy claiming. Like he's trying to pour his soul into mine.

And I'm down for that. I want all of it. I want his soul, if he'll share it with me.

After I don't know how long, he lifts his head. We're both breathless. He presses his forehead to mine.

"Just to be clear." I clear my throat. "That was a no to this being a Netflix and chill situation and a yes to this being a mutual, in-love-with-your-best-friend situation, right?"

He nods without lifting his head from mine, so that we're both nodding together. "Don't get me wrong, I am down for Netflix. But I am absolutely done being chill where you're concerned." He steps away from me and crosses his arms over his chest to scowl down at me in a way that might just spark every naughty school girl fantasy I've ever had. "I thought that was clear last night."

I bite down on my lip, tempted just for a moment to say "yes, sir" and ask if he needs to punish me. But there will be time for fantasies later. Now, I need to make sure we are exactly on the same page. Emotionally.

I hold up a finger. "In my defense, last night you talked a lot about wanting me physically. You didn't say anything about love. You didn't say anything to indicate you wanted our relationship to change in any way."

He shoves a hand through his hair. "That's because our relationship is perfect, except for the fact that I've basically had a hard-on twenty-four hours a day for the past year or so."

My mind trips over that image for a moment, but then circles back to the first part of his sentence. "So then you do just want friends with—"

He gives me another hard, fast kiss. This one clearly designed to shut me up.

"Stop it," he says.

"Stop what?"

"Stop looking for a loophole in my words. Yes, I think our relationship is just about perfect. And yes, I want more sex. Hopefully, a lot of it. But I want more of everything. I want more time with you. That's why I'm changing jobs. I want more nights at your place. Or at my place, if we can make it less soulless and horrible. I don't ever again want to finish a movie and then have to leave and go home alone. I want to move in together. To get married, if you're still into that kind of thing. To have kids together. Or cats or corgis or parakeets or whatever the hell you imagine having someday."

He cups my face, brushing his thumbs across my cheeks. He kisses me again, and it's not until I taste salt on his lips that I realize he was wiping away my tears.

"I want all that, too," I say breathlessly.

"Thank fuck," he says on a groan, before kissing me yet again. "Then what was all that shit about? After last night, I thought we were settled. And then this morning you basically bolted. What the hell, Glasses? Because you scared the shit out of me."

I know I sound pitiful and pathetic, but I can't help asking a question in response. "So why weren't you with me? Before now?"

He studies me for a second, before one side of his lips twitch up. "As far as I was concerned, I was with you. I haven't been with another woman in ..." He huffs out a breath and shifts his eyes, like he's doing the math. "A couple of years now. Three, at least, since I've dated anyone."

"What?"

"I realized I was in love with you, and I wasn't interested in being with anyone else."

I just stare at him. "How is that possible? What about Selah?"

"That was three years ago." His gaze hardens, and he huffs out another breath, stepping back a little. "I'm trying really hard here not to be the jealous asshole who demands to know if you have been with other guys since Ollie, okay? I know I don't have the right to ask that. I get it, but—"

I yank him back to me. "I haven't been with anyone else since Ollie. I swear. Be the jealous asshole if you need to be."

The muscle in his jaw stops ticking, and the tension eases out of him.

Maybe the jealous asshole shouldn't work on me, but it totally does. I love that he clearly hated the idea of me being with someone else, just as much as I love the idea that he's been celibate all this time.

Which ... wow ... a celibate Keegan? Who would have thought?

Biting down on my lip again, I ask, "Exactly how private is this room?"

"Why?"

I look around, then tug him a little closer. "I was just noticing that it seems pretty private."

His lips twitch. "You always have had a good eye for details."

"True. And how long do you think we have before someone comes looking for us?"

"Don't you have to get back to work?" he asks. "I thought you had a big presentation to work on."

I wrap his tie around my fist as I contemplate my next words. Slowly, as I tug his mouth down to mine, I say, "I think I might need to quit, anyway."

He stills and pulls back. "Seriously?"

I huff out a breath. "I'll tell you about it later, okay?"

When I tug on his tie again, he resists, tipping up my chin until I meet his gaze. "Is that why you rushed over here? Because you decided to quit and you panicked?"

I tip my head to the side, trying to unravel the mental roller coaster of my day. "No. One hundred percent of my panic today has been about our relationship, and I haven't decided anything about my job. Not yet. Because you know how cautious I am."

He gives a snort of laughter. "Yes. Painfully aware of how cautious you are."

I poke a finger in his side. "Hey!"

He gives me another long, serious look. "I don't want to be your second choice."

I nearly laugh out loud until I realize he's serious. "Keegan, I think I've been in love with you since college. You have always been my first choice. I just didn't see it until now."

He growls as he tugs me closer to him. Just before he kisses me, he says, "Same, Glasses. Same."

twenty-four

ONE YEAR LATER....

You might think I would never get tired of having people tell me I'm brilliant, but you'd be wrong.

Okay, it's not that I'm tired of the compliments, because I'm not. But the party to launch The Langley Complex seems like it's going on for days rather than mere hours.

I glance down at my watch. Okay, it's after midnight.

So it has officially been going on for days now. Sort of.

There was a groundbreaking ceremony and cocktail party this evening, timed to take advantage of the amazing views of the hill country sunset, followed by an "after party" on the top floor common room in the building where Keegan lives, for investors and people who've already put down a deposit on property in the development.

So far, everything about the project is a huge success, and I've never once regretted the decision I made about my career.

Working for McQuade Development is my new dream job.

Was I worried at first about leaving Forester+Blake and putting all of my eggs in the Keegan basket?

Yes. A little.

But I love working side by side with him. Neither he nor anyone else in his family is my direct superior and my contract is ironclad. Reb found me some hot shot lawyer to go over it. Not that I'm worried about any of that at all. After all, McQuade Development is a family business. And now I'm family.

Of course, all this success is also the reason I'm trapped at this party. Being lavished with praise, yes, but still ready to get out of these heels.

I'm in the middle of a conversation with one of the investors about some of the green initiatives in the project when Keegan catches my eye from across the room. He quirks an eyebrow in question as he tips an imaginary drink in my direction, clearly asking if I want another drink.

I give a slight shake of my head in response.

This time, he raises both eyebrows, tipping his head ever so slightly in the direction of the door.

Beside me, Reb gives a sigh.

"What?" I ask her under my breath.

She loops an arm through my mine and grins over at the investors. "Never mind us. I'm just going to borrow Meg for a moment."

After leading me away, she whispers, "As adorable as it is when you and Keegan have entire silent conversations from across the room, y'all should really just get out of here."

"I can't leave yet. There are still all these people here."

She pauses beside Tad. When I left Forester+Blake, Tad

followed a few months later to come work under me. Turns out I wasn't the only one tired of being upstaged by Teresa. Now, Reb taps him on the shoulder. "Hey, superstar, go chat with the investors. I'm going to sneak Meg out before she falls asleep on her feet."

He nods and gives her a jaunty salute. "Got it."

I look over my shoulder as he heads towards the investors. "I can't just–"

"Yes, you absolutely can. It's called delegating. Tad is great with investors, and midnight is still early for him. He and I can hold down the fort."

"If I didn't know better, I'd think you were in cahoots with Keegan."

"Who? Me?" She pastes on an over-exaggerated look of shock, pressing her hand to her chest. "That is an audacious accusation, Meg!"

"No," I shoot back, hands on my hips. "It's not. You two are thick as thieves and—"

A hand slips around my waist, palming my hip before lightly brushing the sensitive place below by belly button.

"What's going on here?" Keegan says, his breath tickling the hairs at my neck.

"You should know." My tone is accusatory, but I know it's belied by how I move slightly back, pressing my ass against his thighs.

Reb plants a hand on each of us and practically shoves us toward the door. "Now's your chance! Just sneak out." To Keegan, she says, "Mission accomplished. Now take your girl home and do unspeakable things to her instead of just making googly eyes at her all night."

He grins. "Yes, ma'am."

Before I can protest, he's guiding me out the door. The

second the elevator closes behind us, he backs me against the wall.

"What are you doing?" I gasp as his teeth rake against the sensitive skin of my neck.

He's got one hand buried in my hair and the other is already lifting my skirt to cup my ass as he grinds against me. "I'm following directions. What does it look like I'm doing?"

"But someone could—"

I don't have a chance to finish my sentence because the elevator door opens with a ding.

Keegan grabs my hand and leads me out into the hallway outside his condo. "I assume you want to stay at my place tonight, since it's closer."

"Yes, please." Even though we basically live together, we haven't quite gotten around to selling his condo. Mostly we stay at my place still and rent his out on Airbnb, but every once in a while we stay at his place.

"Thank fuck," he mutters, his mouth on my neck again. "Because I don't think I want to wait to get home."

"You don't?" I ask in mock innocence.

"Nope." He pushes me against the wall beside his door. "Because I love watching you work a room when you're in badass, marketing mode. It's so fucking hot."

I press my hands to his shoulders so that he pauses long enough to look up at me. "Y-you do? I mean, it is?"

He grins down at me. "Fuck yeah, it is." After a second, his expression shifts and he suddenly looks serious. "Do you realize this spot right here is where we had our first kiss?"

I bite down on my lip as I nod, remembering how nervous and confused I was. How uncertain of everything.

I run my hand up from his shoulder to cup his jaw. "I don't ever want to be back in that place."

A frown flickers across his face. "You don't ever want me to kiss you in the hall again?"

"No. In that emotional place. Where I'm uncertain of your feelings and confused and so afraid of losing you."

"Same, Glasses. Same."

And then, because Keegan is incapable of being too serious for too long, he pulls what has become his favorite move. He picks me up and tosses me over his shoulder as if I weigh nothing and carries me inside. I squeal in protest and he gives me a playful pat on the ass.

"Shush. You'll wake the neighbors."

Once we're in his condo, the door slamming behind us, I playfully smack his ass. "Put me down!"

I'm not sure how he's able to lower me without straining a muscle, but he does, and with a little oof, I land on his oversized sofa, which is arranged near floor to ceiling windows overlooking the cityscape of Austin.

"Now be a good girl and take off your clothes."

"Excuse me?" I sass back.

He raises an eyebrow at me, licking his lips as those Caribbean blue eyes of his rake slowly down my body as he unbuttons his shirt. "You heard me."

I quickly shimmy out of my clothes, then lift up and slide my panties off my bottom and kick them on the floor. His own clothes follow a moment later.

"Open your legs, Meg, let me see you."

"You first." I point to his boxers.

He doesn't even hesitate. He just rolls them down. Then his hand is gripping his thick erection. Please don't let me be drooling on myself.

"Open. Your. Legs."

I slide my thighs apart, the leather cool on my skin.

He licks his lips again, stepping forward, then lowering to his knees, so he's kneeling between my splayed thighs. Still, his hand is stroking his hard cock. "Touch yourself."

His voice is low and full of sexy gravel. This side of Keegan, this side of him that only I ever see, stern and commanding in the bedroom, is just about the sexiest thing I've ever seen.

At the first brush of my fingertips to my clit, I jerk and moan. I am soaked. Embarrassingly so. Still, I begin a slow circle over the hood.

His hand slides up his dick and then down. "Are you getting close? Your breathing is tightening," he says.

"Yes." I can't tear my eyes away from his hand and that long, perfectly veined dick of his.

He shakes his head. "Stop. Hands up above your head. I want you to come on my face or my cock. Nothing else."

My breath catches.

"I want your cock. Now."

"Hands up," he orders.

I move my hands obediently above my head, gripping the back of the sofa. I'm so turned on, my entire body is vibrating and I'm pretty sure all it will take is for him to blow on my clit and I will detonate.

"I'll eat that pussy later, Glasses. Right now I've got to get inside you."

"Yes," I say. I open my thighs wider, dropping his pelvis into the right position.

He notches himself at my entrance, and then slides all the way inside me. He angles my hips just so, knowing exactly how to thrust to hit my g-spot, exactly how to touch my clit, exactly the rhythm I need to get there.

My orgasm hits hard and fast and seems to last forever.

As I shudder around him, he doesn't stop. Instead, he pulls me closer, so I'm part sitting on the edge of the sofa, arms braced around his shoulders and neck. I wrap my thighs around his waist, thankful and shocked that they're not totally boneless.

"Fuck," He says, as he pushes into me. We're closer this way. He slides deeper, almost bruising in the most delicious way. "Fuck, you feel so good."

I can't think, can't speak. I just rake my teeth over the shell of his ear, mindless to pleasure as he thrusts in and out of me, pulling more and more pleasure from me.

Without warning, he twists, pulling me fully off the couch and laying me on the plush carpeted floor. His hand finds my wrist, and he drags it between us. "Come for me again, Meg."

"I don't think I can," I say, but my fingers are already finding the overly-sensitive nub. My fingertips brush against his dick as he slowly pulls out, then pushes back in. I barely contain a hiss as his teeth find my neck, scraping the side of my throat.

"You can," he says, his fingers finding my breast, tweaking the tip. "I want to feel you shatter on me again."

I flick my fingers over my clit as he pinches my nipple and thrusts into me. God, it feels amazing. Planting my heels, I arch, meeting his thrusts, and *oh*.

Ohhhh, that's it.

His pace quickens, and his fingers trail up to my neck, wrapping around my throat. He doesn't squeeze or push. He just holds me there, pinning me gently as he stares down at me, his gaze locked with mine. And God, he's beautiful. His hair is tangled, and his mouth has a gleam of wetness from kissing me. His shoulders bunch and flex as he moves inside me, and as my fingers circle just right, he thrusts faster, rubbing my g-spot. "Come with me, Meg."

And, on command, my whole body comes apart. As every fiber of my being explodes into a kaleidoscope of color and pleasure and feeling, my thighs tremble, tensing in almost-pain as I tumble over the edge. He pushes into me once, twice, and then his body tenses, my pleasure igniting his as we freefall together.

Moments or maybe minutes later, I'm floating back to consciousness. Keegan's lying on top of me, and his weight is delicious. I trail my fingers up and down his back, which is slightly damp with sweat. His head is braced on his forearm on the floor next to my face, and his breath is hot against my cheek as he catches his breath.

I run my tongue over the ridge of his shoulder, where the muscle meets his neck, enjoying the salty-sweet taste of him. "Mmmm."

"You're a minx," he chastises, but there's nothing but appreciation in the tone.

"Maybe," I admit with a small laugh, letting my head loll to the side, inhaling the cooler air as I look over to the wall. When I catch sight of what's leaning against the wall, its cord haphazardly wound around its hook, my mood instantly shifts from pure contentedness to utter amusement. Hilarity, even.

I start laughing, and Keegan lifts up a bit to look down at me. "What?"

"That," I say, nodding toward the wall. His attention follows mine, and his grin is quick.

"What?" He repeats, all innocence, but his smile is knowing, as if he knows exactly what I'm laughing at. "Just trying to make your fantasies come to life, Glasses."

I pull him down for a kiss, but I can't stop the laughter

now. I'm in a fit. "Did you honestly buy a two thousand dollar vacuum as a joke?"

"Hey now," he says, nipping my bottom lip playfully. "I'll have you know that is a Butler *steam vacuum*. It sanitizes *and* vacuums, all at once." He shifts, moving to my side and tucking me against him, so now we are both staring at the avocado green steam vacuum leaning against the wall. He runs a hand over the carpet in front of my belly, forcing the fibers in the opposite direction so they make a pattern. "Does a pretty good job, too. I don't think this carpet has ever been this white."

"You're ridiculous, Keegan."

"What can I say? I'm a sucker for a good ad."

Later, after Keegan has cleaned us both up and brought me a glass of water, we climb into bed and he snuggles against me. I think back to that moment in the hall. To the reminder of our first kiss. And also of another hall and another first. That dark, dank hall in the co-op where we first met, when I was wrapped in a towel and Keegan rescued me.

"You know," I murmur, tracing the back of the hand he has cupped around my breast. "I used to think I had a good imagination."

"What?" he asks sleepily. "What do you mean, used to? You have a great imagination."

"Nah." I roll over just enough to look up at him. He pushes himself up on his elbow to gaze down at me. "Because none of the fantasy versions of my perfect life could have measured up to this."

I hope you *loved* Meg and Keegan's story.

If you did, how would you feel about some bonus content from Keegan's point of view?

I've got two bonus scenes up for grabs if you sign up for my newsletter. Follow the link in the qr code below to get them now!

Follow to read a bonus scene from
Head Over Feels

Also, fair and honest reviews (wherever you leave them) are always welcome! And don't forget to keep reading for a sample chapter of one of my other books!

acknowledgments

My best friend, Kat Baxter, loves friends to lovers stories.

She's the one who read an early draft of the beginning of this book—that was supposed to be a work place, boss/employee romance—and said, "Why the hell doesn't she end up with Keegan? What is wrong with her?"

Thank goodness for Kat. Once she pointed it out, it was obvious to me that Keegan was in love with Meg and that I was as much as a dumbass as Meg was.

So, Kat, you were right, as you usually are. Thank you for helping me see past my ideas about what the story should be to the real story.

And also, Kate Johnson, my amazing and talented editor. Thank you for pushing me every time I tried to take the easy way out. Without you, this book would be shorter and decidedly less satisfying.

IAN

It shouldn't matter to me how beautiful she is—Savannah, this woman who is my personal chef and living on my property. It shouldn't matter at all, but somehow, now that I've seen her, it does.

For the life of me, I don't know why it does

I almost never even notice what other people look like.

After nearly six months of dating Ava, I couldn't even remember what color her eyes were. I objectively knew she was beautiful because other people kept telling me she was. Now, after two months of not having seen her at all, I have only a vague recollection of blond hair. And a lot of high heels. I only remember her name being Ava and not Eva because that's how my assistant saved her contact on my phone.

So trust me when I tell you, I don't normally study women, let alone notice their beauty.

Despite that, I can't stop looking at this woman. Maybe it's because she's here in my kitchen, dressed in a tank top and impossibly short shorts. Barefoot, for fuck's sake.

Maybe it's because I only just woke up and my brain is

281

still foggy with theta brain waves and the wash of hormones that accompany morning wood.

Maybe it's because I haven't even actually met her, but I've already held her in my arms, tight against my body, her ass rubbing against said morning wood.

Or maybe it's just her. Just some primal, gut level reaction to this particular woman.

Whatever the reason, I seem to take in everything about her all at once, and she is stunning.

Long legs that are tan and lean and shapely, despite the lack of heels. Hips and tits that are full of soft, enticing curves. Hair that is brown and half piled on her head in some kind of sloppy knot. Eyes that are the most stunning blue-green I've ever seen.

I swear I've never once even noticed another person's eyes before. I've never just stared into them, lost in the pale green flecks scattered amongst the blue. The dark ring around the outside of her iris. The way her eyes dilate as she studies me in return.

Everything about this woman tugs at something deep inside me I would have sworn didn't even exist until this moment. Something that makes me want things I've never wanted before. Not like this, at least.

I'm a grown man. Obviously I've felt physical attraction before. The simple, base reaction to another human's body. But not like this. This is something different. This sudden need to ... what?

Pull her back into my arms? Feel her ass bucking against my dick again? Get another lungful of her hair?

"Show me," she blurts. Her words jolt me back into the moment. Show her?

Show her all the things I want to do to her?

No.

That can't be right.

"If you're really Mr. Donovan, then show me your ID."

A beat passes as her words sink in.

Right.

She doesn't believe I'm … me. And I offered to get my wallet and show her my ID. But all I want to do is stand here and stare at her like a fucking moron.

Jesus H. Christ. What is wrong with me?